Praise for A. Bello and

'A. Bello represents the long-awa
literature world. Creating a character like Emily Knight who provides
YA readers of colour their own heroine to look up to! Really excited
about this series!'
The British Blacklist

'An exciting adventure with a wonderful heroine you can't help
but root for'
Katherine Webber, author of Wing Jones

'...radical and rebellious yet touching and empowering. A must read!'
Style Biblio

'A perfect novel for any kids that fell in love with the Harry Potter
series. That includes any kid at heart!'
Popthebutterfly Reviews

'A fun read for children 9+. It's great to read a fantasy novel with
multicultural characters'
Fantastic Reads

'Once you start on the Emily Knight journey you do not want to stop!'
Helen Lewis, Director of Literally PR

'A book that will keep teens and pre-teens happily turning the pages.'
Madhouse Family reviews

'If you like Harry Potter and The Hunger Games'
Stressed Rach Reviews

'A. Bello has written a children's book for the 21st century. It's
representative, inclusive and plays a vital role in teaching young
people that our heroes are not just one race or gender. It's also fun,
entertaining and truly imaginative. I hope others follow in A. Bello's
steps and ensures that children's literature is more representative and
culturally diverse.'
Jared Garfield

Also by A. Bello

Emily Knight . . . I am

For the latest news, competitions and exclusive material
from A. Bello visit:
www.a-bello.com

EMILY KNIGHT

I am...Awakened

A.BELLO

Hashtag PRESS

Published in Great Britain by Hashtag Press 2017

A CIP catalogue for this book is available from the British Library.

ISBN 978-0-9957806-4-4

Typeset in Garamond Classic 11.75/14.5 by Blaze Typesetting
Printed in Great Britain by Clays Ltd, St Ives plc

 PRESS

HASHTAG PRESS BOOKS
Hashtag Press Ltd
Kent, England, United Kingdom
Email: info@hashtagpress.co.uk
Website: www.hashtagpress.co.uk
Twitter: @hashtag_press

Acknowledgements

All praise goes to the most high. Thank you for helping me create this book. This book was finished years ago so it feels AMAZING to finally have it out!

Thank you to those who helped to make this book so gorgeous in the inside and out. The best people I could have for book 2—Ale, Jem, Tiffany, Kate, Rachel and Helen.

Thank you to my agent Val, Paul, Chris and the entire Treehouse Digital team for understanding my world and helping to take it to the next level. Literally PR for all the fab press and of course my family and friends for the endless support. This author life is not easy!

And lastly to every single person who has read Emily Knight. You are amazing!

To Leanne
Who shows me what it means to be brave every single day

PROLOGUE

Rose

The window shutters swung to and fro, creaking nosily in the quaint farmhouse. Rose Moore, a little girl with two neat plaits wrapped in red ribbon, sat at the kitchen table swinging her skinny legs back and forth to the sound of the creaking. She began to hum tunelessly, a song she had heard on the radio.

May Moore was making brownies, and her wrinkled hands were covered in chocolate. Her blue almond eyes, enhanced by her round-framed glasses, were staring intensely at the brownie mixture, and her chubby cheeks were red from the heat of the kitchen.

"That smells lovely," Jack Moore said, as he hobbled into the kitchen. He bent down and kissed his granddaughter's nose. She giggled and he walked to his wife, sticking out his finger.

"Hey!" May said, slapping his blue-veined hand away from the brownie mixture. She poured the mixture into a circular baking tray and handed Jack the bowl. "Share it with Rose but not too much!"

Jack kissed his wife on the cheek. May smiled and he

winked at his grinning granddaughter. Rose placed her finger in the bowl and scooped up the mixture. She swirled the chocolate and sugar around in her mouth.

"Yum," she said, as she scooped again. Jack watched Rose adoringly as she cleaned the bowl. "Finished," she squealed triumphantly.

"Good, you can wash the bowl. Come on," May said, when Rose pulled a face.

"Are these for tomorrow?" Jack asked, noticing the white roses on the table.

"Yes, we'll leave them in the morning. We're going to visit your parents' grave tomorrow, Rose."

"Can I put the flowers down?" Rose asked, as she rolled up her sleeves and turned on the tap.

"Of course you can, lovely," May said, kissing her forehead.

That night, May locked up the chickens and ducks that lived in the back garden and chased the rooster that crowed at sunrise into its cage. Jack, as usual, locked up the doors and windows, before sitting at Rose's bedside to finish her bedtime story. His voice was calm and gentle. He stopped constantly to show her the pictures in the book. This particular picture was of a tiny girl the size of a thumb who was staring into the giant face of her mother. The tiny girl was questioning why she was a different size from everyone else.

"Would you still love me if I was different?" Rose interrupted.

Jack looked up from the book. "Of course I would, Rosie Posie. Why do you ask?"

Rose turned away from him. "What if . . . I could do things?"

Jack closed *One Tiny Girl* and frowned at his granddaughter.

"What sort of things?" Rose hesitated. "Come on, Rose, you can tell me anything."

Rose stared at him with her eyes wide. "What if I could fly?"

"Fly?" Jack asked frowning. "Why would you be able to fly?"

A shrill scream came from downstairs.

"May?" Jack shouted.

He jumped up from his seat, and moved with the alertness of a young man. Rose went to follow him, but he shook his head. She sat back on her fairy-covered bed and pulled the duvet over herself, so that she was hidden. Rose heard shouts, and deep voices she had never heard before. Her grandfather was yelling. Rose had never heard her grandfather raise his voice before, and it frightened her.

She curled into a ball and began to loudly hum a song she had heard on the radio, to block out the screams. Then she smelt it. Fire. She threw her fairy duvet on to the floor, and shot out of bed. She jumped the stairs two at a time and stopped when she saw shadows moving in the smoke.

"Grandpa?" she yelled, as she looked around.

Shouting and laughing echoed around her. She watched helplessly as three figures ran out of her house, congratulating each other on their accomplishment. Rose screamed when she saw two bodies slumped on the kitchen floor motionless, surrounded by red flames that were licking her grandmother's cream wallpaper.

The smoke was filling up Rose's young lungs. She began to heave and cough. She kneeled over and put her pyjama top over her mouth. Rose walked slowly towards her grandparents, but her bare feet scratched on the shattered glass on the floor. She fell, clutching her pale foot as the blood spread over it. Her head felt light. She couldn't breathe.

"Help," she said desperately, before everything went black.

SEVEN YEARS LATER

The bathroom door swung shut behind her. Rose fumbled at the taps, but she couldn't get a firm grip. The smoke from her hands was getting stronger. Rose bit down hard on her lip to stop herself from screaming in pain. She finally managed to turn the stiff tap, and the cold water shot down on to her hot hands. Her hands sizzled and the smoke and pain slowly began to disappear. Rose looked at them in awe. Apart from the scars from the fire, they were okay.

"Thank God," she sighed.

She looked up and caught her reflection. Her large, sad brown eyes stared back at her through her long black hair. Her pale cheeks, engraved with burn marks, were flushed. She poured water into her cupped hands, and dabbed the water on to her cheeks until they were pale again.

Rose returned to her English class, where the students were sitting in silence, writing an essay. Mrs Draught glanced up as Rose entered the room, then she continued to mark her papers. Rose sat in her seat, and tore off a piece of paper from her exercise book. She wrote on it quickly, scrunched it up, and threw it to the desk next to hers. Her best friend, Max Jacobs, a skinny boy with a long brown fringe and glasses that were too big for his face, opened it up on his lap.

Smoky hands. What does it mean?

Rose could see from the corner of her eye that Max had opened his backpack and pulled out a book that he placed on his lap. He turned the pages quickly, and Rose glimpsed pictures of famous warriors. When he stopped, he wrote down something on the back of her note, scrunched it back up, and threw it to her.

Rose glanced up but Mrs Draught was still marking her papers. Rose opened up the note and it read in messy writing:

That means you are officially a warrior!

Rose gasped. Her eyes immediately started to well up and she shook her head from side to side.

"No, no, no!" She tore the note into little pieces and threw them in the air.

"Rose!" Mrs Draught was on her feet with her hands on her hips. "What is going on?"

Rose pushed back her desk with so much force that it toppled to the floor. The class watched in shocked silence as she ran out of the classroom, slamming the door behind her.

"Are you okay?" Max asked, sitting beside her on the bench in the playground. "Why did you get so upset?"

"Because I hate them," Rose spat.

"Why?" Max asked.

"They're evil," she replied. "And I don't want nothing to do with them."

They watched the other children playing games and chasing

each other around the school playground. Rose couldn't remember the last time she had felt happy. After her grandparents' death, there was a part of her that died with them and she felt empty. Since then, the days seemed to merge into one long stretch.

They were under the oak tree, Rose's favourite spot in the entire school. The shade from the tree hid Rose and Max from the other students. She felt like they were invisible to the world.

"But how are warriors evil?" Max asked her. "I mean, Tainwo Kena saved loads of people's lives." He pointed to the book on his lap. There was a photograph of a young Korean man, with biceps bulging through his t-shirt, firing a blue fireball up into the sky.

Rose sighed and hit Tainwo Kena's face in the book with her finger. "People like *him* kill people. These warriors set fire to my house and killed my grandparents when I was six. They enjoyed doing it. If it wasn't for the neighbours calling the fire brigade, I would be dead too. Look at me! They left their mark."

She could feel Max staring at her face. Her face was destroyed because of people like them.

"Do you know who they were?" Max asked, turning away.

Rose shook her head. "I wish I did." *I would kill them,* she wanted to add, but she didn't want to scare away her only friend.

A football gently hit Rose's foot.

"Hey, patchwork!" James Dunce shouted. "Pass us the ball."

Rose ignored him. She ignored anyone who called her names. The only person she didn't ignore was Max.

James walked towards her. He was a tall, lean boy with

spiky black hair, blue eyes, and a beauty spot on his right temple. All the girls at St Peter's Secondary School thought there was something special about James and they all fought over him. Rose thought he was an idiot.

"You deaf or something? I asked for my ball."

She looked at him through her long black hair. "You called me patchwork, when my name is Rose."

James looked down at her, scrunching his round face up like there was a nasty smell under his nose. "Well, you're the ugliest rose I've ever seen. You're more of a weed, a disgusting, burnt one." He let out a loud roar of a laugh and sat himself down between Max and Rose.

"Come on," Max said hurriedly as he got up from the bench. Rose followed him, and James followed her.

"You should join a freak show!" James shouted, as he deliberately stepped on the back of Rose's battered shoes.

She fell down on to the concrete floor and scraped her skinny knees.

"Leave off!" Max shouted at James, who laughed.

"What are you going to do, puny? Puny and ugly, what a tag team!"

"GO AWAY!" Rose screamed, as she whipped around to face him.

James's eyes widened as he was lifted high into the air. He elevated for a few seconds before he was thrown into the oak tree. He banged his head hard on the wood, and slid down the trunk. He slumped helplessly on to the ground, with his head resting on his chest.

Carolyn Smith, James's jealous girlfriend, had been watching from across the playground. She screamed when she saw James fly through the air and collide with the tree. She sprinted towards him, shouting his name, catching the attention of the other students who ran after her.

Rose stared at her scarred hands, breathing fast. Max looked at her with his eyes wide.

"This is not good," Max said, as he watched the students charging towards them, screaming James's name.

Rose glanced at James but he was still knocked out.

The headmaster hurried out of the school doors in his tight, shiny suit. Frown lines were imprinted in his face. Students were running towards him, pointing at James. Rose got up slowly. She took a step backwards and when no one looked her way, she took another. She glanced over her shoulder at the school gates. In that moment, she was grateful that she was good at blending into the background. With all eyes on James, she turned around and walked normally to the gates, breathing faster than usual.

"You can't go!" Max said horrified, grabbing her arm. "What should I say happened to him?"

"I don't know . . . tell them I'm sorry," Rose whispered, before she ran out of the school gates.

Rose ran and ran, even though her side ached. She ran until she came to her home on Broad Street. The tears that rained from her eyes blinded her as she fumbled for her keys. She managed to open the front door to hear her aunt Janet singing 'Summer Holidays' in the kitchen. Rose raced up the stairs, hiding her tear-stained face in her long hair.

"Rose, is that you?" Aunt Janet called, but Rose slammed the door, and buried herself under the duvet, where she cried and howled into the mattress.

Tap.

Rose pulled the duvet of her face and looked at her watch. Five hours had passed. Rose brushed her hair out of her face, realising that she must have cried herself to sleep.

Tap.

She looked around the room to find out where the sound was coming from but it was too dark to see. She caught her reflection in the mirror and jumped. "You should be in a horror film," she said to herself, as she stared at her scars, highlighted by the glow of the moon.

Rose squinted her eyes. There was a small circular light on the mirror that shook from right to left. Rose stood up and moved closer to it.

Tap.

A small rock was thrown on to her windowpane. Rose moved cautiously towards the window, and looked down at the bright lights.

"There she is!" a voice cried.

Rose ducked. She sat on the floor, holding her knees to her chest, rocking back and forth. The crowd began to chant, "Freak." An avalanche of rocks was being hurled on to her window. One broke through the glass and Rose screamed. She covered her ears, and hummed tunelessly a song she had heard seven years ago in her grandparent's kitchen. The louder they chanted, the louder she hummed.

"Rose?" Aunt Janet called from behind the door. She fiddled with the doorknob, but it was locked. "Rose, open the door!"

"No!" Rose shouted. "Why can't everyone just leave me alone?"

"Is the freak show coming out to play?" James called, from beneath her window. "I'm going to make you pay for what you did."

"James," Rose whispered, relieved that she hadn't killed him.

"She must be wetting herself, James," a voice she didn't recognise said. "Where's that brick? Let's chuck it!"

"Rose!" Aunt Janet called louder. "Open this door now!"

Rose put her hands over her ears. She hummed the tune louder and louder until the noise around her made her feel like her head was going to explode. "LEAVE ME ALONE!"

The unbroken windows smashed. Shards of glass rained on the crowd of people outside her house. They instinctively covered their heads and ran away screaming. The door to her room blew open. The impact knocked her large aunt off her feet, and she fell with a heavy thud to the floor. Rose opened her eyes slowly. She jumped when she saw Aunt Janet unconscious.

"Oh no, oh no," Rose said to herself.

Out of the corner of her eye, she saw her school bag. Without a second thought, she picked it up and threw the contents on to the floor. She grabbed her purse and hurriedly stuffed clean clothes and underwear. Rose pulled on a grey hoodie and used a spare trainer from the floor to carefully brush the glass off the window. She dropped the trainer, and climbed on to the ledge.

"I'm sorry," Rose said to her aunt before she jumped and landed gracefully on her feet.

"Where are you going?" a voice called in the dark and Rose froze. She was surprised to see it was Max, still in his school uniform. "I wanted to make sure you were okay because of the people outside."

Rose turned away from him. "I'm going somewhere safe. Far away from people so I can't hurt them." She shook her head sadly. "I didn't mean to hurt James. I don't know how I did it."

"You're like the warriors in my book," Max said, smiling to himself.

"I am nothing like them," Rose hissed and Max recoiled as if he had been hit. "I just need to figure out what's happening to me, so I can stop it."

"You could use your powers to help people," Max suggested.

Rose shook her head. "Max, look at me. I need rescuing. I can't play the part of the hero." Tears fell from her eyes, and she angrily wiped them away. "I don't want this power. I don't want to be like the people that killed my grandparents. It makes me sick. I hate warriors. They shouldn't exist. They're dangerous, they're careless and they left me with no one. I cared when I hurt James, but they didn't care about my family! I'm going to get rid of all of them. I swear on my grandparents' graves, I will kill them, every last one of them."

"But you are a warrior, Rose," Max said softly.

"Please stop saying that," Rose whispered.

Max walked towards her and wrapped his arms around her waist, stroking her long black hair. "I could come with you," he whispered. "I'll help you figure this out."

Rose gently pushed him away. "I don't know how long I'll be gone for." She looked back at the empty, dark house. "I might never come back. What should I do about my aunt? She's unconscious."

"I'll make a private call to the ambulance. Let me help you, Rose. You don't have to do this alone," Max said desperately. "We can get out of here, together. You know I've been reading about warriors for years. I can help you control this."

Rose looked at him. She didn't want to take him seriously, but she knew he meant it. Rose stared out ahead of her. She knew in her heart she couldn't do it by herself.

"What about your parents?"

Max laughed. "They wouldn't care. Too drunk to even remember my name. They wouldn't even notice if we went to the house to get some money."

Rose stared hard at Max. He wasn't big and strong. If they got into any trouble, she knew she would be the one to protect them. But no one knew more about warriors than Max. Plus, he actually cared about her and Rose didn't have anyone else.

"Okay," she eventually said. "Let's go."

The chirps from the robins awoke Rose. Her head was rested on Max's lap and his arms were around her. She sat up and shook Max, who looked around wildly mumbling, "Where am I?"

Rose pulled her hood over her unwashed hair, and shielded her eyes from the sun. The train was slowing down as it reached Necises Green. A chubby woman with her hair in a big, blonde bun, pulled her trolley up to them. "Anything from the cart, loves?"

Rose and Max looked hungrily at the sandwiches, buns and cakes.

"We'll have four sandwiches and a cake, please," Max said, handing her some pound coins.

The woman stared kindly at Max as she handed him his purchases. He put them on the table in front of them and opened a sandwich wrapping.

"You alright, love?" The woman said to Rose. "It's just that I saw you sleeping and you were tossing and turning. Are you meeting some family?"

Rose smiled at the woman's consideration, but it was quickly replaced by a frown as she noticed the woman was no longer looking in her eyes, but over her scars and burns. Rose pulled down her hood further, so that it covered the majority of her face.

"We're meeting our grandparents, thanks," Rose replied frostily. She put the sandwiches and cakes in her school bag.

"You didn't have to sound so rude," Max hissed when the woman walked on.

"Well, she should know staring is rude," Rose retorted.

The train stopped at Necises Green station. Rose and Max left the train to curious looks from the other passengers. Rose breathed in the country air and sighed while she admired the fields and trees that stretched out before her.

"Welcome to my home, Max."

The farmhouse was a couple of miles away from the station and they set out straight away, stopping only once so Rose could eat a sandwich. On the journey, Rose spoke excitedly about where she had visited as a child. They crossed the familiar bridge and passed the little pond, where she used to feed the fishes with her grandfather and the farm up the road where she had played with a little lamb with her grandmother. She came to a halt when she saw the farmhouse with its broken windows and the door off its hinges. She assumed that someone would have fixed it up, maybe Aunt Janet because it was her parents' house, but she now knew that no one cared enough. The entire house was covered in black soot and half of the roof had fallen in.

"Whoa, that's not pretty." Max said frowning.

"It is to me." Rose smiled, as she walked towards it.

Max grabbed her arm. "I don't think it's safe to go in there."

She shook him off, but paused to look back at him. "I'm sure it'll be fine. Come on, I'll show you around."

Rose stepped inside the house. The smell of fire still clung on to the walls, so she had to cover her nose to block out the smell. Everything was burnt and ruined. She began to climb the stairs, inspecting each one carefully as some were broken. She brushed the cobwebs that had gathered outside of her bedroom door. Her old room didn't look too bad. The mattress was still in good shape although it was covered in soot and the paint had melted off the walls.

"Oh, wow," Rose said with her eyes wide.

On the floor, beside her bed, was the copy of *One Tiny Girl* that her grandfather had read to her. They never got to finish the story. Rose flicked through the beautiful illustrations. The tips of the pages were slightly singed, but other than that it was in great condition. Rose handed the book to Max who was staring around her room in fascination.

"One Tiny Girl?" Max said, turning the book over.

"It's a great read," Rose said. "Max, can I look at your warrior book?"

"Yeah sure," Max said, pulling it out from his rucksack

A Gift Not A Curse, read the title. Rose flicked though it and randomly stopped at a middle-aged woman called Su Ling Li, who was holding a small yellow fireball in her palm. Two paragraphs on the page were highlighted with a green pen.

Abilities can only be inherited, but it is common that two parents who are warriors will give birth to a child who is not a warrior. However, that child can go on to have children who will inherit the warrior gene. It is known that the warrior gene can appear generations later.

Fireballs are an important part of battles. A fireball is when you transfer your energy into a ball. The first step is producing a Baby Ball; a basic fireball, the same size as a tennis ball. The way to start is to think of something that makes you angry, focus all of that anger and want it to appear in your hand, then it should in the form of a Baby Ball.

Rose closed the book and looked at her hands. "I attacked James and hurt Aunt Janet because I was angry, but if I understand this power, I can control it, then put a stop to it before it's too late. Before I turn into them." She clasped her hands into tight fists. She looked up and Max was staring at her.

"But if you inherited it, then it's a part of you," Max said delicately.

Rose shook her head. "It will never be a part of me. I'll be right back."

Rose went into the back garden. It was hard to remember a time when it was beautiful. The roses her grandmother planted used to grow over by the fence and the swing her grandfather had installed for her stood rusty in the middle of the garden. Rose slowly faced the kitchen window. The kitchen where they had died. Where the fire had consumed them and Rose had done nothing to help. *Why did I have to have this life? Why does everyone I love die?*

"WHY?" Rose threw her head back and screamed.

Her chest rose rapidly. Her body felt hot and sweaty. She was shaking with anger, so blinded with rage, that she was oblivious to the huge red fireballs in her hands.

"Rose!" Max called. He quickly ran across the garden.

Rose saw Max coming towards her, and held up her hands. "Leave me alone!" she yelled, but it was like a bigger force was controlling her, and the fireballs shot at Max, who looked on horrified.

It felt like everything was in slow motion. The fireballs were glowing a bright red, the air smelt like smoke, bringing Rose back to that night, where she almost chocked from the fire. For a second, she thought she was trapped in the farmhouse, and she couldn't breathe.

Max's loud screams brought her back to the present and he ducked his head and used his arms to shield his face. The fireballs hit Max with a loud boom and erupted into a blinding white light. Rose shielded her eyes until the light had cleared and then she sprinted towards him, hollering his name. Rose skidded to a halt and gasped.

Max was standing perfectly still, with his eyes closed tight, but his entire body was frozen in ice.

"Max?" Rose whispered, but he didn't move.

Slowly, Rose walked towards the frozen Max. She was confused. In the book it hadn't said that fireballs could freeze people. Her heart stopped. *What if I killed him?* She was in front of him now, breathing heavily.

"Max?" she said louder.

Max's eyes opened and Rose screamed and fell over. The ice melted from Max's body and he looked like he had taken a shower fully clothed.

"It's okay, I'm okay," Max shouted over her screams, as he reached for her hand and squeezed it.

"How—how did you do that?"

He ran his fingers through his wet hair. "I don't know. I just saw your fireball coming towards me, and I tried to protect myself, and I felt . . . nothing."

"Did you have the hands burning thing as well?"

Max nodded. "That's why I brought the book."

Rose hit his arm. "Why didn't you tell me?"

Max looked away embarrassed. "Because I couldn't do anything the warriors in the book could do. I thought my powers were . . . faulty or something! And I know you don't like being a warrior, and I didn't want you to not be my friend anymore."

"Oh, Max," Rose said hugging him, but she jumped away because he was so cold. "We will always be best friends."

"Promise?"

Rose nodded and then she frowned. "So, what does this mean?"

The corners of Max's mouth, curled upwards. "I guess you're not alone anymore."

CHAPTER ONE

The Life Line

Emily Knight watched as the forest erupted into bright amber flames. The dry leaves crinkled and withered as they were licked by the fire. The air was covered in a grey smoke that caused Emily to cover her mouth, and cough harshly as her throat dried up.

The red-haired warrior, Scarlett, lifted her pale arms and with a seductive smile, she flicked back her long hair, and shot a white fireball that soared towards Emily.

Emily caught it with her bare hands. She closed her eyes and embraced the heat, just as Master Zen had taught her to do at school. She was in control and the fireball couldn't hurt her. She looked up at Scarlett and threw her arms back, but the fireball didn't move. She stared at the fireball in disbelief. She shook her hands viciously, but the fireball wouldn't budge.

"No way," Emily whispered, as the fireball in her hands began to shrink in size.

A soaring pain shot sharply through Emily's arms and she screamed as the fireball entered her body. Emily fell on to the grassy floor and writhed in pain as the fireball travelled through her chest and dropped to the pit of her stomach. She could faintly hear Scarlett's laughter.

"Get out! Please get out!" Emily cried.

She shook violently, tears pouring down her face, as she watched the fireball travel from her stomach, and back up to her chest. A bright, white light beamed through her training kit. She scratched at her chest, drawing blood. It felt like a fire was trapped inside her body. Emily threw her head back and roared, as her body swelled up. Everything went black and the fireball and her body exploded.

Emily opened her eyes. She was breathing hard. Her head was banging and her ears were ringing with Scarlett's laughter. She pulled open the top of her pyjama shirt and saw no scratch marks and no fireball trapped in her body. Emily reached over to the other side of the bed and felt cool sheets.

"Cathy?" Emily called anxiously, looking around the large room for her blonde-haired foster sister. Emily kicked off the duvet cover and sat up. She put her head in her hands and groaned. It was the second nightmare that night. "Cathy?" she said louder.

"I'm here," Cathy Lee said, as she closed the bedroom door behind her. Her blonde curls tumbled messily down her back. She handed Emily a cold glass of water, which Emily gulped down in one go. Cathy sat next to her, and rested her hand comfortingly on Emily's arm.

"Thank you," Emily said. "I guess you recognise the signs now?"

Cathy nodded. "The constant punching while you're asleep is a good give away. At least I didn't get hit tonight." Cathy looked around the room, covered with posters of battles and trophies that Lox had won. "I still don't get why you want to sleep in here."

Emily put the glass down on the bedside table. She collapsed back on to the bed, allowing the cool air to tame her overheated body.

"It makes me feel closer to him," Emily mumbled.

Emily knew Cathy didn't understand. Nor did her godparents, Sally and Michael Meran. When Emily had started sleeping in her older brother, Lox's bedroom, Sally had pursed her lips and remained silent, but Emily had overheard Sally and Michael arguing in the kitchen.

"Maybe she wouldn't have nightmares if she wasn't sleeping in his bedroom!"

Michael sighed and said warily, "If it brings her comfort, then I don't see the problem."

"Comfort!" Sally screeched. "He tried to kill her!"

"He tried to save her life," Michael retorted.

Sally scoffed. "Please. She saved *his* life. If it wasn't for her, Neci would have killed them both."

Emily had lost count of the nightmares she'd had since her encounter with Neci, the deadliest warrior to exist. Those born with the warrior gene usually got their powers at aged thirteen and they can fly, breathe under water, create fireballs and are very strong. Neci had all of that, but she was also very powerful, cunning and ruthless. She was the only warrior to challenge the elite Five Warriors and she famously murdered two of their members in battle—Cecil Archinia and Niles Thompson.

Only a few months ago, Emily learnt that when Lox had run away from home as a young boy, Neci had persuaded him to train with her. Lox had just became the youngest warrior in history to win the prestigious Warrior Tournament, defeating warriors double his age and Neci wanted to take him under her wing. They bonded over their shared hatred for Lox and Emily's father, and leader of The Five Warriors, Thomas Knight. Neci wanted to train Lox and use him as a weapon against Thomas, the only warrior to ever defeat her. With Thomas Knight dead, Neci would once again be the most powerful warrior in the world.

Last year, Neci sent Lox to the Osaki Training School, where Emily attended. Lox's mission was to recruit Emily to their team, and if she refused, he was instructed to kill her. Emily didn't want anything to do with Neci and Lox couldn't carry out his assignment—so seconds before she appeared, Lox warned her that Neci was coming to finish his mission. Neci and her warriors attacked Emily and Lox, but Emily was able to create a light beam that temporarily blinded them. She got herself and Lox back to safety, but Lox had disappeared again the next day and had not been seen since.

During the big England vs. Germany Dojo match at the end of last term, Neci had hijacked the TV station, interrupting the match and revealed to the world that she was back. She announced that she was on the hunt for her missing warrior to complete her fighting team and then she would declare a war against anyone that didn't support her. She was going to kill Thomas Knight, Roberta Taniana and Hubert Jenkins— the remaining three members of the Five Warriors. No one had any idea who the missing warrior could be.

Everything had been a blur since that encounter. News reporters and the paparazzi had followed Emily from school all the way to her front door, snapping endless pictures and asking numerous questions. The press had been calling the house phone asking for an exclusive interview with her. No one cared that she was tired, traumatised and upset, all they wanted to know was what she was going to do now that Neci was back.

The only topic on the news was about the potential war, so Emily didn't watch TV, or read the newspapers. She had no idea what was happening outside of the four walls of her room, which she had been cooped up in since the summer holidays began. She felt like she couldn't speak to anyone about how she was feeling, not even her best friends—Michella Kinkle, Wesley Parker and Jason Notting—who she had ignored all summer. Unlike them, Neci had put a target on her back because she was a Knight.

The only thing Emily looked forward to was going back to school in a few weeks. School is a word that most kids don't like to hear whilst on their holidays, let alone something to get excited about, but the Osaki Training School was not an ordinary school. It was a school that teenagers from all over England were invited to attend if they had inherited the warrior gene. They were trained to control and develop their powers, such as flying, breathing under water and creating fireballs. There were six teams in Osaki named after the leaders of the Warrior Revolution—Bernard Ogragon, Joseph Berbinin, Arthur Linktie, Ce-Ce Pentwon, Rose-Marie Mentorawth and Idris Jenkint. All warriors were placed into a team based on their family history. Emily and her best friends were in Ogragon. They stayed at the school during the week, whilst Emily preferred to go home at the end of each day.

Sally and Michael were at a loss with how to help Emily, who refused to open up to them. Sally insisted that Emily should continue her counselling sessions with Jenny Li. She prayed that Emily would open up to Jenny, but so far Emily would sit in silence until the session ended.

Emily had lived with her godparents, Sally and Michael Meran and their four foster children since she was seven years old. Her father had moved them into the family mansion before leaving to find Lox after he ran away.

Emily hadn't seen her father in years, as he had promised her deceased mother that he would bring Lox home, and he was still searching for him. Emily had gone through a phase where she would purposely steal, so that she could get on the cover of every worldwide newspaper, in the hope that her father would see that she needed him. But Thomas hadn't returned and even after Neci's announcement, there had been no word or sighting of him.

Usually, Emily could share her thoughts with her foster sister, Cathy Lee, but Cathy had wanted to hear all about Lox and Emily's encounter with Neci—all of the things Emily didn't want to talk about, so Emily had stopped speaking to Cathy. Only recently, Cathy had offered to stay in Lox's bed with her after Emily had complained of not sleeping well. They still hadn't spoken properly about that night, but her presence had helped. Some nights, Emily would sleep without any nightmares.

She turned to her clock. Midnight. Midnight was the time she had agreed to meet Lox, three months ago. And when she did, he had almost allowed Neci to kill her. She found it strange that she didn't resent Lox for coming back into her life and deliberately taking her to Neci. Maybe because he had many opportunities to kill her all year, and he never did. All she wanted to know was that he was still alive.

"Em?" Cathy said, as she lay down next to Emily. "I know you don't want to talk about it, but I just want to remind you that in this war, if it does happen, you do have a choice if you want to fight."

Emily stared up at the cream ceiling, wishing she could disappear. "I don't have a choice."

Cathy searched in the dark until she found Emily's hand and grabbed it. "You always have a choice, babe."

Emily closed her eyes and squeezed Cathy's hand tight.

A rustling noise woke Emily up the next morning. Emily opened her eyes and looked around the room. She was back in her own bedroom. Someone had moved her in the night and opened the curtains on her four-poster bed. The room was bright from the sun that she had been avoiding. Cathy was gone and in her place was a note that Emily picked up.

It may be just a coincidence
but you sleep much better in your own room
C x

Emily jumped when she heard a thump from underneath her bed and a loud, "Ow!" She looked down the side of her bed and saw a person in blue denim jeans, a white t-shirt and a red baseball cap turned backwards. It was one of her best friends, Wesley Parker, and he was rubbing the back of his sore head.

Wesley's hazel eyes lit up as he saw Emily. "How's it going?"

Emily stifled her laughter. "What are you doing?"

"I was looking at your new phone and it rolled under your bed. What's this?" Wesley pulled out a black bra from underneath the bed and quickly dropped it as Emily turned away embarrassed.

"Is she awake?" Michella Kinkle asked, opening the door. Her long braids were piled on top of her head in a high bun. She was wearing a red summer dress and gold sandals. She frowned when she saw the bra at Wesley's feet. "Err Wesley, there's a—"

"I know," Wesley said, cutting her off. "Let's not make it more awkward than it already is." He reached back under the bed, grabbed the phone and placed it next to Emily. "Who got you that?"

"Sally and Michael for my birthday. I haven't even looked it at properly. But what are you two doing here?" Emily asked confused.

"What does it look like we're doing?" Michella said. "We're here to get you back on track. To rescue your poor excuse for a summer! We've been calling you for weeks to see how you are, and your family kept telling us that you weren't up to talking, so we decided to come ourselves."

"How did you even get into the Village?" Emily asked.

Emily was aware that the paparazzi were once again camped outside Legends Village. Even opening her window to get fresh air was deemed front-page news, based on how quickly they grabbed their cameras when they saw a glimpse of her.

"We flew," Michella said. She smiled as she picked up a picture frame with a photo of Emily as a baby playing on a sandy beach. "We landed on your doorstep. Because they're not warriors they couldn't sense us coming, so we were inside super quick. The paps could do nothing but take pictures of our backs."

"It's so weird flying outside of school," Wesley confessed.

Michella put down the picture frame and laughed. "Wes thought we would get swallowed by the propellers on the plane that we flew alongside!"

Emily laughed and Wesley shot Michella a dark look.

"But we were stopped by the flight controllers," Wesley said defensively.

"The what?" Emily frowned.

"They check that you've passed the basics in flying," Michella explained. "We got sent a FLY card that says that we passed at Osaki, and we have to carry it at all times. You must have got one too?"

Emily shrugged. "It must be in that mountain of post downstairs . . ."

Wesley snorted. "It's pretty pointless though. People fly even if they don't have a FLY card."

Michella nodded in agreement. "But since Neci's come back, everyone is being more cautious and now people are getting fined if they don't carry it. Warren got fined the other day."

The three of them sat in silence. Emily wondered what else had changed since Neci was back on her warpath.

"What did you do for your birthday?" Michella asked, as Wesley sat on the edge of Emily's bed. "Gosh, Warren and Pete had this house party that went crazy. Mum was so mad."

"What was the party for?" Emily asked.

"Warren's birthday," Michella said. "Even though they're eleven months apart, they always celebrate each other's birthday like it's their own. They're more joined at the hip than the twins. Anyway, there were so many drunk people. I found a couple kissing in Mike and Madison's room, which was disgusting. Mum said when they come home to visit from school, they aren't allowed to see any friends."

Emily sighed. "Unlike Warren, I didn't bother celebrating my birthday. I spent my fourteenth birthday at home. Michael ordered me this amazing red velvet cake, and I barely ate any. I've spent all summer thinking about what I'm going to do when Neci decides to attack, and I still have nothing."

"There's still time, Emily," Michella said, as she joined Wesley on the bed. "We're going to be pushed to a next level at Osaki. You'll be ready when she comes."

"But we don't know when she's coming," Emily protested. "She could come right now, teleport into my room if she wanted to without a moment's notice, and I'll die, and it . . . it frightens me."

The room fell silent again. Wesley stood up and stared at Emily with a determined expression. "We're not going anywhere. We'll be ready when it happens. Everyone's scared, I definitely am! But at least we'll be fighting her together."

Emily smiled. "I know, thank you. Where's blondie?"

Michella laughed. "He's on holiday in the South of France. He said he wrote to you. Didn't you get his postcard?"

Emily shook her head. "I haven't read any mail."

"I guess you don't know about the Survival Training then?" Wesley asked.

"The what?"

"It's some tradition the second years do every year. We're going to Redrook Forest for a week to train. It should be a laugh, and apparently a celebrity always comes to train the students."

"Camping?" Emily said sceptically. "I hate camping. I was actually looking forward to going back to school until you said that."

"Emily!" Sally hollered from downstairs. "Get your butt in gear. Your aunt is coming."

"All right," Emily shouted back with no intention of leaving her bed.

"Have you been sleeping okay?" Michella asked.

Emily shook her head. "I've been having nightmares. For some reason, I just keep seeing that red-haired warrior, Scarlett, and this fireball. It's so weird, it goes inside my body, and then I explode. Can that even happen?"

"I heard about some man who consumed so much energy he exploded," Wesley said earnestly.

Michella snickered. "What man?"

"I don't know," Wesley snapped. "It was in the paper."

"Today's?"

"No . . . it was ages ago. What? Do you think I'm lying?"

"I don't think that's possible," Michella said, crossing her arms. "You're trying to tell me that if I was really powerful, and had too much power in me, I'll kill myself? It just seems a bit out there."

Emily's mind flashbacked to a conversation she had last year at school with their headmaster, Mr Davon. "Actually, Wesley's sort of right."

"Thank you," Wesley said smugly as Michella frowned.

"If you have a lot of power and you can't control it, or your emotions, the two can merge together, and you can become uncontrollable," Emily explained. "So uncontrollable that you could potentially kill yourself. I've really got to step up my training."

The doorbell rang. Emily looked at the clock. It was midday.

"One of the kids will get it," Emily said, referring to her younger foster brother and sisters, James Evernham, Rosy Lang-Sheen and Yvonne Saunders.

The doorbell continued to ring. Emily waited a few seconds and when she couldn't hear any footsteps, she huffed and threw off the duvet.

"Nice pyjamas," Wesley teased, looking at Emily's teddy bear print. She stuck her tongue out at him.

The three of them ran down the steps towards the door.

"Sally?" Emily called, but no one responded. Emily opened the front door.

"No way," Wesley said, as he looked at the visitor up and down. "Pinch me."

"Pinch me first," Michella said, with her mouth hanging open. "This is unreal."

"You're—you're," Wesley stammered.

"Yes, I am," the woman said in a husky voice. She smiled at them. She was used to this particular reaction. "Hello, Emily."

"Hi, Aunt Roberta," Emily said, wishing she wasn't in her teddy bear pyjamas.

"Aunt?" Wesley mouthed to Michella behind Emily's back.

The three of them stepped aside, and watched Roberta glide into the room. Her elbow length black hair was tousled around her face, which made her almond-shaped green eyes pop. Her pale skin was sun-kissed from her recent trip home to Italy. Her full lips were painted red and when she smiled she revealed perfect white teeth. She was dressed in a figure-hugging red top and a black pencil skirt that clung to her curves. Emily understood why she was consistently voted the world's most beautiful woman. She had an aura that was spellbinding.

Roberta Taniana was the only female in the legendary Five Warriors and was one of the strongest warriors in the world. She was married to her fellow teammate, Hubert Jenkins and Emily had lived next door to them all her life.

Emily noticed how peaceful it sounded outside. She looked out of the door and the paparazzi were gone. "Where are they?" she asked amazed.

"Oh, Jenkins has made an illusion of me on the other side of the Village."

"Jenkins!" Michella mouthed to Wesley.

Emily caught Michella and Wesley's excited faces and her mouth twitched. "These are my friends, Michella Kinkle and Wesley Parker. They go to Osaki with me."

"Kinkle?" Roberta asked, shaking hands with Michella, who looked down at her hand in awe and nodded. "Are you related to Janette Kinkle?"

"She's my sister," Michella replied, looking up at Roberta adoringly.

"Really? My eldest son, Xavier loves her. He thinks she's the best Dojo player and the more tattoos she gets, the more obsessed he is." Roberta giggled, before she shook Wesley's hand. He stared at her with his mouth hanging open. "And it's nice to meet you, Wesley."

Michella clutched tightly on to Emily's arm and whispered, "Oh my gosh, Roberta Taniana's here, oh my gosh."

"Be cool," Emily whispered back.

"Emily," Roberta said, smiling warmly at her. "Can we sit down and talk?"

Emily nodded and led the way to the living room, which was surprisingly tidy. Everything had been wiped down and smelt faintly of vanilla incense. The TV was still on in the background. Emily could feel her hands sweating and rubbed them on the front of her top.

Roberta perched herself in the middle of the black couch and Emily, Michella and Wesley sat opposite her, huddled up together. Roberta crossed her toned legs, and rested her chin on her hand.

"How have you been, Emily? Jenkins and I have tried to see you, but we were told you weren't feeling well."

Emily shrugged. "I'm fine now."

Roberta raised a perfectly arched eyebrow. "How have you really been? And the truth would be very helpful."

Emily fell silent. When she spoke, she was surprised to hear her voice shaking. "I've been scared. Scared that Neci is going to come, and I won't be ready to fight her. I never thought she would be back, I thought she disappeared forever. I'm scared of the expectations people have on me. I don't want to fail and disappoint anyone. I want to protect my family but I don't know if I can. Cathy and James kind of know what's going on, but Rosy and Yvonne don't. How do you tell two little girls that their sister might die?"

Roberta stared intensely at Emily. Michella put an arm around her shoulders and Emily smiled at her gratefully.

"There's a lot to discuss and we have our work cut out for us, but for you, Emily it might be different," Roberta said. "Since Neci's announcement during the Dojo match, a group of warriors that support us have been attempting to follow her movements. We've been trying to figure out who this missing warrior is. When Neci was at large before, she never had a team of warriors fighting alongside her, so we don't have any idea of who she's looking for, but judging by the team she currently has, we know it will be someone very powerful with a rare hidden power. Someone who will definitely give her an edge."

"If she doesn't find the missing warrior, do you think she will still go to war?" Wesley asked.

Roberta shook her head. "Neci wants to win and she will not battle Thomas again unless she is absolutely certain that she will defeat him. Since that battle, Thomas's fame has soared, there are a lot of people, warriors and non-warriors, that will fight for him, but if Neci has a team of those with hidden powers . . . it will make our job much harder."

"What can the warriors on her team do?" Michella asked.

"We know Scarlett can create fire, Dion manipulates time, Maggie can heal and Lox has unlimited strength."

"That's some team," Michella said looking impressed. "What can our team do?"

"I have visions, Jenkins can create illusions and Thomas has unlimited strength."

Michella frowned. "Is that all we've got? But Thomas Knight isn't even here!"

Roberta smiled. "That's why we need to find more strong warriors with hidden powers. Lox is not with her at the moment, so he could be the missing warrior she's searching for, but the other night, Jenkins found a kids' TV channel that Neci and her warriors had hijacked. She sent out a message to you, Emily."

"To me?" Emily looked confused from Michella to Wesley. "What did she say?"

"She said she was giving you a way out."

"A way out?" Emily echoed.

"Neci said that she would find Lox and reunite you both without any harm, as long as you both promise not to get involved in the war."

"What about my dad?" Emily asked hopefully.

Roberta shook her head. "She would never let Thomas walk away. He's the only warrior to ever beat her."

"That doesn't make sense," Wesley said frowning. "I thought Emily was a main target?"

"That's what we all thought," Roberta said.

"So there's no way Lox could be the missing warrior if she's giving him a way out," Wesley said.

"But it's a trick, isn't it?" Michella said aggressively. "Neci wouldn't keep the kids of Thomas Knight alive! That would be stupid. Didn't she train Lox so that she could have him fight with her?"

Roberta pointed at Michella. "You're right, it would be stupid, but my theory is Neci is scared of what Emily can and will do. She fears Emily will have unlimited strength like Thomas and Lox and the three of them together could be deadly. She's offering a strange olive branch, using Lox to bribe Emily, but this woman can't be trusted. You're right, she did train Lox, so why would she suddenly be okay with him not fighting with her? At the same time, no one can make Emily fight in a war she doesn't want to be part of. Emily doesn't have to fight just because of whom she's related too. It's completely her choice."

The three of them turned to look at Emily, who was staring blankly into space.

Wesley gently nudged her. "Emily, were you listening?"

"Lox," Emily said, with a desperate look at Roberta. "Did she say anything about, Lox? Does she have any idea where he is?"

Roberta shook her head. "Only what I told you but Emily, Neci is not to be trusted. She's only out to kill, steal and destroy. When she attacked you in the forest, she didn't expect you to release the power that you did. It would make her job a lot easier if you weren't in the picture. Do you understand?"

"Yes," Emily said.

"I'm sure I know the answer, but I need to know that you are all on the Five Warriors team, and that we have your full support."

"I'm definitely team Five Warriors," Wesley said without hesitation.

"Me too," Michella said.

"Emily?" Roberta asked.

Emily looked down at her hands and sighed deeply. She knew that the Five Warriors was the right team, but what if Neci wasn't lying? What if this was a golden opportunity for her to be with her family? Emily looked up into Roberta's green eyes, and saw a wave of panic shoot through them.

"Five Warriors," Emily eventually said, and Roberta smiled beautifully.

"Obviously, my children, Xavier and Antonio are being

targeted as well . . . oh, look, there's Alice!" Roberta was pointing at a beautiful teenage girl on the television. She seemed to have modelled herself on Roberta with her full make up on her heart shaped face and big, tousled, almost white-blonde hair. She was talking directly to the camera.

"Ooh, I love this show," Michella said, reaching for the remote and turning up the volume.

Emily looked confused at everyone.

Wesley caught her expression. "It's *Life with Alice.* She's Cecil Archinia's granddaughter. Her reality show is huge."

"Don't you remember her?" Roberta asked, and Emily shook her head. "You used to play together, when you were little girls. Alice is only two years older than you."

". . . so unfortunately because of this whole Neci thing, my godmother, Roberta Taniana, thinks it's not cool to keep the show going," Alice drawled. She had a posh voice, but when she spoke, it came across with an 'I don't care' type of attitude. "It's been brill sharing my amazing life with you guys, and hopefully season four can start as soon as we win this war. Ciao for now!" Alice blew a kiss to the camera, and it went into the end credits.

"Oh—no more, Alice?" Michella asked, looking crestfallen.

"It's not safe with Neci being back. We had to pull the plug," Roberta explained. She stood up, and straightened out her black pencil skirt. Wesley stared transfixed at her smooth legs. "I just want to let you know that we are searching everywhere to find Neci's missing warrior before she does, and we're doing everything in our power to persuade warriors to fight with us. This time, we will make sure Neci is gone for good, and we can continue to co-exist with non-warriors in peace."

"Have you heard from my dad?" Emily asked.

"Thomas was in Bosnia a couple of days ago," Roberta explained. "We had a call saying that Lox was spotted in a village there, and your dad went to check it out. Thomas has spent many years making secure connections around the world. He was preparing for a time like now where we can use all the help we can get. Don't worry, Emily, he's coming home soon to see his favourite girl."

Roberta smiled at her and Emily couldn't help but smile back. The prospect of Lox and her father, all three of them together again was an excitement and happiness she hadn't felt in a long time.

"What will happen when we catch Neci?" Michella suddenly asked.

"We will kill her," Roberta said and Emily felt Michella tense up beside her. "Something I wished Thomas wasn't so noble about last time. I have to go, but thank you all for your time. Keep strong and keep your faith. We will win this war. Emily, do you mind walking me to the door?"

After Roberta had hugged Michella and autographed Wesley's arm, Emily and Roberta left the room.

"You have lovely friends. Keep them close to you."

"I will," Emily replied.

"Emily, do you trust me?" Roberta asked.

"Of course," Emily said automatically.

"I'll have to remind you of that because there may be a few surprises at Osaki. I have had a few visions this summer. I can't really make sense of them, but I saw you in every one, so I want to give you some advice. Niles's brother, Gabriel is joining the school this September. He's the complete opposite of Niles, and I need you to keep an eye on him for me. Alice is transferring to Osaki, but I think you should keep that to yourself, as Michella seems to be a big fan. And Emily, if something doesn't feel right, don't ignore it."

"Okay," Emily said uncertainly.

Roberta kissed Emily's cheeks and walked to her mansion next door. Emily closed the door, and leaned on it. She couldn't believe Neci was giving her a way out, but only if she didn't get involved. Emily sighed. *How can I not be involved if she's after Dad?*

"You okay?" Michella asked, walking up to her.

"Yeah . . . I just . . . let's go in the pool."

"The pool?" Michella frowned. "You hate swimming."

"But I need to tackle breathing under water, so no time like the present, right? Come on." Emily pulled on Michella's arm and led her downstairs.

"Emily, are you okay?"

Emily gulped down her glass of water and coughed heavily.

Wesley frowned at Michella. "I knew this was a bad idea. Does she look in the right state to be training?"

"Don't shout at me," Michella snapped. "She persisted, and fair enough, I should have realised she was under water for a long time, but I thought she was doing it!"

"Stop arguing," Emily croaked. "It's my fault, I wasn't focusing."

"But you passed your Water Studies exam, so you must have breathed under water?" Michella asked baffled.

Emily coughed. "I cheated. I just held my breath for a long time."

Wesley grabbed Emily's arms. Emily couldn't help noticing how the water from the pool was dripping down his toned torso. There was one drop that was travelling from his neck down to the middle of his chest. Emily felt a sudden urge to trace its journey with her finger.

"Hey," Wesley lifted her chin so their eyes were locked and Emily was grateful that Wesley wasn't telepathic. "There's enough time to train and get prepared. You don't have to start today, okay?" Defeated, Emily nodded. "I think you need a change of scenery. Let's fly to my house for a few hours. My nan makes the best lemon cake." Emily's eyes lit up and Wesley laughed. "I'll let her know we're coming."

CHAPTER TWO

The First Attack

"You found it?" Wesley asked.

"Not yet," Emily responded.

She couldn't believe how much post she had received. Ever since she had saved Lox from Neci, fan letters had been arriving at her house, and they were sprawled out on the floor around her, making it impossible to see the letters from Osaki. A picture of a beach stared back at her, and Emily picked it up to see Jason's neat handwriting, wishing her a happy birthday. She placed the postcard on top of the pile, and kept searching, until she found the letters from Osaki. One was information on the start of the new term and the other was about the Survival Training. Emily placed them on the dining room table for Sally. She spotted a small envelope that had her FLY card.

"Got it," Emily called, as she placed the letters into a messy pile on top of the nearest cabinet file.

"How long will it take you to get ready?" Michella asked, with a towel wrapped around her wet hair.

"Just give me ten minutes. Do me a favour and leave a note for Sally saying that I'm with you guys and I'll call her later."

Whilst Emily was in the shower, she thought about Gabriel Thompson and Alice Archinia, who would be joining Osaki. She wondered if they felt the same pressure she did, to live up to the Five Warriors' reputation. Emily frowned. Alice didn't look like the kind of girl to stress out about her powers. She was riding the Five Warriors' wave and creating a career out of it.

"Are you really going out like that?" Emily heard Michella say in a disapproving tone, when she walked down the stairs, dressed in denim shorts and a vest top.

Wesley was back in his jeans, with his red baseball cap placed backwards on his head, but he was still topless. Emily deliberately avoided looking at him.

"What? It's boiling outside!" he protested.

"Emily, are you seeing this?" Michella asked and Emily blushed.

"Let's just go," Emily said, quickly walking out of the door.

Michella raised her eyebrows and followed her.

Emily smiled when the sun hit her face. She sighed pleasantly and stretched out her arms. She didn't realise how much she had missed being outside. The village looked picturesque with its beautiful mansions and neat gardens.

"We better get a move on. Jenkins' illusion may have gone," Wesley pointed out.

They bent their knees and soared up into the air. Emily agreed with Wesley, it was very weird flying outside of the stadium at school, without the flying teacher, Ms Macay's watchful eye. Emily closed her eyes and felt a soft breeze hit her face. She forgot how good it felt to fly.

"You live next to Michella, right?" she asked Wesley.

"Just up the road." He grinned wickedly at her. "Race you?"

Emily laughed. "You're on."

Wesley shot ahead of her. Emily tensed her body, locked her arms to her torso and pressed her legs close together to increase her speed.

"Hey! Wait for me!" Michella called behind them.

They were flying so fast that everything seemed to merge into one. Wesley was just in front of her and Emily reached out and grabbed his foot. He turned around and Emily smiled innocently, before pulling him back. Wesley soared behind her whilst Emily flew ahead laughing loudly.

"I'll get you for that one, Emily!" Wesley shouted.

"If you can even catch me!" Emily yelled back. She flew head first into something solid. "Ouch," she said, rubbing her head. A man dressed in all white, with FLY printed across his shirt, stared at her coldly. "Sorry," she added.

Wesley and Michella appeared next to her. The man's eyes never left Emily. He was olive skinned with a sculptured face, and his black, wavy hair peeped out from under his white hat.

"FLY cards, please," he said, with a Cockney twang to his accent.

The three of them pulled out their cards and the man grabbed them. Emily opened her mouth to say something, but Michella held her arm, and shook her head.

"I'll be back in a moment," the man said before he teleported.

"Where the hell is he going?" Emily asked Michella.

"I don't know. I've never seen this happen before," Michella said anxiously.

"How do we know he hasn't just teleported to Neci?" Emily said, looking troubled.

"With our FLY cards? What would Neci do with that?" Wesley protested. "All it does is prove that we're allowed to fly."

"There's something off about him. He could be on her team!" Emily said.

The FLY man appeared in front of them, looking transparent. They watched him until he became solid again. This time he was smiling. "Sorry about that, guys. I had to take it to the chief. A lot of fake cards these days." He handed their cards back to them, but his brown eyes still hovered on Emily. "Where are you all heading?"

The three of them stayed silent. Emily hoped that no one was going to say a word.

"Just enjoying the weather," Michella said sweetly. "If that's all, can we continue with our journey?"

The man opened his mouth, then closed it. He eventually nodded, looking rather defeated, and the three of them flew off. Emily glanced back, and the man was staring after them.

"Weirdo," Wesley said. "This is exactly why we should learn to teleport in our first year. Let's get to mine quick, yeah?"

They flew in silence until Wesley shouted that they were almost there. A few minutes later they could see Wesley, Michella and Jason's neighbourhood. They dived and landed outside Wesley's front door. Emily couldn't help looking back up to the sky in case the FLY man had followed them, but it was clear, not even a cloud was in sight.

Wesley opened the door and Emily followed him into the living room. His house was smaller than Michella's, but what surprised Emily was how bare it was compared to her own home. It seemed like there were only the essentials in the living room. Two couches, a small television, and one coffee table. Wesley caught her looking around.

"My mum sold a lot of our stuff to pay for her alcohol . . . we never seem to get round to replacing it."

Emily nodded, and noticed above the TV, the only picture of Wesley and his family on the pretty, floral wallpaper. Wesley was sitting beside his mum, a beautiful black lady with long, dark dreadlocks and brown eyes and on the other side of his mum was Wesley's little sister, Cammie. She was mixed race with big hazel eyes and had long, curly, blonde hair.

"When is your mum coming back from rehab?" Emily asked.

"Very soon," Wesley said as he stood next to her, staring at the picture of his mother.

"Ah, Wesley, there you are," a lady with a faint Jamaican accent said.

Emily turned and saw a chubby lady, wearing a long, salmon coloured skirt and a white cardigan, walk slowly into the room. She had a short, grey Afro and round glasses.

"Hey Nan, you okay?" Wesley asked, as he greeted her with a kiss.

"Your sister is driving me mad! She's asking me for this new Dojo kit in pink. What does she need a pink Dojo kit for? Hmmm? The girl is only eight years old, and she's so demanding."

Wesley laughed. "Nan, this my friend, Emily Knight."

"Hello," Emily said, holding out her hand and Wesley's grandmother shook it.

"Ah, Thomas Knight's daughter? A fine man he is. It's nice to meet you, Emily, you just call me Nan everyone—," she stopped and stared at Wesley, as if seeing him for the first time. "Boy, where's your top?"

"Ah Nan, it's so hot, man."

"I don't care! You don't walk on road looking like that, bringing shame to my door." She walked out of the door and came back with a grey t-shirt. "Here, put this on. Michella, why did you let him come out like that?"

Michella shook her head. "He ignores me."

Nan tutted at Wesley, who smiled cheekily at her. "Michella, come help me get some lunch ready. I can't deal with these kids today."

Michella followed Nan into the kitchen while Wesley put his t-shirt on. A small, blonde-haired girl came into the room carrying drinks on a tray. She was walking very slowly, staring down at the drinks as if she was scared she would drop it. When she had almost reached the table, she looked up and saw Emily, who was sitting on the couch.

"Oh my gosh!" she screeched before she knocked over the tray and spilt juice all over the floor and Wesley.

"Cammie!"

"I'm so sorry, I'm so sorry—I'll get a cloth," she said before she ran out of the room with her face red.

"For goodness sake," Wesley muttered. He whipped off his top again, that now had orange juice stains over it.

Emily glanced at his toned torso and felt a small shiver that seemed to start in her stomach and travel through her body. When she realised that she was staring so obviously, she quickly looked away, but Wesley had seen her. A slow smile spread across his face. Emily surprised herself with how much she wanted to glance again at his muscular physique. Wesley walked towards her and bent down, so his face was level with hers.

"I'm flattered," he said.

"As if, Wesley," Emily scoffed, but even to her own ears it sounded forced.

Wesley continued to smile. His eyes never left hers and Emily couldn't help but stare back at him. She knew Wesley was cute, but now he seemed to have a different effect on her. Emily couldn't help thinking about the time they had held hands before her first Dojo match and the way her heart raced, like it was racing now. She wanted to feel more than just his hands. She wanted to know what it felt like to have his lips on hers. As if reading her mind, Wesley moved closer towards her and slowly, Emily did the same.

"I've got a towel. Cammie is in awe of Em—," Michella said, as Wesley jumped away from Emily. He looked down at the floor and rubbed the back of his neck with his hand. Emily suddenly looked interested at the soap opera playing on the TV.

Michella narrowed her eyes and looked from one to the other. "What's going on?"

"Nothing," Emily and Wesley said simultaneously.

"It kind of looked like you two were—"

"Doing nothing," Emily interrupted. She stood up abruptly. "I'm just getting some air." She walked out of the door, deliberately avoiding Wesley and Michella's eyes. When she was outside, she took a deep breath and sighed. She wasn't sure if she was happy or irritated that Michella had interrupted them. Kissing Wesley would change their friendship and she had no idea if it would be for the better.

Emily sat down on the bricked wall and kicked the back of her trainers against it.

"Hey!"

Emily looked up. A group of girls stormed towards her with hostile faces. Emily jumped off the wall quickly.

"You're Emily Knight, yeah?" one of the girls asked. She was white with short, brown hair and she was wearing jeans and a cropped top that showed off her flabby belly.

Emily noticed her hands were in fists. "Yeah," she said cautiously.

The girl grabbed Emily's top and pulled her roughly towards her. "My dad has been missing for a week now. He worked on Kids Net, one of the channels Neci hijacked, and that's all because your stupid dad is hiding."

"My dad isn't hiding," Emily said, annoyed. She pushed the girl off her, so she toppled back into her group of friends.

"Let me handle this, Zoë." A large black girl with streaked red hair smiled at Emily before she swung a punch at her. Emily grabbed the girl's fist and held it tight, crushing it. The girl screamed and dropped to her knees, begging Emily to let go. Zoë and her friends stared at Emily with their mouths open. They held up their hands as if surrendering and walked backwards.

"Anyone else want to have a go?" Emily hollered.

"Emily, stop!" Michella cried, running out of the house.

Emily let go of the girl, who crawled away, holding her fist and whimpering. Michella and Wesley appeared bedside her.

"This isn't over, Emily," Zoë said, helping her friend up from the ground.

"Yes, it is," Emily said, before she punched down into the

concrete and the ground heaved and rippled towards the girls, who fell over as the concrete moved under them.

"Stop it," Michella hissed. She grabbed Emily's arm and pulled her roughly towards the house. "What if the press were here? You can't afford to lose your rag every time—"

"What did you say?" Wesley asked. He was staring at the group of girls.

Emily and Michella turned around and the large girl who had tried to punch Emily was struggling to her feet, as her friends were still on the ground.

"I said . . . they say she's meant to be the good one." She pointed an accusing finger at Emily.

"Come on," Michella said, hustling Emily inside before she could react. Michella slammed the door behind them and stared at Emily accusingly. "You were out of line."

"Excuse me?" Emily said, breathing hard. "Those dumb girls tried to attack me while I was minding my own business. If you think I'm going to sit there and take their insults then you obviously don't know me that well."

"But she was right, you're meant to be the good one. You're the only Knight around. People are looking at you for some hope," Michella said.

"I didn't ask for this!" Emily snapped, before she stormed into the living room.

Emily, Wesley, and Michella ate their lunch in silence. Nan didn't seem to notice as she was humming to herself.

Cammie looked at the stony faces of her brother, Emily and Michella and asked in a small voice, "Is everything okay?"

"Yeah, Cam," Wesley responded, forcing a smile. "Nan, lunch tastes great, thanks."

47

"You're welcome, child. You know today when I woke up, I was thinking what should I cook today? And . . ."

Emily tuned out of what Nan was saying and instead thought of the hostility of the girls. *How many people will be like that? How many times will I have to take the fall for Lox and my dad?*

". . . but I think my favourite one is Tahama Kena. Ooh that girl is beautiful."

"Tahama Kena?" Emily asked, looking at Nan.

"Yes, child. Lorraine, their mum, was an artist. She used to do portraits of people, sometimes celebrities. I was saying my favourite portrait was of Tahama Kena, Tainwo Kena's daughter. Lorraine used to love watching her battle." Nan pulled a distasteful face. "Their father used to take her to watch."

"Is Tahama Julian Kena's mum?" Emily asked Wesley.

"Yes," Wesley said sharply, staring at his food.

"I wonder why no one makes a big fuss of Julian? He has a famous family," Emily said.

"I think enough girls fuss over Julian," Michella said and Emily raised her eyebrows, surprised. Michella knew that she fancied Julian. Michella noticed and covered her mouth. "Sorry, I wasn't having a dig."

"Well Tahama and Tainwo Kena are great, but they're nothing on your dad," Wesley explained, looking up at Emily. "I mean, Thomas Knight is the biggest celebrity in the world. It's on another level."

"But Tainwo Kena created light beams," Cammie chipped in.

"Thomas beat Neci and leads the Five Warriors," Wesley replied. "It's not the same."

"Have you got the picture?" Emily asked intrigued.

Nan laughed. "Oh no, it's in one of them art museums. All the rest of Lorraine's stuff is in storage. She used to sell the pictures to fund her drinking habit, so we moved them out of the house. When the kids are older, they can take them."

As Nan and Cammie cleared the table, she heard Wesley cough loudly. Emily looked up and he was staring at Michella, talking to her with his eyes and nodding his head towards Emily.

"I'm sorry," Michella eventually said to Emily. "I wasn't thinking about how difficult this is for you, and you're right— you didn't ask to be a poster girl, so why should you be? If a girl swung for me on the street, I would defend myself too."

Emily smiled. "Thank you."

Wesley sighed dramatically. "Finally! The world is balanced again. Can we go to yours, Mich? We'll take some of Nan's cake with us."

"Yeah sure," Michella said, pushing back her chair. "I think Janette might be home and Emily you can finally meet my dad."

"Oh cool, just give me a second," Emily said, running from the table.

She found Cammie in the kitchen, washing her hands at the sink. Emily tapped her on the shoulder and when Cammie turned around, she gave her a big hug. Cammie squealed and squeezed her back.

"Oh my gosh, I can't believe you just hugged me!"

Emily laughed. "Why don't you come with us to Michella's? You can see the twins."

"Yeah, that sounds good," Cammie smiled. "I'll just tell Nan."

The streets were empty when they left Wesley's house.

Nevertheless, they kept vigilant as they walked the short distance to Michella's. Michella opened the door and some of the Kinkles were relaxing in the living room with the television playing in the background. The eight-year-old twins, Mike and Madison, ran up to Emily, hugging her excitedly before dragging Cammie up to their room.

The eldest Kinkle, Janette, was sitting on the sofa in a blue dress that showed off her tattooed arms. She played professional Dojo for the London Flyaways and England.

Dojo is an aggressive, fast-paced fighting game, where each team has to battle each other over five rounds. It was normal to leave the stadium with a broken bone or a concussion. A team can only win if they defeat all the Fighters on the opposite team. The Distracters are usually female and they have to distract the other team by attacking them. Fighters aren't allowed to hit Distracters. Janette is the lead Distracter for her teams and she is arguably the most unconventional Distracter because she uses her tattoo-covered body to distract her opponents.

Janette was sitting beside Lenny and they had a bunch of official looking forms between them.

"Hey," Michella called.

Lenny and Janette looked up and Janette beamed when she saw them. "Hi guys! Wesley, Emily, how are you?"

"Good thanks," Emily said.

Wesley opened the tissue that his cake was wrapped in and offered some to Lenny and Janette.

Lenny tapped his stomach. "I'm in training," he said.

At the same time, Janette said, "Yum, yes please."

"Aren't you the Dojo star?" Wesley teased. "Why are you allowed to have cake and not Lenny?"

Janette placed a manicured finger in the icing, scooped it up and put it in her mouth. "Didn't you know I'm a rebel? Besides, Lenny is training to be a future Dojo star himself. Keeping it in the family."

"What do you mean?" Emily asked in between bites of her cake.

"He has got a trial next year to play for the London Flyaways," Janette announced proudly, with one arm around Lenny's shoulders.

Emily almost dropped her cake. "You're leaving Osaki?"

Lenny nodded. "This is my last year."

"Oh," Emily said disappointed that Lenny wouldn't be her Dojo captain anymore.

"Aren't you scared to audition?" Wesley asked.

"He's got to fly off sometime," Janette said before Lenny could respond. "Have I ever told you guys the story of the eagle tattoo on my back?"

"Not this again," Michella sighed.

"I'm out," Lenny said. He stood up and left the room.

"I've only said it twice!" Janette said. "Anyway, the reason why I got the eagle tattooed on my back is because of what it signifies." Emily and Wesley exchanged confused glances and Janette rolled her eyes. "Come on, it represents courage and strength. If Lenny, or any of you want to achieve anything great, you have got to think you're an eagle."

"There was me thinking I was a warrior," Wesley whispered to Emily who laughed.

Janette gathered the forms into a neat pile looking unfazed. "You'll understand it one day."

"Hi Emily, Wesley, any news on Thomas?" Michella's

brothers, Warren and Pete walked into the living room. Michella elbowed Warren hard in his stomach, making him double over.

"What? I was just asking!" Warren said, rubbing his stomach.

"No, nothing yet," Emily responded.

"Ignore them. Let me introduce you to my dad," Michella said, grabbing Emily's hand whilst shooting Warren and Pete a dirty look.

Emily followed Michella up the stairs and to a room next to the bathroom. Michella knocked on the door then opened it. It was a small, cream room, with a light brown carpet and a white sofa. Next to the window was a computer and a man was sitting at it, staring at the screen through his glasses.

"Hey, Dad," Michella called.

Mr Kinkle looked over. He took off his glasses and smiled. He stood up from the chair and Emily was surprised to see how tall he was. He had dark brown skin and a shaved head. He had a neatly trimmed black goatee and the whitest teeth Emily had seen.

"Hi girls, you must be Emily Knight? I've heard a lot about you," Mr Kinkle said, holding out his hand, which Emily shook. He had a nice entrancing voice. A radio voice, as Sally would describe it.

"What are you working on?" Michella asked, peering at the computer screen.

"Oh, just a proposition letter for a new training school in Mexico."

"Mexico?" Emily said, surprised. She never thought about training schools in other countries.

"Dad manages a company that builds training schools," Michella explained, sitting down on her father's chair.

"Figured I've got to fit in somehow with all the warriors in this house," Mr Kinkle said, winking at Michella, who giggled.

Emily couldn't hide her surprise. "You're not a warrior?"

Mr Kinkle shook his head. "The kids got their warrior gene from their mother, although we've still got to see who Mike and Madison take after. But I always wanted to be one. I used to love watching your dad compete at the warrior tournaments. His speed, power, charisma—he knew how to work a crowd. He had so much energy and passion that would fill up the stadium. The crowd would be chanting his name and if his opponent hit him, they would boo and throw food on the battle floor. He could battle against twenty warriors and he would still look like he hadn't broken a sweat. I hear you're pretty powerful too?"

"I'm okay," Emily said.

Michella scoffed. "She's more than okay."

"So how are you feeling about Neci's threat of a war?"

"Dad," Michella said sharply, standing up. "Emily didn't come over here to talk about that."

Emily smiled gratefully at her.

"Sorry," Mr Kinkle said. He bent down and kissed Michella's hair. She looked up at him adoringly. Emily looked away wishing she had her father to share these gestures with.

"See you in a bit," Michella said, grabbing Emily's hand and leading her out of the door. Emily waved at Mr Kinkle and closed the door behind her.

"Your dad's really nice," Emily said.

"Yeah, he's great, but what was that with you and Wesley earlier?" Michella asked, as they walked down the stairs.

"Nothing," Emily said, avoiding her gaze.

"Really?" Michella said, sounding unconvinced. "Do you think he's cute?"

Emily shrugged. "Yeah, I guess . . . I don't know."

"But you still like Julian Kena?" Michella asked frowning.

Julian Kena was a student at Osaki and Emily had fancied him from the first time that she saw him. The most interaction she had had with Julian was beating him in her first Dojo match at school. She hoped this year she would actually get to have a full conversation with him.

"Your dad builds training schools? Tell me more," Emily said, linking arms with Michella, who laughed.

"Okay, okay, I get the hint. We'll talk about it later," Michella said. She glanced at Emily. "But I will be watching you and Wesley closely."

The Kinkles, Emily and Wesley spent the rest of the evening watching a comedy and eating bowls of popcorn. Emily fell asleep on the couch, halfway through the film.

"Where is our Knight to save us all?" a woman's high-pitched voice rang loudly in Emily's ear. She slowly opened her eyes and saw the Kinkles surrounding the television screen that showed a house covered in fire. Emily shot up in her seat and gasped. The Kinkles looked at her and then looked back at the screen. A bulletin reading 'Five Warrior's house burnt down' flashed quickly across the television. Emily's heart stopped.

"Whose house is it?" Emily demanded.

"Niles Thompson's," Michella replied desolately. "His brother, Gabriel is still in there."

"What?" Emily cried, running towards the television.

Her eyes darted to and fro searching for Niles's brother. She spotted a couple clutching each other tightly. The woman was screaming as if in agony and was reaching out towards the house, suggesting that she wanted to go inside.

"That's his parents," Lenny said.

Emily threw her hand to her mouth and shook her head. "Do you think it was Neci and her lot?"

"Who else?" Lenny replied sadly.

Emily watched in dismay as the firefighters hosed down the aggressive flames. The police were stopping people from entering the house by creating a human wall around it.

"Those people aren't even warriors! Where are the bloody warriors?" Warren shouted at the screen.

"There has been no sign of Gabriel Thompson, the younger brother of Five Warriors legend, Niles Thompson," the high-pitched news announcer said. "What we need are some warriors to come . . . is that? Roberta Taniana and Jenkins are flying towards us, right now, as I speak."

"Oh, thank God," Mrs Kinkle said, putting her hands on her racing chest. Mr Kinkle had his arm around her and Madison leaned over to them. Mrs Kinkle kissed her on the forehead and hugged her tight.

Emily held her breath as Jenkins flew straight through the third storey window, leaving broken glass behind him. Roberta took two hoses from the fire brigade and flew swiftly around the top of the house. The fire began to burn out and a couple of minutes later, the fire had gone. The crowd cheered loudly as Roberta flew down to Niles's parents and hugged them tight. They all looked up to the third storey window.

A moment later, Jenkins flew back out of the house with an unconscious Gabriel Thompson in his arms. The crowd cheered even louder when Jenkins landed and gave Gabriel to a member of the ambulance team, who strapped him onto a stretcher. Gabriel's parents ran over to him as Roberta kissed Jenkins.

Emily finally breathed again.

"And there you have it. The Five Warriors once again saved the day from a suspicious attack by Neci. But it still beckons the question, where is Thomas Knight? This is Saundra Dawson, over to you, Jeremy."

The television screen went black. Pete pressed numerous buttons on the remote control, but nothing happened.

"Check the batteries, maybe they're dead?" Mike suggested.

Pete pressed another button and the screen changed to a music channel, but when he went back to the news channel, it was still black.

"What is going on?" Michella asked, as the screen flickered and a message flashed on to the screen in big, bold, white letters, 'PROPERTY OF NECI'.

"Are they serious? Are they just going to hijack everything?" Lenny protested.

Madison screamed. Emily looked away in shock and disgust. The picture had gone back to the news studio and there were bodies scattered over the floor, all of them dead. In the centre, were the news reporters tied together with thick ropes and scarves wrapped around their mouths, so they couldn't speak. Their faces were streaked with tears and blood. They looked pleadingly into the camera. Manic laughter was heard in the background as the handheld camera swayed slightly and then the screen went black again.

The Kinkle household was silent, the only noises coming from Madison who was crying in her mother's arms. Cammie ran across the room to Wesley, who hugged her tight. Wesley and Mrs Kinkle were reassuring them that everything was going to be all right. Emily didn't realise that she had been squeezing her own arm tight, but when she released it, there were nail imprints in her skin.

CHAPTER THREE

Home

Emily awoke to the smell of fried bacon. She rubbed her eyes as she sat up in Michella's bed. Sally had called her a few minutes after the footage of the captured news reporters, asking her if she was okay. Emily was lost for words and had no idea how to process what she had seen. She wanted to cry, throw up and have a hug all at the same time.

"Stay with Michella and let me know when you want to come home," Sally said hurriedly. "Emily, I know that was horrible what they showed tonight but I can't have you retreating back to your room. Roberta said you seemed okay today? Do you feel a bit better?"

"Yeah," Emily said quietly. "It helped seeing my friends."

"Okay sweetie, you call me if you need me. Give the phone to Michella's mum. I love you."

"Love you too," Emily said before she went to call Mrs Kinkle.

For the past two nights, since the fire at Gabriel Thompson's house, Emily had stayed up late to see how many channels had been hijacked by Neci and so far, she had found eight channels. The media had taken the slogan, 'Where is our Knight?' and it had trended worldwide. Emily was also beginning to wonder why her father was still absent. She had come face to face with Neci who had announced to the world that she wants to go to war. *What else needed to happen for him to return home?*

No one knew what had happened to the news reporters who were tied up at the studio. Supportive warriors had broken into the news studio to rescue the captives, but it was deserted, even the dead bodies were gone. They didn't have a clue where Neci was.

"Bye everyone," Mr Kinkle called from downstairs before he shut the front door and Michella jumped up awake.

In a few hours, Mrs Kinkle was taking Emily and Michella to get their camping gear for their Survival Training trip.

"Breakfast!" Mrs Kinkle hollered.

"Why is everyone so loud this morning?" Michella groaned, holding her head in her hands.

By the time Emily and Michella were dressed and went downstairs, all of the Kinkle kids, except Janette, were at the kitchen table. Emily took a seat and Mrs Kinkle placed a stack of blueberry pancakes, sausages and bacon in front of her.

"I hope none of you have plans for today because we have to collect your school things," Mrs Kinkle said.

Pete and Warren glanced at each other. Pete gave Warren an encouraging nod.

"Err . . . Mum, can me and Pete–"

"No," Mrs Kinkle interrupted, as she put away the clean pots in the cupboard.

"But you didn't hear me out!" Warren protested.

"If the question has anything do with animals, fireworks, anything you know I'm going to say no to, but you're asking me anyway, hoping I'm going to say yes, but I promise you, Warren, the answer will be no."

Warren looked helplessly at Pete.

"No, Mum it's nothing like that," Pete said smiling charmingly. "It's actually . . . err . . . a present. Yeah, a present for Nicholas at school. We just want money to get him something. It is the big 1-6."

Mrs Kinkle narrowed her eyes. "If you're lying, Pete—"

"We're not, we just want to get him a present. Innit, Warren?"

Warren nodded. Emily saw that he had crossed his fingers behind his back.

After breakfast, they drove to Sia's Avenue, which was covered in cobbled roads and was popular for its fancy restaurants and vintage shops. When everyone had evacuated the car, Mrs Kinkle gave Pete extra money towards Nicholas's present, which he took eagerly.

"I better see a receipt!" Mrs Kinkle shouted after them. She turned to Emily and Michella. "Why don't you two go and get some ice-cream from Shake City? I can get your camping bits."

"Thanks, Mum," Michella said. Mrs Kinkle handed Michella some pound coins.

"We'll be back in half an hour," Mrs Kinkle promised.

They watched Mrs Kinkle walk off with Mike and Madison by her side. Emily and Michella walked the opposite way and Emily tucked her hair back and pulled her baseball cap low over her face.

"You are fighting for our side, aren't you?" Michella demanded.

"What?" Emily said off-guard. "Of course I am." When Michella still looked sceptical, Emily added, "I know I hesitated, but after the fire at Niles's house and the hijacking . . . I mean, they're serious about this, aren't they?"

Michella nodded. "She's been gone for years. I dread to think how much stronger she is."

They reached Shake City and it was noisy and crowded with children. Emily fidgeted with her hat, pulling it down even lower.

"You wait here and I'll get the ice-creams," Michella suggested. "What flavour do you want?"

"Whatever you get," Emily said.

Michella went inside and Emily leaned against the wall, keeping her head down.

A few minutes later, Michella handed her a cone with four massive scoops of chocolate ice cream with caramel sauce and sprinkles.

"This looks amazing," Emily said before she licked it and grinned. "It's so good."

"I know, it's the best," Michella said. "I never come to Sia's Avenue without getting one."

They walked slowly back to the car. Emily looked around at the families that were walking down the cobbled streets. A group of girls walked past them, with their arms linked and they were laughing and talking loudly.

"So many people are going to get murdered," Emily said sadly. "But for what? Just to be number one again?"

"She was the best before the Five Warriors came along."

"So everyone that's a threat to her has two options—to die, or fight for her?"

Michella shrugged. "I think Lox is the one you really need to talk to. He must know Neci's plans."

They were silent again.

Emily was fighting herself, trying to stop her mouth from saying the words she secretly feared. "What if she wins?" They stopped and locked eyes and Emily saw the same fear she felt reflected in Michella's eyes. "What if she kills my dad?"

Michella blinked and whatever uncertainty she felt seemed to have disappeared. "She won't win," Michella said confidently. "He's Thomas Knight! If he beat her once, he can do it again."

Mrs Kinkle was true to her word. She arrived back thirty minutes later and bit by bit the other Kinkles returned to the car. Emily was gazing out of the window, up at the clear sky, thinking about Neci. She remembered how strong her presence was. Emily had used most of her power to create a fireball but Neci had swatted it away easily, like it was nothing. Emily shuddered at the memory. Something heavy bumped into her leg.

"Sorry, Emily," Pete said, sitting down at the back of the car, carrying a black rucksack that he didn't have before. Mike looked at it and edged closer towards Pete.

"That stinks," Mike exclaimed. He moved back sharply and pinched his nose. "What's in there?"

"Your head if you don't move," Pete said menacingly. Mike huffed and turned away from him.

Warren was entertaining them all with a joke book he had brought from Bonkers and Madison was passing around a packet of Macnocs' famous liquorice, which had her beautiful face plastered across it.

"Is that the best part? Being the face of Macnocs?" Emily asked, taking a piece of liquorice.

"No way," Madison said. "It's all the free sweets!"

"Hey, Mikey," Emily heard Pete whisper behind her. "Come here, let me show you something?"

Mike grinned and looked at the bag eagerly. Pete picked up the rucksack and went to open it. Warren spotted Emily watching them curiously.

"Now, now Emily, wait your turn," Warren said in a singsong voice, wagging his finger mockingly at her.

Emily reluctantly turned around. She heard the zip moving across the bag.

"AAAAHHHH!" Mike screamed.

Pete zipped up the bag and dropped it quickly on the floor. Everyone fell silent and looked at Mike.

"Michael Sean Kinkle! What in heaven's name are you screaming about?" Mrs Kinkle shouted angrily from the driver's seat, glaring at him from the rear view mirror.

"They have a—" Mike stopped suddenly. His face transformed from petrified to pain. Emily saw Pete twisting Mike's wrist. "They have a really great present," he finished lamely.

The summer holidays rolled by quickly and before Emily knew it, it was the last night before she would return to the Osaki Training School. Sally was elated that Emily was no longer confined to her room and as a special treat for the children, she had hired a chef to cook them a feast for dinner. Sally had suggested cooking herself until all the kids imitated throwing up and she swiftly changed her mind.

Emily was sitting opposite her counsellor, Jenny Li, in one of the many rooms in the house. It was empty apart from two comfy beige armchairs and a bookshelf in the corner. Jenny was sitting in an armchair with her legs crossed. Her red floral dress was hanging over her knees and she was writing down notes in Emily's file. Her long, dark hair was hiding her face. Emily had been counselled by Jenny for years and she loved and hated her sessions. Sometimes there was so much she had to say that she would feel frustrated when their time ran out and other times, she wished Jenny would stop forcing her to talk.

Emily glanced at the clock. An hour had almost passed.

"Okay, Em, last question. If you could ask Lox anything, what would it be?"

Emily hesitated. "I guess I'd want to know who he would fight for."

Jenny nodded and chewed on the pen lid. "Do you believe he would pick Neci over you?"

Emily shrugged her shoulders. "I can't work him out. He plots with Neci to recruit me, and because I refused, he was supposed to kill me, but he doesn't. Then he kidnaps me because Neci told him to and then warns me at the last minute that she's coming to hurt me. Now he's gone again and I don't know if . . ."

Jenny leaned forward with the pen lid now in her hand. "What is it?"

"I don't know if *he's* the missing warrior Neci is talking

about. One—he is missing, two—he has a hidden power and three—Neci trained him to fight Dad."

Jenny put down Emily's file on the floor and placed her pale hands on her lap. "Emily, do you really believe your own brother would join a war that could kill you and Thomas? You're his only living family."

Emily threw up her hands in exasperation. "The problem is Jenny, I don't even think Lox knows what he's doing. Maybe he's the missing warrior and is staying away to prevent the war from happening, but he did train with Neci because he *wanted* to fight Dad. You didn't hear the way he spoke about Dad. It was so hateful. I just want to understand where his brain is at."

"Don't give up hope," Jenny said, clasping her hands together. "Lox came through for you before. Don't write him off just yet."

Dinner that evening was perfect. The chef made all their favourite things. There was coq au vin for Sally and Michael, carbonara for Emily and Cathy and wedges and burgers for the younger kids. For afters, there was homemade vanilla ice cream with a chocolate fondant. It was the happiest Emily had felt all summer.

Cathy came into Emily's room as she was packing her school bag for the morning. She jumped on to her four-poster bed. "I can't believe they're making you go camping." She peered at the rolled up tent. "If my school made me do that, I would go mental."

"Lucky for you, you're not a warrior and you're not forced to do annoying stuff like this. I'm so not looking forward to it," Emily said sighing. She stopped packing and stretched out her neck from side to side. "Cath, have you ever heard of Alice Archinia?"

Cathy's eyes widened. "Alice Archinia? From *Life with Alice?* Duh, everyone knows who she is. She has like millions of followers."

"Well, she's coming to my school."

Cathy's mouth dropped. "Shut up."

Emily laughed. "I'm being serious. I know I don't know her, but she seems so . . ."

"Superficial?" Cathy suggested and Emily nodded. "Yeah she is, but that's why everyone loves her. She's pretty and rich and she tells everyone that she is. Not everyone is like you and is resentful of their status. She's a warrior, right?" Emily nodded again and Cathy laughed. "Oh my gosh, I need to see her battle. What will she do when her nail breaks?"

Emily tutted. "Neci is not going to care how pretty she is before she kills her."

Cathy reached out and grabbed Emily's hand and Emily looked at her surprised. "Thomas will come back. He will not let a war happen, I know it."

Emily shook her head. "To be honest Cathy, I don't know anymore."

"Well, I do," Cathy said confidently. She suddenly smirked. "How's Wesley?"

"Why?" Emily asked too quickly, thinking of the last time they had hung out together and she couldn't stop staring at him and thinking, *has he always been so hot?*

Cathy threw her head back and laughed. "Emily, you are so transparent, it's ridiculous."

Emily's face turned red and ignoring Cathy's gaze, she continued to pack her bag.

That night, Emily fell asleep as soon as her head touched the pillow. She shivered in her sleep and pulled up the covers, but the air around her seemed to feel cold, icy even. Emily sat up and opened her eyes. She whipped back the curtain around her four-poster bed and looked at her closed windows. For a split second, Emily was sure that she had felt something. An energy she had never sensed before. She looked around the dark room, but only Cathy was there. Emily wrapped the duvet around her like a cocoon, and snuggled next to Cathy. She closed her eyes, but she couldn't get back to sleep.

Emily was staring into the mirror, looking at her tired, light brown eyes. She buttoned up the last gold 'O' inscribed button on her school uniform. She brushed her hair out with her fingers as she searched for her hairbrush, which she eventually found on top of her school bag. She picked it up and began to brush her long, dark hair.

"Emily?" Sally was standing at the door with fear in her grey eyes. "Come with me."

Emily dropped the brush and followed Sally downstairs. Cathy was standing in front of the television, but she moved out of the way, so Emily could see. On the television was a motorway that was congested with cars. Angry, frustrated drivers were honking their horns, swearing and shouting at one another. Some of them were standing with half their bodies out of the car using rude hand gestures.

"What's going on?" Emily asked confused.

"Neci's lot have blocked up the motorway and they're not letting anyone through unless they accept the chip they're injecting into people, that proves they support Neci," Cathy explained.

"How does that prove anything?" Emily asked.

"Look," Cathy said. She pointed at Maggie, a short, frog-eyed woman and Dion, who had a black Mohican, that Emily had met that night in the forest. They were holding some form of device that they were scanning on people's arms. When a red light appeared on the device, they would let those people through. "What else is she going to block off?"

"This is unbelievable. Why are they still in their cars? They need to leave," Emily said.

"Look at the ones that tried," Cathy said.

Emily gasped when she noticed the people lying face down on the road. Emily wasn't sure if they were dead or alive.

"A bit of a coincidence they do this on the first day back to school," Sally said furiously.

"What are we meant to do? Should I fly to school?" Emily asked in a shrill voice. She had no idea how to get to Osaki if she flew.

"No, she probably has warriors in the skies," Sally said marching to the television and pulling the plug out from the back. Cathy and Emily silently watched her as she put on her coat over her oversized shirt and leggings and placed her handbag on her shoulder. "We're going to Osaki right now."

"But how are we—" Emily started before she was interrupted.

"Mummy, what's for breakfast?" Yvonne Saunders asked, still wearing her flower print pyjamas. Her Afro hair was coming out of its bun.

Sally stroked Yvonne's face gently. "Cathy, please watch the kids. I'll be home in a few hours."

"Okay," Cathy said, grabbing Yvonne's hand and hurrying her out of the living room.

Emily hadn't seen Sally look this fierce in a long time.

"If that evil cow thinks this will stop you from getting to school, she is messing with the wrong woman. Let's go."

Emily quickly ran up the stairs, grabbed her stuff, hurried back down and followed Sally out the door. She automatically ducked her head as the paparazzi snapped endless pictures and called out to Emily to turn towards them.

"How are you getting to Osaki?"

"Neci has blocked the roads!"

"Where's Thomas?"

"GET OUT OF THE WAY!" Sally roared.

The press fell silent for a few seconds before they went back to snapping pictures. Emily quickly shut the car door. She buckled her seat belt and Sally moved the car off so fast that Emily feared she would run over the paparazzi, but they managed to jump out of the way.

"Are we going to the bus station?"

"No, I'm going to take a different route and get you to school. Put the radio on for me. I want to hear the updates."

Emily fiddled with the radio, trying to find the right station. Out of habit, she glanced out of the side mirror to check for the press, but instead she saw a sleek, black car behind them. Emily stared intensely in the mirror and a familiar woman with red hair was staring hungrily back at her.

"Sally," Emily said slowly. "We're being followed."

"What?" Sally screeched. "Are you sure?"

Emily nodded. "Her name is Scarlett. She was there with Neci that night."

"Oh my gosh, oh my gosh," Sally said, looking at the car through her mirror. She brushed her brown hair out of her eyes. "We'll have to try and lose them." Sally accelerated and swerved in and out of the traffic, overtaking drivers who beeped their horns angrily at her, but the black car stayed on their trail.

"They're still there!" Emily said.

"Hold on!"

Emily held on to her seat, as Sally accelerated so fast that everything seemed to merge into a blur. CRASH. A fireball shattered the back window into a hundred pieces. Emily and Sally ducked as the glass sprayed on them. A truck honked, coming directly at them and Sally swerved just in time that they avoided a collision.

Emily unbuckled her seat belt and began to climb over the passenger seat.

"Emily, leave it!" Sally screamed, using one hand to pull her back.

Emily brushed her hand off and sat on her knees on the back seat. Scarlett blew a kiss at her. Emily shot fireballs at the front tyres and she caught Scarlett's shocked face before the front tyres blew up and the car span wildly.

"Yes, yes, Roberta—we need you right now!" Sally screamed into her phone.

A vision in black flew out of the driver's seat and Scarlett hovered in the air. In her hands, a red fireball was slowly growing bigger. Emily went to fly out, but she felt someone jerk her back by her leg.

"Oh no you don't!"

Roberta Taniana pushed Emily back into the car and flew up to Scarlett. Scarlett shot her fireball at Roberta who caught it and threw it back with such force, that it hit Scarlett in her stomach, making her recoil, so all Emily could see was red hair and smoke.

Roberta flew back to the car, held out her hand and Emily grabbed it. Sally, the car and the road faded away. Emily shut her eyes tight and held on to Roberta. Everything felt light as if she was floating. She landed hard on solid ground and when she opened her eyes, she was standing in front of the Osaki Training School. She breathed a sigh of relief when she saw the familiar tall, white, five-floored building. Roberta squeezed her hand and smiled at her.

"I'm going to sort out Sally. See you in a bit," Roberta promised, before she teleported.

All around her, people were teleporting on to the school grounds. Everyone seemed to be arriving with an adult. It was clear by everyone's faces that they were shaken up.

"Emily!"

Wesley and Michella broke away from the Kinkles and grabbed her in a tight hug.

"How crazy was that?" Michella said. "Are you okay? How did you get here?"

"We got followed and Aunt Roberta came and helped us out."

"You were followed?" Wesley asked in disbelief. "Where's Roberta now?"

"I think she's taking Sally home. I don't know what would have happened if she didn't come."

"Who was it?" Wesley asked.

"Scarlett. She fights for Neci," Emily said. She felt sick that she was that close to Scarlett again.

The two wide front doors opened and the deputy headmaster, Laton Chin, came out wearing a cream-coloured training kit. He did not seem the least bit surprised that there were students and parents standing on the school grounds hours before their arrival time. The talking stopped instantly when they saw him. Laton Chin stepped aside, encouraging them to go into the dining hall.

"Are you okay, love?" Mrs Kinkle asked Emily, hugging her tight. "You look drained."

"I've felt better," Emily confessed.

Mrs Kinkle led the way into Osaki carrying Michella's suitcase. Emily could feel hundreds of eyes staring at her and she deliberately looked down at the floor as she walked in. When she had sat down, Emily looked around anxiously for a blond-haired boy, but she couldn't find him.

"No Jason," she said to Wesley and Michella, who were also scanning the room.

"I hope he'll be okay getting to school," Michella said looking anxious.

"His parents are warriors, he'll be fine," Wesley said, squeezing her arm.

Emily was sitting next to Warren Kinkle, who was tapping his foot impatiently. "I can't see Summer anywhere," he said, looking for his girlfriend and Dojo team mate, Summer Wind.

The dining hall doors burst open and Mr Davon, the

headmaster of the school, walked confidently down the aisle and stood at the front of the hall. He waited patiently until he had captured everyone's attention. His midnight blue training kit made his blue eyes look brighter than usual.

"Thank you all for bringing your children back to Osaki. It has become clear that Neci intended for all warrior students to not return to their training schools, through the fear and disruption she has caused throughout the summer, as well as this morning," Mr Davon said, looking grave. "As well as the roads, Neci and her team were in the sky blocking warriors from travelling unless they accepted the chips in their arms. Please do not be alarmed at the missing students. There are some who made it to St Bertudes and are safe on the coach, which is taking a less dangerous route and has the best warriors chaperoning it. They should all be here by late afternoon. Others will still be teleporting on to the grounds, which is being guarded by the teachers, but please note that there are a few who may not come back." Emily felt her insides tighten. "There are some who may have been captured by Neci, or may have joined her side."

"Are we safe here, sir?" Warren Kinkle asked. "I mean, Neci won't come here again, will she?"

"Neci teleported into the forest at the end of last term and not into Osaki, Mr Kinkle. We have the strongest warriors that teach at this school, who are on high alert, for any intruders. Everyone is safe at Osaki. On a happier note, breakfast will be served soon, so please remain in the dining hall. Parents, thank you and you're welcome to stay."

Mr Davon smiled and walked back down the aisle. The dining hall doors stayed open after he left, so every few minutes people would turn to look at the doors to see if anyone they knew and loved had arrived safely.

Students arrived frequently on to the school grounds. A chubby, dark skinned girl, Ola Ade and a horse-faced brunette, Fiona Corn, were seated on the far side of the dining hall. Their parents had left them as soon as they had arrived and they were huddled together, staring transfixed at the oak doors.

Emily was surprised to see Tanya Frank walk into the dining hall a few minutes later. Her dark hair was pulled into a tight ponytail and it swung as she walked. Tanya caught Emily's eye and for once, Tanya didn't greet her with a dirty look. Ola and Fiona ran up to her and hugged her tight.

"I was convinced she would have ran over to Neci," Michella said, watching Tanya.

"There he is!" Wesley exclaimed loudly.

Emily spun around and saw an effortlessly handsome, sun-streaked, blond haired boy with a dark tan standing at the entrance of the dining hall in between a round lady with bouncy, blonde hair and a dark-haired, lean figured man, who Jason resembled. Jason's dad looked over at them and waved. He nudged Jason, who broke into a big smile and ran towards them.

"I'm so glad you're here," Michella said, devouring him in a big hug.

"Where else would I be?" Jason asked laughing, holding her tight.

He hugged Wesley next, slapping his back and ruffling his hair and then he hugged Emily. Emily couldn't help but notice that over the summer, Jason had grown taller and muscular. She also noticed that a lot of the girls in the dining hall were looking over at him with interest. Emily raised her eyebrows when Tanya Frank let her hair loose and flicked it over her shoulder as she watched Jason. He brushed his long fringe out of his deep blue eyes and stared at Emily.

"You look a bit off colour. Rough night?"

Emily nudged him. "More like a rough summer."

"Dude, how was France?" Wesley asked eagerly. Obviously ecstatic to have more testosterone back in the group.

"It was great," Jason said, as he sat down and waved at the Kinkle family. "We stayed in this big house overlooking the beach. Six weeks of seeing beautiful French girls in small bikinis, what's not to love?"

They all laughed. Mrs Notting shook her head disapprovingly at her son's comment and continued her conversation with Mrs Kinkle, whilst Mr Notting stared at Emily in awe.

"Emily Knight," he called in a loud, commanding voice, as he leaned over the table and firmly shook her hand. "It's nice to finally meet you. I'm Daniel Notting and this is my wife Saundra. Saundra?" He tapped his wife on the shoulder.

"Hello, dear," Mrs Notting said sweetly, before turning her attention back to Mrs Kinkle.

"It's nice to meet you," Emily said politely. "Was your holiday good?"

"It was excellent," Mr Notting said, stretching out his arms and placing them behind his head. "Six weeks of bliss that I got to spend with my boy. He's growing up quickly, into a handsome young man."

"Dad," Jason said blushing.

Emily laughed. She always found it amazing that Jason couldn't see how beautiful he clearly was.

"What do you think, Emily?" Mr Notting asked, suddenly

leaning forward, so that his face was almost touching hers. She pulled away quickly. "Do you think my boy's handsome?"

Michella sharply looked up from the conversation she was having with Wesley. She looked back and forth from Emily and Jason with an odd expression on her face.

"Dad!" Jason said looking at him darkly. "Stop."

"What?" Mr Notting said, looking confused by his son's angry expression. "What girl were you talking about on holiday? She's a fine girl, Jason and she's powerful too."

Emily caught Wesley's eye and they both burst out laughing. Mr Notting looked perplexed, as Emily explained, "Jason and I are just friends."

"Really?" Mr Notting asked in disbelief.

"Yes, really," Jason snapped. "I wasn't talking about her." Jason glanced at Emily. "No offence."

"None taken," Emily said.

"But who was it then?" Mr Notting said looking frustrated. "Just think about it, son—you could be going out with the daughter of the best—"

"Mum!" Jason said, cutting of his father. His mother, who was oblivious to the situation, looked over at him. "Can you please tell Dad that he's already late for work?"

"Work?" Mr Notting said scowling. "Breakfast is just being served, boy."

Emily looked towards the kitchen doors and saw the cooks trooping out with platters of food and jugs of juice.

"Oh, kill me now," Jason moaned, sinking into his seat, so only the top of his streaked hair could be seen. Emily patted his shoulder sympathetically, but stopped when Jason whispered, "Don't. You'll only give him ideas."

And sure enough, Mr Notting was looking ecstatic at the pair's clear display of affection.

It wasn't until late that afternoon, when all the parents had gone that Emily, Michella, Wesley and Jason managed to get alone time together at the table and they were able to fill Jason in on everything that had happened throughout the summer.

"Please tell me you took a picture of Roberta?" Jason pleaded to Wesley.

"Oh no," Wesley said, holding the sides of his head. "I completely forgot. Don't worry I'm sure we'll see her again," he added, when Jason looked disappointed.

"But didn't you hear about the hijacking in France?" Michella asked confused.

Jason shook his head. "Like I said, I was on the beach the whole time and Mum and Dad didn't want the television on. I mean, I knew stuff would kick off, but not like this. I can't believe it! What are the Five Warriors planning to do?"

"Well, Roberta and Jenkins are gathering warriors for our side and my dad . . ." Emily paused.

Julian Kena had just appeared in the dining hall. Emily sat up straighter and ran her fingers quickly through her hair. She tried not to look surprised when she saw Ambria Appleton from Berbinin embrace him with a kiss on the cheek.

"My dad, according to Roberta," Emily continued, looking away from the pair. "Has secured connections with warriors around the world that will fight with us if needed."

"So do you think that's why he has been gone for so long?" Jason asked. "To search for Lox and to create stronger ties?"

Emily nodded.

Several people in the hall ran up to the large windows, pressing their faces into the glass.

"What's going on?" Michella asked Daisy Atam, a blonde-haired bubbly girl from Ogragon.

"The bus is here!" Daisy said excitedly.

The four of them watched the doors, waiting to see which students would arrive. A few minutes later, hundreds of students trooped into the dining hall to loud cheering. Emily saw Summer Wind, Raquel Davis and Rosa Martin from the Ogragon Dojo team and waved at them as they took a seat at a nearby table. Warren hurried over to them and embraced Summer with a kiss.

"Oh, Harmony's back," Wesley said happily, when he saw Harmony Loving-Dale, his co-commentator for the Dojo matches. Her long blonde hair was covered in multi-coloured beads.

It was clear by the empty chairs that there were a few elder students missing, but none that Emily was close to.

"Here they come," Jason said.

The hall erupted in applause as the first years walked to the front of the hall behind Laton Chin. Most were so small, Emily couldn't believe they were thirteen.

"How come they're not having their tour of Osaki like we did?" Emily asked Jason.

"Maybe they're going to have it tomorrow because of all the drama," he responded.

One dark-haired boy had red blotches on his face as if he had been crying. Wesley pointed him out and was convinced that he looked just like that on his first day. Emily spotted Gabriel Thompson from afar. She remembered his face from the news broadcast.

He was a lanky, pale boy with a small, pointy nose, brown hair and black, square glasses. He wasn't as handsome as Niles, although there was a slight resemblance. He walked with his head hung low and his hands clasped tight behind him. People were standing out of their seats to get a better look at him.

"At least he hasn't got any burns from the fire," Michella whispered to Emily.

"Can I have everyone's attention, please?" Laton Chin said and everyone fell silent. "Traditionally the first years have a tour of Osaki and are put into their teams, but because of the disruption this morning, they were sorted into their teams as soon as they arrived and they will be given a tour of the school in the morning. Please be helpful to any of them who may be lost . . ."

"Emily, over here," a voice whispered urgently.

Emily looked over at the table behind hers and saw blonde-haired Lisa Fowler, waving madly at her.

"Tell Jason I like his tan," she whispered.

"What?" Emily frowned. "Why?"

"Just tell him," Lisa said sharply.

Emily tapped Jason on the arm and whispered what Lisa had said. Jason looked bemused, but he looked at Lisa and gave her a thumbs up before he looked back at the new students. Emily looked at Lisa to see her smiling smugly to herself.

"What?" Lisa asked innocently, when she caught Emily staring.

Emily had missed the rest of Laton Chin's speech and the new students were sitting down at various tables, but even though everyone was making room for Gabriel and calling out to him, he sat at the table closest to the window, with the fewest people. He looked out of it, as if he wanted to be anywhere else, but at Osaki.

"What team do you think he's in?" Wesley whispered to Emily.

"I bet it's Mentorawth because of Niles," Emily responded.

A tall girl with green, cat-shaped eyes and a heart-shaped face walked into the hall. Everyone turned to watch her. The big, tousled, blonde–almost white–hair Emily had seen on TV had been cut into a short, sharp bob. One side of her hair was slicked back, revealing an ear, heavily pierced with silver hoops and star studs. She wore bright red lipstick on her perfectly made up face. She had the same school uniform as everyone else, but hers seemed to strain on her ample bosom as if it had been customised. She walked down the aisle with an assurance that she was sexy and it was clear by the comments shouted at her, that the boys shared the same view. Most of the girls were talking excitedly and some were trying to take pictures of her on their phones.

"Oh my gosh! Oh my gosh! She's here!" Michella cried.

"This is Alice Archinia," Laton Chin announced, when Alice joined him at the front of the dining hall, with her hand on her hip as if she was posing for the press. "She is Cecil Archinia's granddaughter and due to Neci's return, she has transferred from Stallion Girls Training School to Osaki and she will continue her training here from now on. Please make her feel welcome. She will be joining the fourth years in team Mentorawth."

The applause for Alice was deafening, mainly because the boys were wolf whistling and stamping their feet. Alice smiled and strutted to the table where Julian Kena was. She scooted over Ambria Appleton, who looked at her crossly and Alice instantly engaged in a conversation with Julian. Emily couldn't help feeling jealous as she watched them bantering like old friends. She wished she had the confidence to approach Julian like that.

"Some day, eh?" Wesley said, looking excited when the cooks came out with a late lunch.

"Yeah, some day," Emily echoed as she looked from Gabriel to Alice.

Alice looked instantly comfortable with the spotlight; she spoke to anyone that approached her and flirted with the boys that looked her way. Gabriel avoided everyone's gaze. Emily found herself staring at him and as if he could feel her, he looked away from the window and locked eyes with her. His stare had a hardness that surprised Emily and made her feel uncomfortable. She looked away, but a few seconds later, she glanced back at him and he was still staring.

Over her food, Emily found herself spying on Gabriel as everyone around her was in deep conversations catching up about their summer holidays and discussing Neci and Alice's makeover. She noticed that many people approached Gabriel, but they seemed to only get in a few words before he turned away from them. He didn't touch his food once and he didn't look at Emily again for the rest of the meal.

CHAPTER FOUR

The Six Warriors

Michella's piercing scream echoed throughout the bedroom. Emily jumped up and looked away from the window that faced the stadium to see Michella standing over her suitcase, peering at it anxiously. Sisters, Sydney and Sarah John ran to stand beside her. Sydney's long hair was unravelling slowly from its ponytail as she leaned towards Michella's suitcase.

"Don't!" Violet Hijen, a cute Chinese girl said, grabbing Sydney's arm. "If it runs out of there, we're screwed."

"GET IT OUT OF MY STUFF!" Michella yelled.

"What's going on?" Emily asked, as she tried to look over Violet's shoulder, to see inside the suitcase. "Is that a—"

"Mouse! In my suitcase!" Michella cried.

Lisa Fowler picked up her baht shoe, that they wore to train in, and raised it high.

"Don't do that!" Daisy Atam grabbed Lisa's shoe and threw it on the floor. She reached in Michella's suitcase and picked the brown mouse off Michella's t-shirt by its tail. "You'll hurt it."

"I'm gonna be sick," Violet said, covering her mouth with her hand and running out of the bedroom.

"This is the excitement you miss every morning, Emily," Sarah said and Emily laughed.

"I won't be early again if this is what I have to look forward to," Emily responded.

"Daisy, no one cares if it's hurt," Nicky Johansen said, as she watched the mouse squirm in Daisy's hand. She had wrapped herself in her duvet and was looking on from the safety of her bed. "Chuck it out."

"Yuck, I can't believe you're touching that," Sydney said disgusted.

"I'll take it downstairs and let it out the front door," Daisy said calmly, before she bounced out of the room.

"Why would a mouse be in your suitcase?" Emily asked bewildered.

"That's what I want to know," Michella said, throwing all her clothes on to the floor. "I'll have to wash these now!"

"Okay, now that's been dealt with, let's get on to more important things," Violet said, walking back into the room with her eyes glistening. She jumped on to her bed. "When did Jason get so hot?"

"He didn't," Michella replied swiftly. She smelt the jumper in her hand and wrinkled her nose. "I'm sure it peed on this. Smell." She held it up to Emily who swatted her hand away.

"Set me up on a date with Jason," Lisa begged. "And soon because I know he's getting loads of attention."

"Here." Sarah handed Michella a carrier bag.

Michella threw her jumper into the bag and laughed. "A date? Whatever."

"That's not nice," Lisa said hotly. "I really like him."

"Since when?" Michella asked, with her eyebrows raised.

"Since . . ." Lisa frowned. "Okay, since last night, but that's beside the point. He's so yummy!"

"Yummy?" Emily laughed.

"You laugh now," Sydney said, looking around the room dramatically. "But he's the one to get. He's got this sexy, California, surfer beach thing going on."

"What he's got is a tan that will fade and some bloody streaks from the sun!" Michella exclaimed loudly. "He looks exactly how he has always looked. I'll be glad to tell him that it's definitely his looks you're after. I'm sure he'll be so impressed."

There was an awkward silence in the air. Emily saw Violet and Nicky look at each other in a way that suggested that they thought Michella was jealous. She was definitely aggressive this morning as she continued to stuff her clothes in the bag, at times punching them in, so they would fit.

The door opened and Daisy returned, announcing that she had just seen Julian Kena and Alice Archinia walking down to breakfast with their arms linked. Emily couldn't help the rage that seemed to boil from the bottom of her stomach. Michella looked over at her and Emily tried to look as if the news hadn't affected her. She wasn't sure if Michella was fooled.

"That cow!" Violet said, boldly saying what all the girls were thinking. "She's only been here ten seconds and she's already taking the good-looking guys. You better watch Jason, Lisa."

Lisa suddenly looked worried and Emily couldn't help but wish that Alice had gone after Jason and not Julian.

It was during breakfast when the post was delivered to the students. Usually, the post wasn't given out early in the term, but after last night's antics, everyone seemed to have one that morning from anxious parents hoping that they were okay. Wesley slammed down his letter in front of Michella.

"Would you believe this?" he exclaimed. "Your brother Mike has only gone and asked out Cammie and she said yes!"

"It's only Mike, so relax. At least he's nothing like Warren," Michella said, cutting her bagel in half.

"Well, I need to talk to Mike."

"What for?" Michella demanded. "You've known Mike for years. Cammie and Mike grew up together. He's not going to taking the mick."

"Mike your little brother wouldn't, but Mike, Cammie's new boyfriend might. He just needs to know what would happen to him if his little hands decide to wander."

Michella laughed. "Wander where? To the cookie jar? They're eight for goodness sake!"

Emily knew Jason had entered the dining hall before she had seen him. Every girl in the room was suddenly sitting up straighter and fussing with their hair, even Alice Archinia stopped talking mid-sentence to Julian to watch him. Emily saw Lisa behind him looking disappointed.

"Morning," Jason said, grabbing half of Michella's bagel from her plate. He began to smother it in chocolate spread. "Got cornered by Lisa on the way down. Started shouting at me about Alice. I don't know what she's on. I just managed to leg it."

Michella caught Emily's eye and they both laughed.

Mr Davon walked down the aisle of the dining hall in a

red training kit which clashed nicely with his blonde, grey hair. He was followed by the teachers, who marched in unison behind him.

"What's going on?" Emily asked, as the teachers walked to the front of the hall.

They stood in a straight line with Mr Davon in the centre. The room instantly fell silent as Mr Davon addressed the students. "Good morning all. My sincere apologies to the first years for your tour of the school being disrupted yesterday and I hope you're looking forward to seeing Osaki in all its glory after breakfast. If you have any problems, please do not hesitate to ask a teacher. I would like to remind everyone that flying and fireballs are not permitted around the school and anybody interested in playing Dojo, Mentorawth and Pentwon are both looking for Fighters, so please see their team captains.

"Now second years are due to go on their Survival Training." Mr Davon paused until the cheers from the second years had faded. "This will begin next week for five days where you will camp in Redrook Forest, which is next to Mount Gregory. It is our tradition that a celebrity will accompany you and help to train you. Usually, this is announced on the first day of Survival Training, but these celebrities mean so much to everyone, that I think they deserve a special announcement.

"These two warriors have done so much for us and they have dedicated their lives to fight for peace. They have two sons, nine-year-old Xavier and five-year-old Antonio, whom you may see around Osaki from time to time this year. Please can everyone stand up and give a huge welcome to Roberta Taniana and Hubert Jenkins from the Five Warriors."

Everyone stood up, screaming and cheering as two small

boys with light, caramel skin and silky, black, curly hair entered the room, clutching on to the hands of Roberta and Jenkins.

Jenkins was a very tall and athletic built, dark skinned man with a charming smile. He was extremely handsome with chiselled cheekbones and small cat-shaped eyes.

Roberta was wearing a fitted white dress that emphasised every curve in her hourglass figure. Her black hair fell elegantly around her beautiful face. She caught Emily's eye and winked, although Jason was convinced that she was actually winking at him.

They walked up to the teachers and embraced them. Roberta kissed Mr Davon on the cheek, which caused a few wolf whistles and Jenkins shook his hand. The ghosts of Cecil Archinia and Niles Thompson hovered besides Roberta and Jenkins. They looked at each other lovingly and did a strange group hug, where they weren't actually touching each other, but anyone could see how much they wanted to. Roberta wiped a tear away from her eye and Niles blew a kiss at her.

"This is unbelievable!" Wesley hollered over the noise and Emily nodded.

The applause in the hall was deafening. Four of the legendary Five Warriors were here at Osaki and, for the first time in years, Emily felt that she wasn't alone. She knew that they would do anything to protect her and at that moment, she was grateful that she happened to be the daughter of their leader, Thomas Knight.

Someone at the back of the hall shouted, "Speech!" and everyone began to chant it. Emily saw Jenkins smile at a girl in front of him and she turned beetroot red.

"There will be plenty of time to hear from them. Come

on, let's finish breakfast," Mr Davon said, but everyone was too excited to eat.

"What a hottie!" Violet Hijen said, as she stared at Jenkins.

"His skin is like chocolate," Sarah John said dreamily. "I just want to lick it."

Emily looked over at the table where Alice Archinia was sitting. Her green eyes weren't focused on Roberta and Jenkins; they were looking straight at Emily. Emily couldn't figure out the look. It wasn't dismissive, like how Tanya looked at her, but it wasn't inviting either.

Emily wondered if Alice felt the same as her. Protected by the Five Warriors because she was Cecil's granddaughter. Emily smiled at her, but Alice didn't return it, instead she turned away from her. Emily frowned and wondered what she had done to cause Alice to be unfriendly.

A few tables down, she spotted Gabriel Thompson. He was seated at a table, where everyone was clearly excited about the Five Warriors, but he was staring into space looking glum. It baffled Emily how Gabriel could be sad with these legendary warriors in the room, including his brother, Niles. She went to point out Gabriel to Michella, but she was too busy talking to Sarah John about how gorgeous Jenkins was.

After breakfast was Wilderness class, a special lesson with the head chef and the Dojo flag flyer, Ferguson Cloud. It was in preparation for the Survival Training and it was the first lesson of the term, for the second years, but as Emily, Michella, Wesley and Jason gathered their belongings, Ms Macay stopped Emily and told her to stay behind. Confused, Emily sat back down at the table as her friends waved her goodbye. When the last of the students and teachers had left the hall and Cecil and Niles had teleported to teach a Foughtgon class, Mr Davon beckoned her closer.

"Thank you all for staying behind," Mr Davon said. "Roberta would you care to explain why they're here?"

Roberta nodded. She brushed her glossy hair of her face and smiled. "I think it's clear to us that we will determine the outcome of this war, if it happens."

Emily looked at Alice Archinia, Gabriel Thompson, Julian Kena, Xavier and Antonio Jenkins.

"You all share the bloodline of legendary warriors," Roberta said, looking at each face carefully. "And this shows me that you are the warriors who need special training. If you have hidden power, we need to reveal it before we fight, Neci. I'm aware that there will be more warriors who will be an asset, but you guys in particular will be targeted. Neci said she would go after anyone that supports the Five Warriors, but her first target will be our families." Roberta turned to Julian. "I know you're not related to the Five Warriors, but when she finds out that you're Tainwo Kena's grandson, who is a legend himself, I'm certain she will come after you too."

Julian nodded, but Emily noticed that his hands were shaking. When he caught Emily looking, he placed them behind his back.

"Jenkins and I are going to do extra training classes with you to prepare for the war. It will be a long process, but you will be better warriors for it."

"Wicked," Xavier Jenkins said excitedly.

"My sons, Xavier and Antonio are already displaying powers, even though they are only nine and five. Antonio is an illusionist like his father." Roberta tickled him under his chin and Antonio giggled. "It's very important that we get everyone's powers under control. We are the ones people will look too to save the world from Neci and technically you are all the new Five—or should I say Six—Warriors."

Everyone looked at each other. Gabriel looked petrified, Julian looked scared but was trying to disguise it, Antonio was oblivious to the situation and Alice was leaning against the wall, studying her fake nails with great interest. The only one who looked excited was Xavier. Emily didn't know how to feel. She knew that because she was Thomas Knight's daughter, she would immediately have responsibility in the battle, but the thought of fighting an army of warriors was not something she was looking forward to. Then she remembered. Neci had given her a way out, as long as she and Lox didn't get involved in the war.

Gabriel waved his hand in the air. "When will the classes be?" he asked in a small voice.

Roberta looked up at her husband Jenkins who replied in a deep, smooth voice, "We're going to do them at random, so you may be called out of lessons. We are living in dangerous times and we have to be aware that not everyone at this school can be trusted, so please keep what we're doing to yourselves. But I need to stress that we are now one team and we need to trust each other."

A snort came from the back of the group and everyone looked at Alice, who was standing with her arms folded. "Who's going to be the leader of this new team?"

"The leader?" Roberta asked frowning.

"Yeah," Alice said, rolling her eyes. "You guys had Thomas, so which one of us will be the new Thomas?"

"How did Thomas even become the leader?" Julian asked.

"He was the strongest one and he put the Five Warriors together," Roberta explained. "I don't think having a leader is important right now, Alice."

"Why not?" Alice demanded.

Jenkins smiled, but his stare was hard. "We will come to that when it's time. So shall we begin?"

"What, now?" Emily asked, suddenly feeling nervous.

"No time like the present," Jenkins said, waving his arms, so the tables and chairs flew back and landed by the wall. Roberta knelt down and whispered something in Antonio's ear, who nodded and closed his eyes. Suddenly, the dining hall was covered in ten-foot-high, pink teddy bears.

"You'll have to excuse my son, he has an active imagination," Roberta smiled. "But a little warning—watch out for the bears."

"Good luck," Mr Davon said, and the adults teleported.

The only sound was from Antonio who was sitting on the floor, twirling his hair, singing a nursery rhyme. Xavier was standing next to a bear and when he noticed, he moved swiftly away and walked on ahead of everyone else.

"Xavier, where are you going?" Emily shouted after him, but Xavier ignored her.

"Xavier, wait!" Gabriel called, but it fell on deaf ears. He sighed loudly. "So much for the team work."

"What's so scary about this?" Alice asked, touching one of the bears and suddenly they were all growling at them. She took a step back and the four of them huddled together as the bears surrounded them. Emily raised her arms to shoot a fireball at one until someone pushed her back and she fell on the floor.

"Move out of the way. I've got it," Alice said, positioning her hands.

Emily stared at her with resentment before she jumped up and pushed Alice, so she stumbled. Alice stared angrily at Emily.

"Don't push me," Emily said fiercely.

"I can do what I want, Knight. You can't tell me what to do!" Alice shouted back.

"Guys stop, we're meant to be working as a team," Gabriel stressed.

"Oh, shut up," Alice muttered.

"Alice, cool it," Julian said sharply and Emily suppressed a smile that Julian was defending her.

"We're supposed to be on the same side," Gabriel said, standing in between Emily and Alice. "This is part of the test."

"I don't give a crap about the test," Alice shouted, rounding on Gabriel, who took a step backwards. "Let's not act like this is equal ground. I can take any of you on and you know it!"

"Really? And break your nails?" Emily scoffed. "Just get over yourself."

"Get over myself? Has everyone forgotten that you were a low life thief? Disgracing yourself on the cover of every newspaper looking like a spoilt brat!"

"Me? Spoilt brat? I had my reasons for acting out but wise words from the reality star and her cancelled series."

Sparks began to come out from the both of them as they squared up to one another.

"STOP FIGHTING!" Gabriel suddenly shouted, looking upset.

"Baby," Alice spat.

Everything began to disappear and the pink bears vanished. Antonio was still humming from the floor and twirling his hair. Xavier was on the other side of the room, looking irritated. The adults teleported back into the dining hall.

Mr Davon was looking at his watch and shaking his head in disappointment. "Five minutes before you turned on each other."

Jenkins picked Antonio up from the floor, who finally seemed to realise where he was and smiled at his dad. "You were meant to get rid of the bears together, like a team," Jenkins stressed. "This is going to be much harder than I thought."

Emily couldn't help but silently agree with him. Julian and Gabriel came and stood beside her. Everything in Emily's body felt aware that Julian was standing so close to her. The three of them looked at Alice, who was already staring back at them, with her sharp, green eyes.

"She's just hard to work with," Emily confided in Michella, Wesley and Jason.

They were sitting on the floor in the Ogragon living room. She knew she was meant to be keeping the training group a secret, but she also knew her friends could be trusted to keep it to themselves.

"Have you told Roberta or Jenkins?" Jason asked.

"What? Tell on her?" Emily asked frowning. "Sounds a bit primary school, doesn't it?"

"She seems so fun on television," Michella said, looking genuinely upset.

"It's great editing," Emily replied. "Trust me, she's an idiot."

"But how is it spending all that extra time with Julian?" Michella grinned. "Silver lining, right?"

Emily glanced at Wesley, whose jaw looked tight.

"It's okay," Emily mumbled.

They fell silent. The only noise came from the cards that Wesley was shuffling aggressively.

"Careful," Jason said, when one card ripped.

"I would take mad training sessions with Alice than another stupid Wilderness class, learning about fishing and deer," Wesley said, dealing out the cards.

Emily laughed. "Fishing and deer?"

Jason nodded. "Apparently, that's all there is to eat at this training thing. Emily, it's your go."

"Oh yuck," Emily muttered, picking up a card.

"How's everyone else at training?" Michella asked, looking at the cards she was dealt.

Emily sighed. "Well, apart from Alice who keeps attacking me for no reason, you've got Xavier, who doesn't understand the concept of teamwork and he goes off by himself. Julian's great, but he's getting frustrated with the lack of progress. Then there's Antonio. He's super cute, but because he's young, he gets easily distracted and when he's scared he brings out these stupid bears and then Gabriel . . ."

Emily hesitated and everyone looked at her.

"What's wrong with Gabriel?" Jason asked.

Emily looked around the living room. It was more or less empty, but she still lowered her voice. "He's . . . weird. I mean, he's off in his own little world and he always looks so troubled. Like the last session, I kept catching him just staring at me, but it was freaking me out. Then we had to partner up and do sparring and he was my partner, but when I touched him, he was freezing."

There was silence. Emily saw Michella and Jason exchange a 'so what?' look.

"He was freezing?" Wesley asked, but by his tone it suggested that he didn't understand why it was a big deal.

"You didn't see his face when I asked him why he was so cold. He looked frightened," Emily explained, remembering how Gabriel had quickly taken a step away from her. She tried to talk to him, but it was like he had shut down. He refused to look at her, or speak to her and in the end Emily had to spar against Xavier, while Gabriel excused himself from the lesson. When her friends didn't say anything, Emily said defensively, "You didn't see his face," before she put down a Black Jack and Wesley had to pick up five.

It was six o' clock on a Monday morning, when Emily's duvet was yanked away. Instantly, Emily drew her knees up to her chest and hugged them.

"Get up sleepy head, we're leaving for Survival Training in one hour," Michella said excitedly.

Emily moaned and slowly got up. She looked around the dim room. She had almost forgotten that she had stayed the night at Osaki. Her head was throbbing. Every time she closed her eyes, she was back in the forest, but it was on fire. Scarlett was in front of her, holding a white beam and when she shot it, Emily woke up. She had slept on and off all night.

The girls were putting on hoodies over their training kits and gathering their belongings, apart from Sydney John, whose hair was sticking up in different directions and her bag looked like it had exploded over the floor. Emily climbed out of her bed and dragged herself to the bathroom.

Breakfast was eerily quiet. Even though some second years were clearly excited, most like Emily, could barely keep their eyes open. Wesley poured water into his cereal and didn't seem to notice. Emily perked up when Roberta and Jenkins entered the hall. Jenkins caught her eye and walked over to her.

"Oh my gosh, oh my gosh!" Michella said nervously, running a hand through her braids.

"Emily!" Jenkins said, bending down and embracing her in a tight hug.

"Hey, Uncle Jenkins."

"Are you ready for today?" he asked, with his eyebrows raised. He knew better than anyone how much Emily hated camping.

"Ecstatic," Emily said drily, which made him laugh, revealing perfect white teeth.

Roberta was waving Jenkins over, so he squeezed Emily's shoulder before walking away.

"Why is he so gorgeous?" Michella asked wistfully. Wesley let out a loud wolf whistle as he stared at Roberta in her red training kit. "She's not a piece of meat, Wesley," Michella whispered angrily to him.

"Ssh," Wesley replied. "Go back to drooling over her husband."

"Can we please have everyone's attention?" Roberta shouted over the noise in the hall, which fell silent. "Good morning, we'll be leaving in five minutes, so I hope you have everything.

Seeing as Redrook Forest is so close to us, we will be flying there, so please act maturely and stick together."

"Emily, where's your sleeping bag?" Jason asked.

Emily looked down at the floor and only her rucksack was there. "Oh shoot, I'll be back in a sec."

Emily hurried out of the hall and up the flight of stairs. She ran down the corridor until she reached the Ogragon Team Room. The living room was dark and silent and her sleeping bag was next to the door. Emily grabbed it and when she opened the door to leave, she bumped into Gabriel Thompson. His dark hair was wet and matted to his forehead and his glasses were stuck together in the middle with tape, which wasn't there before. He was already dressed in his school uniform. He looked just as surprised to see Emily.

"Gabriel, what are you doing up so early?"

"Oh, Emily—I thought you were going to Survival Training?"

Emily frowned. "I am, but why are you here? Aren't you in Mentorawth?"

Gabriel looked around anxiously. "Yeah I am . . . I was looking for Niles."

Emily stared at him silently. Under her gaze, Gabriel looked more and more uncomfortable. "Why would he be in Ogragon? Isn't he in Mentorawth?" Emily challenged him. Gabriel looked down at the floor and didn't respond. Emily moved closer to him and Gabriel took a step back. "What happened to your glasses?"

Gabriel looked up at her with a hard stare. "I fell. See you later."

Emily watched as Gabriel walked away from her, until he had blended in with the shadows in the corridor.

It wasn't long before Emily and the rest of the second years were soaring through the windy sky. Emily had missed flying, but she soon changed her mind when the cold air was slapping her face and her rucksack was digging into her flesh. She couldn't get her mind off Gabriel. She knew he was covering up something, but what was it?

They had only been in the air for ten minutes, when Harmony Loving-Dale shouted, "There it is!"

Emily gasped when she saw Mount Gregory and all thoughts of Gabriel disappeared. The climate seemed to drop dramatically and her body began to shake. Jenkins beckoned for them to fly down, so Emily dived towards Redrook Forest. As soon as she had landed, she threw off her heaving bag and rubbed her shoulders, wincing from the pain.

"Right, all hoodies and jackets off," Roberta said, rubbing her hands.

"Are you serious?" a shrill voice called from the back. "It's freezing."

Emily rolled her eyes when she heard Tanya Frank's voice. Tanya was wrapped cosily in her winter jacket. Her pale cheeks were red from the cold and her dark hair was hidden under a furry hat with flaps on the side.

"You know I almost forget she existed," Michella whispered to Emily.

"And wasn't it perfect?" Emily responded and Michella laughed.

"Your body will get used to it. This is part of the training," Jenkins said. "So only training kits can stay on."

A loud groan travelled throughout the students as they reluctantly removed their coats and hoodies.

"I don't understand how catching frostbite is going to help my training," Wesley muttered bitterly.

As soon as Emily took off her jumper, the cold air hit her body so quickly that her teeth began to chatter. She jumped from one foot to the other and rubbed her arms in a poor attempt to keep herself warm. She didn't understand how Roberta and Jenkins seemed unaffected by the weather conditions.

"Leave your stuff here and follow us," Roberta said, as her and Jenkins began to walk further into the forest.

"Hey, what took you so long to get back?" Michella asked Emily, as they walked through an unseen path, with branches hitting their arms and hidden tree trunks that made them stubble. Emily told her about her encounter with Gabriel and Michella looked at her bewildered.

"What is he up to?"

Emily shrugged her shoulders. "He's in Mentorawth, so I have no idea why he was hovering outside our team room. Seriously, why would Niles be floating around *our* room?"

"Very strange," Michella muttered. "And what's the deal with the glasses? I mean, he could have fallen . . ." Michella trailed off when she saw Emily's sceptical expression.

They came to a stop at the riverbank. Emily peered at it nervously. Even though the water looked clear and inviting, she knew it would be freezing. She prayed they wouldn't have to get into the water. Jenkins stood in front of them. He was wearing a black training kit and his bulging biceps could be seen though the thin material.

"The first test is to strengthen your bodies to get used to the harsh weather conditions. Everyone is going to dive into this river and in the middle, buried slightly in the water bed, are bottles of Reviving Water that you need to retrieve for yourself. If you fail to retrieve your bottle in ten minutes, you will not have any Reviving Water for today."

"Oh great," Emily said. She hated water ever since she had almost drowned as a child. She wasn't the strongest swimmer and she couldn't breathe under water.

"When you see a white beam in the water, that means time is up. So as soon as your shoes are off, you can begin," Roberta said.

Emily kicked off her baht shoes and walked carefully over the forest ground, trying to avoid the sharp twigs and rocks. The mud at the riverbank oozed between her toes and she shuddered. Emily tied her hair up into a bun and ignoring the students around her, who were diving effortlessly into the water, Emily walked slowly into the river. The freezing water went up her training kit trousers, soaking her knickers. When the water had reached her shoulders, Emily began to breaststroke towards the middle of the river.

"Emily, just dive in," Roberta shouted from the riverbank.

"No thanks," Emily replied.

When she was in the middle of the river, Emily took a deep breath and went under. Everything was slightly blurry and eerie. Reluctantly, she dived deeper into the water. She looked around, but couldn't see Michella, Wesley or Jason anywhere.

When she reached the bottom of the river, she saw only a few bottles sticking out of the water bed. She tugged at one and it came out effortlessly. Clutching her bottle, she turned around and was hit hard on her nose. The pain was excruciating and she covered her nose and mouth with her hands, so she wouldn't take in the water. Her bottle dropped from her hand and was caught by a girl with dark hair.

Emily saw that it was Tanya, who smirked at her before she swam back to the surface with Ola Ade and Fiona Corn behind her. They were carrying three bottles of water each. Emily spun around and her heart sank when she saw there were no more bottles left. Her chest began to hurt. Defeated, she swam as quickly as she could back to the surface. When her head was above the water, she took in a big gulp of air and then coughed viciously.

She wanted to scream out loud. She wanted to hurt the three of them, but when she looked at the riverbank, only Jenkins was there, looking tall and handsome, waiting for her. Embarrassment crept over her. Painfully and slowly, Emily began to swim towards him. The water kept gushing up her nose, making her stop to get it out. It felt like hours later when she was finally able to stand up in the water and walk towards the riverbank.

A bemused Jenkins looked down at her. "And why didn't you just breathe under water like everyone else?"

Emily wiped her wet hair of her face. "Because I don't know how to and before you say it, I know warriors are made to breathe under water, I know we have that weird gag reflex thing, but just the idea of doing it freaks me out, okay?"

Jenkins held up his hands as if surrendering. "It's cool by me, whatever works for you."

They walked in silence, only stopping so Emily could put on her baht shoes. Her wet training kit was now a dirty grey instead of white and hung heavy on her body. She was shivering and her teeth were chattering uncontrollably.

"Where's your water?" Jenkins asked.

"Tanya took it from me," Emily replied coldly.

She looked up at him, expecting him to question why, but he was looking straight ahead and his face was blank. A second later, Jenkins reached in his bag and gave Emily his bottle of Reviving Water.

"Thanks, Uncle Jenkins," Emily said, taking the bottle gratefully.

When they reached the campsite, Roberta was in the middle of talking to the students. Emily re-joined Michella, Wesley and Jason, but she couldn't concentrate. She was more than aware that Tanya, Fiona and Ola were laughing behind her. It took all of Emily's strength not to walk up to them and knock them out. Everyone started to walk away as Emily turned to Jason.

"What did she say?"

Jason's hair was stuck to his face and he had removed his top, so his toned torso was on full display and receiving admiring glances from the girls as they walked by. Behind Jason's back, Emily saw Lisa Fowler watch him longingly. Michella also saw Lisa and purposely stood at an angle that blocked Lisa's view of Jason. Lisa's face turned red and she stormed off.

"Every morning, we're going to get the Reviving Water from the bottom of the river—"

"Oh, great," Emily said sourly, as she sat herself down on a tree stump.

"Right now, we're meant to get food, build a fire, put up our tents and then we're going to climb the mountain and have a battle," Jason finished.

"For goodness sake," Emily said angrily. "This is not what I was expecting."

"It is called Survival Training, Emily. It's not meant to be easy." Michella's eyes suddenly lit up. "Hey, you got your bottle, well done!"

Emily blushed, she was just about to admit that Tanya, Ola and Fiona had taken all the bottles, but she couldn't do it. She wouldn't give them the satisfaction. "Thanks," she replied.

In the end, the four of them agreed that even though they were meant to gather food by themselves, it would be easier if they worked together. So Michella and Jason stayed behind to put up the tents and build a fire, whilst Emily and Wesley set off to get food. They passed bushes covered in pink berries that Wesley picked off. He handed some to Emily, who stared at them suspiciously.

"It's Kyptsu. It's safe, try it."

Emily took one and slowly ate it. It was sweet and delicious. "Mmmmm," she said. "That's good."

"I know, right?" Wesley said, offering her more. "Let's go that way."

"I think we should go this way," Emily said, pointing towards the other direction.

They argued over which way the riverbank was, but stopped when they saw Julian Kena and Natalya Windo from Mentorawth at a small distance in front of them. Like Jason, Julian had removed his top, in an attempt to get dry. Emily couldn't help but stare at the muscles in his back and the way his thick, black hair hung loosely over his broad shoulders.

"Why do you like him?" Wesley suddenly asked.

"What? Who?" Emily stammered. She wished that her

cheeks would stop turning red and Wesley would stop scowling as he looked at her.

"Why?" Wesley asked again. "What's so great about him?"

Emily couldn't help but notice his sharp tone. "I don't know. I just do." She desperately wanted him to stop looking at her. *Was it disappointment on his face?*

They walked in silence until Wesley said, "Just be careful. I've noticed golden boy has a new girl every week."

"What—are you jealous?" She was teasing, but she instantly wished she hadn't said it as Wesley looked at her blankly and then stomped away. Emily mentally kicked herself. She walked quickly behind him in silence.

They followed Julian and Natalya, which led them to the riverbank. Emily and Wesley watched as they both produced a small fireball that floated just at the top of the water and hundreds of little fish swam up to it as if mesmerised by the light from the fireball.

"Wesley, where are you going?" Emily asked as Wesley walked away from the riverbank. He didn't respond, so reluctantly Emily followed him. Julian must have heard her speak because he turned around and waved at her. Emily grinned back at him, her heart thumping so loud that she was certain Julian could hear it, but she instantly felt guilty when Wesley had seen their exchange and walked away from her even faster.

Emily ran to catch up with him, but she suddenly stopped in her tracks. She could feel a strong energy power coming close towards them. She looked around and saw a flash of red. Emily ran up to Wesley and pushed him behind the nearest tree.

Wesley stumbled and shouted, "What are you doing?"

"Ssh," Emily said as she hid behind the tree opposite his and she formed a small fireball in her hands. "Didn't you sense that power? Did you see her?"

Wesley clenched his fists and peeked out from behind the tree. "I couldn't feel anything. See who?"

Emily gulped. "I think I saw Scarlett."

"Are you sure?" Wesley asked urgently.

Emily closed her eyes. All she could sense was Wesley's power energy beside her. The strong power was gone and Emily scolded herself. There was no way Scarlett would be close to her and not attack—her mind must have been playing tricks on her. The fireball in her hand disappeared.

"Come on," Wesley said, unclenching his fists. He moved away from the tree and looked around the forest. "There's nothing here. Let's just get the food quickly. Are you okay?"

Emily nodded, feeling embarrassed.

They walked further into the forest, when Wesley suddenly broke into a run. Frustrated, Emily ran after him. Branches were scratching her bare arms and every time Emily stepped on a twig, Wesley gave her a sharp look. When they were on the other side of the riverbank, Wesley shot out his arm to stop Emily and she ran into it, so it caught her hard on her chest.

"Ow!" she said, shooting him an irritated look.

"Ssh," he whispered, not even looking at her. He smiled to himself. "There it is. Get a fireball ready, I've found us food."

Emily gently put his arm down. Wesley formed a fireball in his hand and Emily copied him. Her stomach rumbled loudly and she looked excitedly at the riverbank. An elegant, beautiful deer was sipping water from the river.

Emily gasped and pushed Wesley hard, so he stumbled

backwards. He caught himself before he fell. "You were going to make us eat the deer?" she shouted.

"Be quiet," Wesley hissed, but it was too late. The deer had perked up its ears at the sound of Emily's voice and ran in the opposite direction.

Wesley threw up his hands. "Are you happy now? That would have lasted us ages!"

"I don't want to eat a deer!" Emily said disgusted. "It's like eating a deer . . . and I like deers."

Wesley stared at her blankly, but then he laughed. "I don't want to eat a deer either. It's gross."

"Why don't we try getting some fish?" Emily suggested and Wesley nodded.

They walked back in silence and the tension was gone, but when they caught each other's eye, there was a sadness in Wesley's that wasn't there before.

After they ate the bland fish and their clothes were dry from the fire Michella and Jason had made, Roberta walked the second years to Mount Gregory. Tanya, Ola and Fiona walked in front of them with linked arms; they kept looking back at Emily and laughing.

"What's their problem?" Jason asked, glaring at them.

"I don't know," Emily lied.

They stopped when they reached the mountain. Emily instantly looked up and sighed when the realisation of how high it was hit her. Roberta clapped her hands to get everyone's attention as the students were loudly talking.

"You will get into groups of four and as a team and with no powers, you will help each other to climb the mountain. We will not be climbing to the very top, but to the middle."

"Thank God for that," Michella said relieved.

"Once you reach there, a person will be waiting for you. As a team, you will have to combine your fireballs together and destroy them. I know it sounds easy, but trust me it's not. Please remember that Jenkins will be doing the illusions. When, or if you defeat that person, you will be able to take a prize each. It can be a thick duvet, a prepared meal, a new change of clothes, a coat, a hot shower, or a big bottle of Reviving Water. You will also get one-on-one training with me. Each group must take a rope and every member must be tied with it. You can begin now."

Roberta walked over to Emily. She affectionately stroked her cheek and whispered, "Good luck,' before she handed Michella a piece of rope, that was thick and dirty.

Michella tied it around her middle, Emily was next, then Jason and Wesley came last. Michella performed fancy knots and was tugging the rope in all directions, that even Wesley looked impressed. Besides them, Tanya Frank was attempting to copy Michella's rope tying, but ended up with her rope in a big knot, which made Emily laugh loudly. Tanya scowled at her.

"Does everyone feel secure?" Michella asked.

They all nodded. Emily began to feel nervous. She had never climbed anything that high before.

"I guess let's go for it," Michella said, leading the way to the mountain.

Michella grabbed on to the hard surface and slowly began to climb. Emily watched her carefully and stepped in the exact places that Michella had stepped. There were sharp edges, slippery surfaces and dust that kept flying into her eyes. Michella showed surprising agility as she climbed up the mountain.

"How are you doing this so easily?" Emily shouted up to her.

"What?" Michella shouted back.

"I said, how are you doing this so easily?"

"I used to do rock climbing a lot as a kid," Michella shouted back.

"Jason!" a girl called from beneath them.

They stopped and looked down to see Lisa Fowler, Violet Hijen, Sydney John and Nicky Johansen. Lisa waved up at Jason, but then lost her balance. The girls screamed as they wobbled on the mountain.

"Grab the rock to your right!" Jason yelled down. Lisa managed to hear him over the screaming and grabbed the rock tightly. The other girls quickly rounded on her, cursing at her. Jason shook his head. "She's so weird."

It took them forty minutes to make it up the mountain. When they climbed over the edge, Emily collapsed on to the hard, dusty floor, feeling slightly dizzy, breathing hard and drenched in sweat.

"That—was—not—fun," she said, in between gasps.

"I agree," Jason said, as he wiped his brow.

Michella was kneeling over and resting her hands on her knees, but Wesley was staring silently at something.

"What's up, Wes?" Jason asked.

Emily followed his gaze and saw a beautiful young woman standing in the middle of the mountain, watching them. She had long, black, wavy hair and light brown eyes. She was wearing a pink jumper and blue jeans on her tall, lean figure. Her body was strong, not how Emily remembered it during her battle with cancer. Emily had only ever seen her look healthy in old pictures. When she caught Emily's eye, she smiled and opened her arms wide. Emily's heart hammered hard against her chest. She slowly got up, ignoring the sharp pains shooting through her legs and stared at the lady in disbelief.

"Who is that?" Wesley asked.

"My mum," Emily replied quietly, but they all heard her.

Wesley helped Jason to his feet and Jason looked from Emily's mother to Emily and back again.

"*That's* your mother?" Jason asked. "But she's dead, isn't she?" he whispered to Wesley, who nodded.

Emily wasn't listening. She was walking slowly towards her mother with tears stinging her eyes. She couldn't believe she was here, so close to her and so beautiful. Everything would be okay now because her mum was back. They could get Lox and her dad. Nothing could hurt her family any more.

"Emily," Michella said softly, grabbing her arm. "She's not really there."

"Yes, she is." Emily smiled. "She's right there. You can see her, right?" Michella hesitated and slowly nodded. "Her name's Leah, I'll introduce you."

"Emily," Michella said sadly, looking at the boys for support. "It's an illusion. Jenkins is doing this. Remember Roberta said . . . we're going to have to defeat her."

Emily stopped walking and turned to Michella, looking fierce. "If you touch my mum, I will kill you," she said, grabbing on to Michella's wrist.

"You're hurting me," Michella cried, pulling her arm away. She took a step back and the boys stood in between the girls, standing protectively in front of Michella.

"None of you will touch her. Do you hear me?" Emily shouted at their shocked faces. Emily looked back around, to see her mother, but she wasn't there. She began to breathe hard and fast. "Mum?" she called, but Leah Knight was nowhere in sight.

Emily sprinted to the middle of the mountain. Wesley went to go after her, but Michella held him back and shook her head. All Emily could see was the mountain stretched out before her.

"Mum! Mum!" Emily screamed, searching for a glimpse of black hair.

She fell on to her knees. It felt as if her heart had broken all over again and with her head in her hands, Emily cried. Strong arms wrapped themselves around her stomach and she could smell Wesley's familiar scent. She buried her head in his chest and he stroked her hair softly.

Lisa Fowler, Violet Hijen, Sydney John and Nicky Johansen, had climbed over the edge and were on all fours and out of breath.

"I think we should call it a day," Jason said when he saw the girls and Michella and Wesley nodded in agreement.

The stars shone bright above her. Emily was lying on her sleeping bag outside of her tent. She was cold, yet she didn't move. She felt numb inside and out, but most of all she felt stupid. Deep down, she knew it wasn't her mum, she knew it was an illusion, yet she didn't realise how much she had missed her.

When Lox ran away and Thomas went to find him, there

was a brief period when it was just her and her mum. "The girls together," her mum would say, until the cancer got worse. She wished she had got close enough to smell her cinnamon scent, or to see her bright, brown eyes.

Emily rolled on to her side. She wanted the Survival Training to be over. She dreaded seeing her mum again tomorrow. She didn't feel strong enough to see her, let alone defeat her. It didn't help that camping in a forest was almost impossible for her to sleep comfortably. Every noise made her jump. She felt too exposed sleeping out in the open.

The mornings followed with the same routine. They had to retrieve Reviving Water, get food and then climb the mountain to defeat an illusion. Other groups had been able to do it and they were able to claim a prize and get one-on-one training with Roberta, but each time Emily saw her mum, she felt weak. There were only a few days left for her to defeat the illusion.

After they had eaten their dinner, Emily excused herself and sat outside the tent. She hugged herself tight and looked up to the dark sky. She found that since she had seen her mum, she desired being alone with her thoughts. It was hard to think in the tent, with her friends around.

"Emily," Michella's small voice called to her. "Are you okay?"

Michella sat beside her and looked up at the sky. There were a million things Emily wanted to tell her. To explain how raw and alone she felt inside, but she knew there was only one thing she had to say.

"I'm sorry again for shouting at you. I wish I could defeat her, but I don't know how to."

"I understand," Michella said. "I was talking to Violet

earlier and she said her illusion was her grandfather. She only just managed to defeat him today, but she's really upset."

Emily sighed. "I know it isn't her, but it is still her. She looks and talks the same. I can't believe Jenkins is doing this to me."

Emily heard a rustling beside her and a second later she felt Michella's hand, rough from the cold, brush against her own. She didn't object when she felt it on top of her hand and they held each other tight, lost in the stars above.

The next day after Michella, Wesley and Jason had retrieved their water (and handed one to Emily), they ate their food and made one last attempt to climb the mountain and beat the illusion. They were now one of two groups who had not completed the challenge. The rest of the students were in another part of the forest, having their own battle with Roberta, whilst Jenkins was waiting for them at the mountain.

The mountain climb was still a struggle, but it was nowhere near as hard to climb as the first day. Now they knew the easiest path to get to the middle and they had grown stronger in the time they had spent in the forest, they managed to climb it in half the time.

When they climbed over the edge, Emily drank down her bottle of Reviving Water and dusted off her training kit. She was doing everything she could to not look at her mother. Jason came and stood beside her. He smiled and held out his hand. She smiled back and took it gratefully and they followed Michella and Wesley to where her mother stood. The closer they got to her mother, the more Emily tensed up and wanted to go back. Jason felt her resistance and he held her hand tighter and kept her walking forward.

"I can't do this," Emily said, trying to turn back.

"You can, come on," Jason replied.

"Let's just do it from here," Wesley said, staring at Emily's mother, who was a few metres away from them.

Emily squeezed her eyes tight. She felt lightheaded and nauseous.

"Emily." Her mother's soft voice carried across the mountain.

Emily took her hand from Jason's and she put her hands over her ears. "No, leave me alone." Tears fell down her face. "I can't do this. I really can't. Please don't make me."

"You can. She's not really there," Jason said, but his voice sounded far away.

"Emily," her mother called again. It sounded like her voice was surrounding her.

And Emily opened her eyes. Leah's dark hair was blowing fiercely in the wind. She was smiling at her and her arms were wide open.

"My darling," Leah said, as she beckoned Emily over and Emily walked towards her as if in a trance.

"Stop, Emily! That isn't your mum!" Michella yelled, but Emily didn't care. She just wanted to touch her, just for a second.

How could she not be real? That smile was real, she was here. She was real. Emily took another step towards her mum and froze. It felt as if a force was blocking her way. Emily struggled, but couldn't move, she couldn't even open her mouth to scream. Out of her control, Emily spun around and with her back to her mother, she saw Jason with his fingers on his temples and his eyes focused on Emily.

CHAPTER FIVE

The First Match Of The Season

"Jason, how are you doing that?" Wesley asked in disbelief.

"I will release you if you help us defeat the illusion," Jason said. His eyes never left Emily's.

"No!" Emily shouted. "I can't do it."

"You can," Jason said kindly. His fingers were still at his temples. "That is not your mum. I'm going to release you and on the count of three, we're going to shoot together, okay?"

"I can't . . ." Emily said, shaking her head.

"One—"

"Jason, please," Emily pleaded.

"Two—"

"You can do this, Emily," Michella said.

"Three."

With her eyes shut tight, Jason spun Emily around and she shot a yellow fireball. She felt the heat of Michella, Wesley, and Jason's fireballs soar past her. The wind blew dust into her face, making her wince and she covered her face with her hands. But she slowly separated her fingers, so she could see though the gaps. Emily let out a gut-wrenching scream as the four different coloured fireballs hit her mum with a deafening boom.

The four of them had been sitting in silence for the past ten minutes. Emily had finally digested the fact that her mother wasn't really there, but Jason controlling her had completely thrown her. Michella was looking at him in a daze.

"When did you know you could do that?" Michella finally asked.

Jason picked up the nearest rock and held it in front of him. He put his fingers to his temples and let the rock go and it floated in the air. Emily, Michella and Wesley watched it in awe.

"Over the summer," he replied, before he dropped the rock on the floor. "I found out by accident. I had read a book about hidden powers and I wondered if I had any. I had this drink on the table and I wanted to see if I could move it without getting up. I was just messing about. I didn't expect it to actually work. I mean, the first couple of glasses broke a few seconds after they left the table, but I just had to focus. A lot of the warriors in the book said they discovered their powers either by accident, or it came out in a time of need."

"What did your parents say?" Wesley asked, looking at his best friend in amazement. "Jeez! I knew there was something crazy about that smart brain of yours!"

Jason laughed. "I haven't told them yet." He looked at Emily. "But I didn't know I could move people."

"If it wasn't for you, we would never have defeated the illusion. I obviously couldn't do it by myself," Emily said, feeling annoyed.

"Hey, we would all be in the same boat if that was our mums, right?" Michella said and the boys nodded.

They sat in silence again but it was broken by a person clapping their hands. Jenkins was grinning and walking towards them. They had barely seen him because he was busy doing the illusions. Emily stood to her feet and clenched her fists.

"What a challenge! Well done, that was brilliant. Jason what an amazing gift you have, we can definitely—"

"Can I speak to you please, Uncle Jenkins?" Emily interrupted.

Jenkins noticed her fists and smiled charmingly at Michella, Wesley and Jason. "If you could please excuse Emily and I for a moment. Roberta is at the campsite, so make sure you claim your prize and of course you can fly down."

Michella hesitated, but Jenkins gave her an encouraging nod and she followed the boys towards the edge of the mountain, glancing back over her shoulder.

"Emily," Jenkins said gently, walking towards her. "The fact that you can look at your mother and push past your emotions to do the right thing is a gift."

Emily's jaw dropped. "A gift? It was evil. You took advantage of my weakness!"

"Of course I did!" Jenkins snapped, making Emily recoil. "Don't you think Neci is going to use what you love against you? Look at Lox. She's not going to fight fair." Jenkins sighed, suddenly looking sad. "Ever since Leah died, I rarely hear you say anything about her." Emily looked down at the floor avoiding his gaze. "What's your last memory of her?"

Emily could remember it clearly as if it was yesterday. The white rose she threw on to the coffin as it was lowered into the ground. Her father, holding her hand and crying. It was the only time she had seen him cry. Everyone had left in dribs and drabs, but Emily and Thomas had stayed until it had become so dark that if she wasn't holding her dad's hand, she would have thought she was alone. She had told Thomas she didn't want to leave her mother alone on her first night. She can remember a sound escaping Thomas's mouth as if he was chocking and he grabbed Emily and held her tight. His tears fell on to her head and she remembered thinking, *it's just the two of us now*. In that moment, she hated Lox with a passion for abandoning them.

Emily felt her knees buckle beneath her and she slumped to the floor, suddenly feeling weak. Jenkins sat beside her and held her tight. Emily allowed her head to rest on his shoulder.

"The funeral," she said quietly. "I always wondered how Lox could miss his own mother's funeral, just to punish Dad."

Jenkins rubbed his hand up and down her arm in an attempt to keep Emily warm from the cold weather. "There was a lot of people that day. Lox could have been around."

Emily scoffed. "I doubt it."

"Leah was his heart as well," Jenkins reminded her and Emily allowed the tears to fall silently down her face. "It doesn't matter how angry Lox was, he would never have left if he knew she had gotten worse."

"But he didn't come back," Emily argued in between tears.

Jenkins sighed. "Sometimes it's harder to go back." He

looked at Emily and wiped at her wet face. "You and Leah had a special bond. She loved you so much. She would never have left you out of choice."

Emily nodded. She knew that, but it still didn't change anything. "That was the hardest thing I've ever done. I know it wasn't really her, but seeing her again . . . reminded me of how much it hurt to lose her."

"But you separated your emotions, something I know you struggle with. Even though it took a while and Jason had to restrain you, you did it. I've heard around Osaki that you are amazing in the Dojo matches, so you have definitely inherited Thomas's fighting skills. If you can keep pushing yourself and you can unlock that hidden power that we know is inside you, you could be one of the greatest warriors of our time."

"Even better than you?" Emily teased.

Jenkins laughed. "Don't push it."

Emily wiped her face with her dirty Dojo kit. "I miss her," she whispered. "Every day I miss her."

Jenkins embraced her tight and kissed her forehead. "Me too," he said into her ear.

As a celebration for everyone completing the illusion task, Roberta and Jenkins had flown back to Osaki and returned with a feast for the grateful students. Emily's stomach rumbled loudly as she eyed the roast chickens, rice, roast potatoes, corn on the cobs, chocolate cakes, biscuits and sweets that Roberta laid out on a long table. Up until now, food had been what they could hunt, so Emily's meals had been pretty limited. She had felt so hungry for the past week and had suffered from stomach cramps. Even her training kit was hanging off her body.

The air was filled with laughter and contentment. The

campsite fire was roaring and a packet of marshmallows was being passed around for people to roast over the fire. Emily's second plate was heaving with a piece of everything.

"I need a drink," Michella said, looking around.

"I got you," Jason said. He put his hand to his temple and focused on the unopened carton of juice that was by Ambria Appleton's feet. It slowly hovered above the ground. It was surreal seeing a carton of juice floating through the air. Everyone was too engrossed in their food to notice.

"I love your power," Michella said, grabbing the juice and drinking it straight from the carton.

"Jas, get those chocolates over there," Wesley said, pointing them out.

Emily looked around the campsite. Everyone was still dirty and bruised, but now the students were smiling and looked relaxed for the first time since the Survival Training had started. She mentally took a picture, wanting to remember the moment.

A flash of red caught Emily's eye by the trees behind Tanya Frank. Scarlett, was the first thought that came to mind. Emily's heart began to race. She closed her eyes, but there were so many strong powers close by, it was hard to pinpoint if one of them was Scarlett's.

"Are you alright?" Michella asked, touching her arm.

Emily leaned in close towards her. "I think I just saw Scarlett."

Michella stood up and looked around wildly. Her plate dropped off her lap and the food scattered over the floor.

"By the trees," Emily said, standing up and pointing to the area. "Roberta and Jenkins aren't here to protect us."

"Where are they?" Michella asked.

"I don't know," Emily said, trying not to panic.

"What's up?" Wesley asked, noticing their alarmed faces.

"Emily thinks she saw Scarlett by the trees," Michella explained.

"Again?" Wesley exclaimed.

"What do you mean again?" Michella asked, looking from Emily to Wesley.

"I thought I saw her on the first day, when we went to get food."

"Why didn't you say?" Michella demanded.

"What is that?" Jason murmured. He was staring at the area which Emily had pointed out.

"What?" Emily said, trying to see, but it was too dark.

"That!"

And Emily saw them. Walking slowly through the darkness were four huge black creatures.

Michella gasped as Jason shouted out, "BEARS! RUN!"

The chatter instantly died down as everyone looked bemused at Jason, but slowly students were looking around to see what the commotion was. Emily watched Tanya spin around and come face to face with one of the bears. Tanya screamed, threw her plate of food in the bear's face and ran. A loud roar echoed through the trees and then the bears started to run towards the students.

One by one the students began to catch on and some shot fireballs over their shoulders as they ran, but they were so aimless, they were hitting other students, knocking them out.

"This is exactly why they should teach us how to bloody teleport!" Wesley shouted, as they ran blindly through the dark forest.

"Fly up," Jason commanded, bending his knees. "Up in the trees."

Emily thought of seeing the second years, happy, ecstatic and enjoying the feast. With that positive thought, she bent her knees and shot up to the sky, watching two bears trample the ground where they were just standing.

"Help!" Harmony Loving-Dale screamed. She was lying on the floor, holding her ankle.

Not far from her, were the other two bears, who turned their heads in her direction when she screamed. Without hesitation, Emily dived to the ground, landing next to Harmony.

"Emily," Harmony said, looking relieved. "I think I twisted it."

"Okay, put your arm around me—oof!" A fireball hit Emily hard on the side of her body and she fell to the floor. The heat of the fireball felt like it was burning her arm.

"Emily, come on," a deep voice said in her ear.

Emily slowly opened her eyes and could make out Julian Kena standing over her. He had a giant gash on his forehead that was dripping with blood.

"Harmony," Emily mumbled.

"I moved her. Put your arm around me."

"What hit me?" Emily asked, wincing as she tried to move her arm.

"A fireball, but I don't know who shot it."

"Scarlett," Emily said, gripping Julian's training kit, but she wasn't sure if he heard her.

The ground seemed to vibrate underneath them. A loud roar came from near by.

"Come on, hurry," Julian said, helping her up.

Emily looked over his shoulder and saw two bears heading towards them. Emily gasped and Julian dropped her painfully on to the floor as he shot a fireball at the bears. It hit one of them in the face and the bear roared. Julian charged at it and met the bear head on and they both rolled on the floor. The bear was snapping its jaws and snarling at Julian, who had managed to get on top of it and was squeezing its neck.

The other bear was heading straight for Emily. Its teeth were yellow and its breath was hot. Emily kicked the bear in the mouth and it stumbled back. The bear shook its large head and roared. Emily slowly stood to her feet, gritting her teeth trying to ignore the pain. It charged at Emily again and she stood her ground, with her clenched fists in front of her. With her good arm, she swung a punch at the bear, but felt air. The bear ran straight through her and Emily felt nothing.

Emily looked down at herself in disbelief. She touched her arms, but they were solid. To her left, Julian was looking around, confused, as the bear he was wrestling was gone.

"Now *that's* how you end a Survival Training," Jenkins announced, appearing out of the trees and clapping his hands. "Great team work you two."

"Brilliant illusion, darling," Roberta said, walking behind him, wearing a red training kit. "Sorry about the fireball, Emily, but you did good." Roberta smiled beautifully at a dazed Emily.

Survival Training was officially over.

It took a while to convince the students that the bears were an illusion and no one found it funny, or appreciated Roberta and Jenkins saying that they should never have let their guard down. All they cared about was that their well-earned feast was ruined.

Emily felt silly overreacting and thinking it was Scarlett. She thanked Julian for helping her, to which he simply replied, "Anytime," and thankfully didn't question her Scarlett outburst.

They flew back to Osaki and there were some parents waiting on the school grounds for the students who didn't stay at the school. Sally was sitting cross-legged on the grass in grey jeans and a blue parka. She had a hand shielding her eyes and waved when she saw Emily. Emily waved back and landed on the grass beside her. Sally stood up and hugged her tight.

"My gosh, I missed you," Sally said, squeezing her. "You don't smell half bad." When Emily didn't laugh, Sally held her at arm's length and frowned. "What's wrong? Was the training awful?"

Emily glanced at the other second years who were within earshot. "Not here," she murmured.

Sally nodded and took Emily's rucksack and sleeping bag and carried it to the car. They drove in silence and Sally kept glancing anxiously at Emily who stared out of the window.

"So how was it?" she asked cautiously.

"It was okay," Emily said. "Much harder than I thought."

"I can imagine," Sally said. "Last night at dinner, Michael was saying—"

"I saw my mum," Emily interrupted and Sally suddenly swerved the car to the far left. Emily clutched on to her seat and screamed.

"Crap," Sally said, pulling over to the side of the road. She turned the car off. Her face looked paler than usual. "How?"

Emily put her hand on top of Sally's because it was shaking. "It was Jenkins' illusion, but she looked so real to me, Sally."

"You saw Leah?" Sally asked.

Emily nodded and Sally put her head on the steering wheel. Emily rubbed Sally's back and waited patiently until she sat up. When she eventually did, Emily explained about her task and having to blow her up. She didn't realise she was crying until Sally wiped a tear from her cheek.

"You are such a brave girl," Sally said, looking teary eyed and Emily shook her head. Sally pulled her close and held her. "You are the bravest girl I know. I was best friends with Leah since we were nine years old. I loved her like a sister and even though it hurts that she's not here, I have you and you remind me of her so much."

"How?" Emily asked, looking up at her with her eyes and nose running.

Sally smiled. "Because she was brave too."

"I miss her so much," Emily said in between tears.

A single tear fell down Sally's face. "I know, darling, me too."

Emily was seated in her favourite armchair in the empty Ogragon living room, attempting to finish her essay for Water Studies, but she kept losing her focus. Earlier that day, Roberta had taken her aside and congratulated her on finding the strength to defeat her mother. Roberta had promised that if she could defeat her mother, she could defeat anyone, but Emily didn't feel that way.

She wished she had her real mother back. Someone she could talk to about how lonely she was, someone who would know what to do. Emily knew she was lucky to have Sally, who loved her so much. She knew that their bond was stronger than ever, but that illusion only reminded Emily that she would never have her real mother again.

"Hey, how was the Survival Training?" Warren Kinkle asked. He sat on an armchair opposite Emily.

Emily hesitated. "It was interesting."

"I'll bet." Warren laughed. "We've got Dojo training today at three."

Emily groaned. She had spent the whole weekend scrubbing her body raw, which amused Cathy, and catching up on much needed sleep. Now, she was back at school and she had been ambushed with essays and presentations, even getting History homework from Mr King, which surprised everyone because he never gave out homework, plus her body was still sore. The last thing she wanted to do was go to Dojo practice.

"But I just got back," Emily moaned.

Warren shrugged his shoulders. "I know, but it's Lenny. He's in desperate need of new tactics or something. Also, while you were away, Davon announced our game against Berbinin. It's in four days."

"Four days!" Emily exclaimed.

Warren laughed. "Yeah, Lenny's face was priceless . . . kind of like yours is now. He requested that you should be called back early to train. Naturally, Ms Macay said no. Summer accused him of being selfish and obsessed with winning. I wouldn't argue with her there."

"Neither would I," Emily grumbled.

"I found a mouse in my suitcase a few weeks ago," a voice said behind them.

Michella was standing with her hands on her hips, staring at Warren suspiciously. Emily looked at Warren and for a split second, she thought he looked worried, but she must have been seeing things as Warren looked as laid back as ever.

"I hope your late night feasts aren't bringing these rodents to our humble home?"

"No, I think they got there another way," Michella replied coldly.

The pair stared at each other in silence looking so alike with their blank expressions. Emily looked from one to the other.

Warren smiled slowly. "Is there something you're accusing me of, sis?" he teased.

"Is there something you need to confess?"

Warren threw back his head and laughed. "I'll see you at three, Emily." He strolled casually to the door before he looked back and blew a kiss at Michella. She flopped on to the chair next to Emily, who patted her arm.

"He is so annoying!" Michella shouted, before she grabbed a sheet of paper and a pen. "I know he's up to something."

"What are you doing?" Emily asked Michella, when she wrote her name on the top of the paper.

"My history essay," Michella replied innocently.

"Why? It's not due for ages."

"So? It will help me to relax."

Emily scoffed. "Writing essays helps you to relax? Sometimes I wonder how we're friends."

At three o' clock, Emily walked down the corridors of Osaki.

By the front doors, she spotted a young boy with shoulder length, black hair, looking helplessly around. He was carrying a stack of books that he was struggling to balance.

"Hey, are you alright?" Emily asked him.

He jumped and she caught one of the books before they fell and placed it neatly back on top of the stack. His large brown eyes stared back at her surprised. "Are you Emily Knight?"

Emily nodded and the boy smiled and held out his hand, which Emily shook. "I'm Jasper Jones and yes, I'm kind of lost. I'm looking for Niles Thompson's room, but I don't know where it is."

"Oh it's . . ." Emily stopped, realising she didn't know where Niles's room was either. "Err . . . I'm not sure. I just assumed he would float around Mentorawth. Is it important?"

Jasper nodded. "It's about his brother, Gabriel."

Emily frowned. "Gabriel? What about him?" Jasper hesitated. "I might be able to help. Do you mind walking with me?" Emily began to walk and prayed that Jasper would follow her. He did. "Are you friends with Gabriel?"

They walked out of the front doors.

Jasper shook his head. "I don't think he likes me very much."

"Why wouldn't he like you?" Emily questioned.

Jasper shrugged his shoulders. "I say hi to him and he sometimes says hi back. At first I thought he was shy, so I kept being nice. I noticed he's kind of a loner. Some of the other kids make fun of him, but he doesn't seem too bothered, but a few days ago, I overheard him talking to someone in our bedroom. I was going to walk away, to give them some privacy, but then she started shouting at him and I thought I heard him crying."

"She?" Emily stopped and looked at him with her heart pounding. "Who was she?"

"I don't know. I opened the door and there was no one there. Gabriel just looked at me and stormed out of the room. I've tried to talk to him since, but he ignores me and he's acting a bit—"

"Strange," Emily finished for him.

Jasper's eyes widened. "Yeah, how do you know?"

"I've spent a bit of time with Gabriel and he's a bit weird." Emily thought of Gabriel being outside the Ogragon team room. "So you have no idea who this woman was?"

Jasper shook his head.

Ms Macay, the team leader for Ogragon walked past them. Emily thought to stop her and tell her of her suspicions, but decided against it. It had to be Neci or someone from her team talking to Gabriel, but Emily had to be sure.

"What should I do?" Jasper asked.

Emily thought for a moment before she said, "Tell Niles, but don't worry. I'll deal with it."

Jasper smiled, clearly relieved. "Thanks, Emily."

"It's no problem. Look, Lenny is going to kill me, so I'll catch you later!"

Emily ran down Gilford's Walk and on to the sandy Dojo pitch. The stadium was a circular shape and was brightly lit, showing off royal red seats. The scoreboard once again read, 'Dojo Champions-Pentwon.'

Lenny Kinkle tapped his watch sharply and yelled, "You're late."

"Sorry, I got held up."

Lenny stared at her in disbelief. "You got held up? We

have a game in four days that we're not ready for and you got held up? If you're not serious—"

"Oh, Lenny, just leave it, will you? She's here now," Jessie Kendaschi said. He was a handsome boy with blond hair, green eyes and an effortless coolness about him. He was the second Fighter for Ogragon, but he had injured his knee last year, so Emily had never seen him fight. It was strange seeing him without crutches.

Lenny shot Jessie a sharp look. "I believe I was speaking to Emily."

"Talk about wasting time," Jessie muttered.

"Listen up," Lenny shouted. "I'm the captain and when I'm speaking—"

"Oh just blow him up, Jessie," Warren said and Jessie laughed.

"Blow him up?" Rosa Martin asked. Her training kit hung on her petite frame.

Jessie opened his hand and in the middle of it was a small fire flame. Unlike fireballs that are formed by the person's energy, fire flames are made out of fire. A very rare hidden power. Everyone crept closer to him, admiring it, even Lenny. Emily had created fire by accident last year.

"How did you do that?" Emily asked.

Jessie shrugged like it wasn't a big deal. "I discovered it over the holidays. I can get it really big too."

"Now, that's a cool power," Pete said, staring memorised at the flame.

"Hello?" Raquel Davis interrupted. She was a striking black girl, with piercings on her ears, nose, and above her top lip. Her hair was now bright red. Emily noticed that it was the same colour as Scarlett's. "It's freezing out here so can we get on with it?"

"Oh my gosh, Raquel I didn't even realise you got your tongue pierced," Emily said surprised.

"Yeah, it killed," Raquel said, sticking out her tongue, so Emily could see it better.

"I could be sleeping," Warren Kinkle moaned.

"You can say that again," Rosa Martin said.

"I could be sleeping," Summer Wind said.

The three of them laughed. Lenny looked frustrated at his team members.

"Right, we have to form a play for Berbinin. We can't keep using the same fighting combinations, or they'll know our next moves before we do it. We also need to figure out new ways to use our Distracters for our advantage and which Distracters should target Berbinin's Fighters. Any ideas?" Everyone fell silent. Lenny raised his eyebrows. "Oh, but everyone was so talkative a minute ago."

Emily's teeth chattered and she hugged herself tight when Warren slowly stuck his hand up.

"We could try this." Warren pulled out a neatly folded piece of paper from his back pocket and handed it to Lenny.

Lenny opened it curiously and as he began to look through it, his eyes widened in surprise. "How did you come up with this?"

"Oh, well . . . we just came up with it together. A pure stroke of genius." Warren smiled.

"We?" Lenny frowned.

"Yeah, me and Pete."

There was a long silence. Lenny suddenly looked very serious. "When did you put this together?" he demanded.

"Hmmm," Warren said, resting his chin on his hand as if he was thinking really hard. "About four weeks ago."

"That's funny because four weeks ago we didn't know who we were playing, so how could you have come up with this?" Lenny asked. "Did you make plays like this for all the teams?"

Warren glanced helplessly at Pete, who suddenly looked very interested in the designs on his baht shoes.

"Well—I mean–it's . . ." Warren stammered, then he shrugged his shoulders. "It was just a lucky guess."

The rest of the team exchanged doubtful looks with each other.

"Warren," Rosa said softly. "I'm not saying you did, but if you broke the rules to make this play we'll be disqualified. This is Lenny's last year. We have to win the cup."

Everyone looked at Warren, who suddenly didn't look as confident. Raquel was staring accusingly at Pete and when he looked up and caught her eye, he turned away swiftly.

"Did you spy on their training sessions?" Lenny suddenly asked and Warren and Pete looked guiltily at the floor. "Wow. You two never fail to surprise me."

"No one knows that we done it," Pete said quietly. "We hid really well."

"Oh, he speaks!" Raquel exclaimed.

Warren began to laugh. "Guys, guys, what is up with the tension? It's a great play and it's *our* play. No one will accuse us of doing anything. Don't you guys trust us?"

Emily couldn't help but smile at the silence. *What a silly question,* she thought.

"You trust me? Don't you, babe?" Warren said to Summer, who hesitated.

"I guess so," she said, sounding defeated.

"Well, there you go," Warren said cheerfully, knowing that Lenny trusted Summer's judgement, except why she had chosen his little brother for a boyfriend. The argument was now over. "Now, let me explain the play to you properly, so you can really see how amazing we are . . ."

Two hours later, when Dojo practice was finally over and Emily's body was screaming out 'overload of pain,' she walked slowly, limping towards the Ogragon living room. As she walked past the dining room, she sensed a power energy from a corridor to her left. The energy was so strong that for a few seconds Emily couldn't move. Slowly, Emily began to walk towards it, trying to stay calm, so her power couldn't be sensed. Her heart was racing at the thought that she could be face to face with Neci again.

"Why is it taking so long?" a female voice asked in an accusing tone.

Emily stopped, surprised. It wasn't Neci. No, this was someone else. Someone very powerful.

"It's not—it's not that easy," Emily heard Gabriel stutter.

"I will kill you personally if you don't get this done. That fire at your house was nothing. How would you like to see your parents die?"

"No! No!" Gabriel screamed. "Please don't!"

Emily heard a scream and the sound of glass smashing. She hobbled towards them as fast as she could. When she rounded the corridor, she saw Gabriel on his knees, trying to pick up his broken glasses from the floor but he was alone. The power energy had disappeared.

"Gabriel, are you okay?" Emily asked, walking painfully

towards him. She rested a hand on his shoulder and he shrugged her off. His eyes were bloodshot and cold. He stood up and pushed her back roughly, making her wince.

"I didn't ask for your help and I don't want it! Alright?" He cradled the pieces of glass in his arms, before storming off, not looking back at a confused Emily.

Emily was standing in the middle of the dining hall for another secret training session. She was opposite Gabriel. He was avoiding her gaze, even though he was her sparring partner. It had been a few days since he had shouted at her and he had not spoken a word to her since.

Emily stood with her knees slightly bent and her hands clenched. One arm was at her side and the other was in front of her face. Gabriel was standing with his shoulders hunched and was now looking at the floor.

"Come on," Emily said. "I'm waiting for you to hit me."

Gabriel sighed and lazily threw a punch at Emily that she barely felt.

"Oh for goodness sake," she muttered. She marched over to him, so they were face to face. "We can't spar if you won't look at me!" When Gabriel didn't respond, she added, "Who was that person threatening you?"

"I don't know what you're talking about," Gabriel said under his breath. His eyes were still focused on the floor.

"Pardon?" Emily asked, crossing her arms.

Gabriel looked at her with a hard stare. "I don't know what you're talking about, so drop it. And if you say anything about me, I'll tell everyone that you're an attention seeking liar."

Emily gasped. "Are you threatening me?" Her fists clenched by her side.

"Why don't you say something and then you'll see," Gabriel said, not flinching.

They held each other's gaze, until Emily let out a frustrated cry and marched over to Jenkins, who was supervising the lesson. She pointed at Gabriel and said, "I need a new partner."

"What's wrong with him?" Jenkins frowned.

"He is—" Emily stopped. She looked back at Gabriel and he was staring at the floor again. His arms were hugging his body, as if he was cold.

"He is what?" Jenkins asked.

"I don't know. Can you talk to him, please?"

Jenkins walked over to Gabriel and Emily stood with her hands on her hips watching the others. Antonio was paired up with Julian, which at first she thought was a silly idea because Antonio was so little, but now she was watching him and she was impressed. He was literally flying in circles around Julian, throwing a kick and a punch in whenever he could. Julian's face was red and he kept trying to grab Antonio, but he was too fast for him.

"Ha!" Julian exclaimed, as he grabbed Antonio and used his knuckles to rub on his head.

Antonio laughed and squealed at the same time. "Get off me," he said in between laughter.

"Not so tough now, huh?" Julian said, smiling.

He put Antonio on the floor, who then ran over to the

Reviving Water bucket that was in the corner of the room and dunked his head in.

"I guess that water's out," Julian said to Emily as he walked towards her.

Antonio lifted his head and shook it, so water sprayed everywhere. He laughed to himself and ran towards Xavier, who was sparring with Alice.

"You had your work cut out with him," Emily said and Julian laughed.

"Don't be fooled by his cute face," Julian said. "What's up with him?" He nodded towards Gabriel. Julian's long, black plait was unravelling and he took it out, so that his hair fell in waves down his back.

Emily shrugged her shoulders. She had a strong urge to run her hands through his hair.

"Do you want to spar?" Julian asked and Emily nodded.

They walked to the middle of the room and they both clenched their fists. Julian walked slowly in a circle and Emily copied him. He threw a punch at Emily's face which she blocked with her arm. She aimed a kick at his stomach, but he pushed her leg down with his hand.

"Do you remember that fireball you shot during the Ogragon versus Mentorawth game? You put me in the sick bay for weeks."

"Yes, I remember beating you," Emily teased.

"I'll win the next time," Julian said confidently and Emily raised her eyebrows.

"We'll see about that," she responded.

Jenkins clapped his hands together and everyone stopped and looked at him. "Time's up, guys. They need to get the dining hall

ready for lunch. We'll let you know when the next training is."
He placed his hand on Gabriel's shoulder. Gabriel was staring
straight ahead at the plain walls, avoiding everyone's gaze.

Alice walked past Emily and ignoring her, she said goodbye
to Julian. Emily rolled her eyes before Julian turned to her
and asked, "Are you going to your team room?"

"Yeah, I'm going to go find my friends."

"I'll walk up with you," Julian said.

Jenkins was walking ahead of them, talking to Gabriel. As
if sensing her, Gabriel looked over his shoulder and stared
directly at Emily with a blank expression.

"How are you liking the training?" Julian asked.

"Huh?" Emily said, looking away from Gabriel.

"The training," Julian said. He headed towards the stairs.
"Do you like it?"

"Yeah, it's okay," Emily said distractedly. She wished she
knew what Jenkins was saying to him.

"You and Alice seem better," Julian said and he laughed
at Emily's horrified face.

"I can't stand that girl!" Emily exclaimed. "It's much better
when we don't talk. How are you finding it?"

"I like it. I'm learning new things and I'm making new
friends. I feel like we're getting to know each other better."

Emily couldn't help but smile. "Yeah definitely."

They got to the first floor where the Mentorawth team
room was.

"Good luck with the Berbinin match tomorrow," he said.

"Thank you. Hopefully we'll win," she replied.

"You're amazing—I mean, Ogragon's amazing." Julian
blushed. "You guys will definitely win. I'll see you later."

"See you," Emily said. As soon as he was out of sight, she punched the air. Remembering where she was, she looked up and down the hall and was thankful no one had witnessed her. With a bounce in her step, she went up another flight of stairs to the Ogragon team room.

"How's training going?" Michella whispered when they sat down for lunch. "How are Gabriel and Alice?"

Emily bent her head close to hers and filled Michella in with what had been happening.

"Oh my gosh, you have to tell Niles what happened," Michella said loudly. "I can't believe he had the cheek to threaten you."

"Ssh, it won't help. Gabriel isn't gonna say a thing to back me up and I can't risk him saying anything about me. Not now when we're trying to get people to fight with us."

"I don't think he'll say anything," Michella said.

Emily tutted. "He sounded pretty serious to me."

"How long have you known about this woman?"

Emily shot her a look. "Only a few days, but trust me, I don't think this is something we should get involved with. Gabriel clearly doesn't want my help," Emily added, as she could see Michella was going to argue back. "We'll eventually see what he's up to."

Michella shook her head. "You better hope you're right, because if anything happens to Gabriel and you knew about it, you're going to be in big trouble."

Emily didn't respond.

At that point, Mr Davon walked into the dining hall, followed by Roberta and Jenkins. They sat down with the other teachers and Mr Davon stood at the front of the hall and said, "Once again, Ogragon open up with the first game of the Dojo season, Ogragon vs. Berbinin at two o'clock. Good luck to both teams."

"Berbinin! Berbinin!" the slow, quiet chant quickly escalated into a booming roar that echoed throughout the dining hall. Students were thumping their fists on the table and drumming their feet on the floor. Some students were looking at Roberta and clapping, but Roberta was waving her hands and shaking her head.

"We're going to bring the cup home for you!" Rio Bryns stood up and pointed at Roberta. He was a Fighter for the Berbinin Dojo Team. Roberta smiled and gestured for him to sit down.

"Is this some kind of joke?" Emily asked bewildered.

Some first year Ogragon students attempted to retaliate, chanting 'Ogragon!' but they were drowned out and eventually they sunk into their seats, looking embarrassed.

"Idiots," Warren Kinkle declared. He stood up and walked out of the hall.

The rest of the Ogragons followed him and the entire hall booed and laughed. Emily passed Julian Kena's table and lowered her head. She hoped he wasn't participating. She wanted to look, but she didn't know what she would do if he was. Emily walked quickly and she heard Tanya hiss, "Break a leg, Emily and an arm and your neck too."

Emily stormed towards History class.

"I can't believe the teachers did nothing. Next time, I'm

going to shoot a fireball during dinner for the fun of it and we'll see if they just stand there!" Wesley shouted.

"I'll join you with that," Michella said, to the surprise of everyone.

"Roberta wasn't even impressed," Danny June said. "She was in Berbinin years ago! Like she really gives a crap about them winning."

"You better knock them out, Emily," Violet Hijen said, followed by cheers.

"Yeah, I will," Emily declared.

"Berbinin my arse," Sydney John spat. "They've never played a decent game."

"They're just getting cocky. They probably think Roberta's going to bring them luck," Nicky Johansen said, crossing her arms over her chest.

Violet Hijen opened the door to the small classroom with its triangular roof and led the way in. Emily almost jumped when she saw that Mr King wasn't slumped over his desk with an empty whisky bottle, or burying himself in a fashion magazine and muttering irritably at anyone who disturbed him. Today, he was standing in front of the black board in smart, clean attire. His trademark trilby hat covered his thinning hair and he smiled at the class.

"Hello Ogragons, please take your seats," he said pleasantly.

"Huh?" Emily uttered, looking at Mr King. "Sir, are you okay?"

Mr King turned to her, smiling slowly, baring his teeth. He looked very bizarre. "Yes, Miss Knight. I'm fine. Can you kindly take your seat?"

Emily nodded and walked towards Michella. "What is he on?"

"I think he's getting assessed," Michella said.

Emily looked around the room, but could only see the Ogragon team. "How do you know?"

"Look at the corner in the back."

Emily looked slowly, trying not to make it obvious. There was a small, plain-faced, middle aged woman, with greying, mousy, brown hair, which was cut into an unflattering bob, sitting on a stool, holding a clipboard and staring at Mr King over her glasses. He glanced at her and nervously wiped his brow.

"Right class, I just want to start off with saying well done for your history marks. I felt you all did very well. However, the school board feels that we could have done better." At this statement, he gritted his teeth. "They feel I didn't teach you enough."

"Doesn't giving fashion advice count as teaching?" Wesley said loudly and everyone laughed.

Mr King's eyes practically bulged out under his black trilby. "There, there, Mr Parker, quite the comedian he is, Martha." He addressed the lady in the corner who nodded wearily.

The entire class turned around to face her.

"This is going to be interesting," Wesley said, with a big smile on his face.

"Who can tell me the full names of the leaders of the Warrior Revolution?" Mr King asked.

No one put their hands up. Emily glanced at Jason, who without a doubt knew the answer, but he was staring back innocently at Mr King.

"We touched on it last year, or we-we-were meant to," Mr King stammered, wiping his brow again. "Anyone?"

Wesley nudged Jason. "Go on, take him out of his misery. He looks like he's about to cry."

Mr King's eyes darted to and fro. Martha's hand moved furiously over her paper. Some of the students started to snigger at Mr King's desperation. Jason sighed loudly and lazily raised his hand.

"Yes, Mr Notting?"

"Bernard Ogragon, Joseph Berbinin, Idris Jenkint, Arthur Linktie, Rose-Marie Mentorawth and Ce-Ce Pentwon and the school teams are named after them."

"That's excellent, Mr Notting." Mr King glanced at Martha, who was now smiling and was writing something down. "Thank you," he mouthed at Jason.

"Sir?" Danny June raised his hand.

"Yes, Mr June?"

"Can we focus today on Joseph Berbinin? And can you tell us why being in Berbinin is so crap?"

"Err," Mr King said nervously. "Crap is not the correct word to use at school."

"What do you mean? You say it all the time," Danny protested and Mr King turned bright red. "Sir, they booed us in the dining hall. Do you know how embarrassing that is? I am seriously pissed off right now."

Emily glanced at Martha, who was staring at Danny with her mouth open.

"Mr June, let's mind the language," Mr King stressed.

"But sir, he's right," Sydney John protested. "That was horrible what happened and Mr Davon did nothing!"

"Don't even get me started on bloody Davon!" Wesley exclaimed.

The class began to talk over each other. Martha stood up so quickly that her chair toppled causing a loud bang when it hit the floor. The noise made everyone fall quiet. "I will be talking to the headmaster about this!" she said, before she marched out of the door.

"Martha, please wait," Mr King pleaded. He ran after her and when he got to the door, he whipped around to face the class, with an ugly frown and roared, "You stupid kids!" He slammed the door on his way out.

An awkward silence fell upon the class until Danny said, "What the hell is his problem?" And everyone began talking over each other.

"I was reading about the Warrior Revolution," Jason said, as they walked outside for break. "It was pretty interesting. It's crazy to think people used their powers to cause that much trouble. Can you imagine what it would have been like if Ogragon and the rest didn't step in?"

"But isn't it history repeating itself?" Emily asked. "It's just what Neci's doing."

"Let's not talk about this now. Why don't we sit under the big oak tree, so you can relax before the match," Michella said.

"I'm fine," Emily stressed, but she was starting to get worried. She had never played Berbinin before and even though Warren and Pete's tactics were impressive, they had spied to get them and if they were caught out . . .

"Emily." Niles Thompson was beside her. His deep dimples clear in his transparent yet comely face.

"Hey, Niles."

It was always surreal seeing legends such as Niles and Cecil Archinia floating around the school grounds, when their faces were plastered across every media outlet worldwide. Emily felt slightly intimidated by Niles. She wasn't sure if it was because he oozed confidence, coolness and was ridiculously handsome, or that he had (and probably still) had no faith in Emily, due to her lack of control over her powers.

"Can I speak to you?" He glanced quickly at Jason, Wesley and Michella, who waved shyly. "In private?"

Emily nodded and followed Niles. She looked back and Wesley pointed at the big oak, where they were heading to. Emily mouthed, 'I'll see you there,' and gave a thumbs up.

Niles stopped when they had reached the koi pond. He watched it for a few moments, looking seriously at the colourful fish and Emily shuffled from one foot to the other, watching Niles, wondering if she should comment on how clean the water looked just to break the silence.

"For a split second, I thought all my family had died in that fire," Niles said softly. He was still looking at the water and Emily instantly stopped moving. "I had never been so frightened in my entire life. Of course, they were shaken up, but everyone seems to have come out of it stronger, except Gabriel."

Niles looked at Emily, his face troubled. "Gabriel isn't like me. He's not confident, or adventurous. He's shy and very humble. He's a sweet kid and the warrior gene in him is almost . . . wrong. I sometimes wonder, why does he have it? He wasn't like me, who didn't want it because I was scared; I thought I was a freak. No, Gabriel doesn't want it cause he hates violence of all sorts."

Niles sighed deeply. "Warriors feed off violence. Something will stir within us, where we'll want to fight. I was the one warriors challenged, I was their target and now I'm like this." Niles looked down at his ghostly figure and Emily could feel his pain. "Gabriel is now the target. That fire at my house was to get to him and he's so scared. He hasn't told me, but I can see it. He walks with his head down, he jumps whenever anyone calls his name. I hate that he has to fight in this war."

"He doesn't have to," Emily said softly. "Roberta and Jenkins can take him out."

Niles shook his head and looked at Emily defeated. "He has no choice."

Emily had a strong urge to hold him, to comfort him, but she knew her hands would go right through him, making it awkward for the both of them.

"Something's changed in him," Niles said, with an urgency in his voice. "There's a barrier to him that I can't . . . I can't break it. I've tried talking to him and he says nothing's wrong. I tried using my powers to get in his head and he shuts me down!" Niles punched his fist into his hand. "That Jasper kid said he's talking to a woman. Who is he talking to?"

"I dunno," Emily said helplessly. "He won't tell me."

"I need to know, Emily," Niles said. His eyes were wide and fearful. "You're the only one I know who's lost a brother. I can't . . . I just can't lose him." Niles' voice chocked and he buried his head in his hands.

The image of Gabriel turning on her, his eyes so cold and full of hate, flashed in her mind.

"I'll find out what's going on," she heard herself say and

Niles reached for her as if he was going to hug her, but stopped at the last minute.

"Thank you," he said. "I really appreciate it."

Seeing as she couldn't keep Lox safe, she was determined to help Gabriel, whether he liked it or not.

Two o'clock. Emily was putting on her black baht shoes. She had to leave a distressed Niles to meet the rest of the team. Lenny Kinkle was pacing up and down the changing room, with his eyes closed, muttering under his breath. Pete Kinkle, who was sitting next to Emily, nudged her and pointed at Lenny. Emily barely smiled. All her thoughts were on Niles and Gabriel.

"Please remember all that we've practiced, guys," Lenny announced. "And not to stress anyone out, but we have to win this to stay in the running for the cup."

"So no pressure," Pete said, rolling his eyes.

"The weathers all right," Lenny continued as if Pete didn't talk. "A bit windy, but that can't be helped. Jessie— surprise them with your fire. Raquel, Rosa—you focus on the Distracters, but Summer—you get the Fighters."

"Got it," Summer Wind said, tying up her long, blonde hair into a high ponytail.

Lenny checked his watch. "Right, let's do this."

When the Ogragons stepped on to the pitch, loud boos erupted from the crowd.

"Just ignore them," she heard Lenny say behind her.

Emily looked up at the commentators' box and waved at Wesley and Harmony Loving-Dale, who both waved back.

"And here's the Ogragon team—Lenny Kinkle, Summer Wind, Raquel Davis, Rosa Martin, Pete Kinkle, Warren Kinkle, Jessie Kendaschi and Emily Knight!"

"Crush 'em, Emily!" Danny June's distinctive voice could be heard over the boos.

The Berbinin team walked on to the pitch in dark purple training kits to thunderous cheers.

"The Berbinin team—Terry Marsh, Felisha Hart, Valerie Silva, Marie Sanders, Andy CarMichael, Gary Coles, Rio Bryns and Ambria Appleton!" Harmony announced.

The two teams faced each other as the audience applauded them. Emily faced Berbinin's fifth Fighter, Ambria Appleton. She was the first person in Foughtgon class to do a Baby Ball last year. She was slightly taller than Emily, with a long nose and almond eyes which were almost hidden behind her dark fringe. She waved at Emily and Emily smiled back.

"Right, guys," Ms Macay said, as she swatted her red hair out of her face. "A clean match is all I'm asking for."

She blew the whistle that rang around the stadium and the teams flew up into the air. Emily looked through the crowds and spotted Michella and Jason waving at her. Lisa Fowler was seated next to Jason, leaning so close to him that she was almost on his lap.

"And they're off," Harmony Loving-Dale reported. "The captains, Lenny Kinkle of Ogragon and Terry Marsh of Berbinin start the match. Kinkle's attacked Marsh with a combo of punches—Marsh has managed to dodge each of them—he's punched Kinkle hard in the face—Kinkle staggers back—Felisha Hart, Distracter for Berbinin has kicked Kinkle in the lower back, but Ogragon's Distracters, Raquel Davis and Rosa Martin have double teamed on Hart. Berbinin need to re-think their team work."

"For once I agree with you, Harmony," Wesley continued. "Kinkle's elbowed Marsh to his chest with so much force that he's collided with the invisible wall—Summer Wind has appeared at Kinkle's side—and what's this? Wind and Kinkle have fired a fireball at each other! Wow, that's huge! What are they doing? They have shot it at Marsh! Ahh, I can't see, there's too much smoke—Harmony, can you see? There he is! Marsh is falling—Berbinin Distracters have just noticed, their teamwork really is rubbish—and he's out! MARSH IS OUT OF THE GAME! 1-0 TO OGRAGON!"

Emily cheered with the rest of the team, but she couldn't help getting distracted by Gary Coles, a stocky, short boy in Berbinin. All throughout the fight, his eyes were glued to Emily. A hateful stare that made Emily nervous.

Andy CarMichael from Berbinin had just stepped out and Lenny was stretching his arms, ready to battle again. Emily glanced over at Gary, who was still watching her.

"What is that guy's problem?" Emily muttered.

"Who?" Jessie Kendaschi asked, following Emily's gaze. Jessie frowned when he saw Gary. "A bit intense."

"Yeah, just a little bit," Emily replied, feeling uncomfortable.

She turned back to watch the fight. Lenny was clearly winning even though he looked a bit tired, when a giant red fireball flew directly towards Emily. Emily ducked and Jessie hit it up into the sky.

"What the—" Emily said.

"Emily, move!" Jessie yelled.

As if in slow motion, Emily watched Gary charge towards

her with a hunger in his eyes. Jessie dived and grabbed him around the neck. Gary struggled aggressively under his grasp.

"Let me get her! Get off me!"

"Gary, what are you doing?" Andy CarMichael cried.

Andy and Lenny had stopped fighting and were flying towards him.

"Do you know how much Neci will reward me if I bring her? Do you know how much she's worth?"

"You're on Neci's team?" Jessie asked in disbelief, although his hold didn't weaken.

"I'm on the right side," Gary spat. "Now get off." He lunged again and Jessie held on tighter.

"You're mental," Warren said, shaking his head. "How can you say stupid stuff like that when the Five Warriors are here?"

Gary laughed. "Neci will protect me. It's all of you that will die and you—" he stared directly at Emily, making her feel cold inside. "You'll be the number one prize."

"Okay, I'm bored of this," Jessie declared, staring at Gary with disgust. "Let Davon deal with this loser. Help me out, Warren."

Gary was trying to pull Jessie's arms from around his neck but Warren grabbed hold of Gary's arms and placed them around his back and they flew him down to the floor. The Berbinin and Ogragon Dojo team followed behind.

Emily overheard Andy apologising to Lenny. "Next time, eh? I didn't see how weird he'd become . . ."

"You okay?" a soft voice said from behind her.

Emily turned to see Ambria Appleton. She never noticed how striking Ambria was, with her brown skin that was a lighter shade than Emily's and her long, thick black eyelashes.

They had never really spoken, even though they had some classes together.

"Yeah." Emily laughed nervously. "That was just a bit . . . weird. I didn't think that people here would be on her side."

"Tell me about it."

They both watched Mr Davon lead Gary towards the exit. Wesley and Harmony were on their feet and were discussing over the microphone why Gary tried to attack Emily. The audience were off their seats, with mixed reactions. Some confused, some were angry and were banging on the invisible walls. A few were cheering and Emily felt sick. She prayed they were happy that Gary was gone. Emily sighed heavily.

"Do you know Cecil's granddaughter, Alice?" Ambria suddenly asked.

"Yeah, why?"

"Is she and Julian, you know . . ."

Emily shook her head viciously. "No way."

"Oh good," Ambria smiled, looking very pretty. "Julian's so hot. I'm definitely gonna ask him out. See you later."

Ambria swooped down towards the sandy floor. Emily looked around the stadium, trying to study the faces of the students and she couldn't help but wonder who else was after her? She watched the Ogragon and Berbinin team talking amongst each other and a few times they looked up at her.

What if they're against me? Emily thought, and a second later she dismissed it and scolded herself. She knew she could trust her teammates. She looked at the commentators' box and caught Wesley's eye.

He mouthed, "You good?" And Emily nodded. He looked

like he was going to say something else when Ms Macay teleported next to him.

"Emily!" Lenny called from below. "Come down."

She flew down to the floor, to rejoin her team as Wesley announced, "Due to Gary Coles' unacceptable behaviour, the Dojo match will not continue."

The students booed loudly and Ms Macay grabbed the microphone and shouted, "We will not tolerate warriors that are in support of Neci and we will not allow a match to continue once the rules are broken. Ogragon will take the win for today."

The Ogragons were on their feet cheering, while the Berbinins looked on with sour-faced expressions.

"Sorry again about, Gary," Terry Marsh, the Berbinin captain said to Emily.

"Thank you," Emily replied.

"Cheers, T," Lenny said and they slapped each other on the back.

"At least something good came out of that," Warren said, once the Berbinins had walked off the pitch. The Ogragons looked at him in disbelief. "What? I didn't mean it like-sorry, Emily."

"Our Emily's tough, right?" Rosa Martin asked, wrapping her arm around Emily's small waist.

"I just want to get off the pitch," Emily confessed.

They walked towards the changing rooms with Rosa holding tight to Emily.

Jessie Kendaschi had his arms folded across his chest and was shaking his head. "Gary Coles, man. I can't believe it."

"I don't know what's more weird. That he follows Neci, or

that he thought he could go for Emily in front of Mr Davon and us and get away with it," Pete said.

"What do you think will happen to him?" Raquel Davis asked.

"He will get expelled for sure," Pete replied. "Maybe even sent to S.U.D.W."

"S.U what?" Raquel frowned.

"The Special Unit for Dangerous Warriors. They should definitely lock him up. I wonder how many people at school have the same motives as Gary?"

"Pete!" Rosa hissed, when she felt Emily tense under her grasp. "I'm sure there's no one else."

Pete scoffed. "Get real. You can't believe that for a second."

Emily glanced at Rosa, waiting for her to disagree, but she didn't and the rest of the Ogragon team remained silent.

CHAPTER SIX

The Hidden Passageway

Emily woke up with her chest feeling tight. She breathed in deeply with her hand on her chest as she searched her room. She had dreamt about that night in the forest, surrounded by Neci's henchmen. Their energy combined was choking the air around her. She was sure she had stopped breathing for a few seconds.

"I'm safe, I'm safe," Emily said to herself, until she felt her body relax.

Cathy was asleep beside her, her blonde curls covering her face. Emily watched her foster sister lovingly. Cathy had stayed with her every night, never allowing Emily to ask. Sometimes Emily envied Cathy's life. All she ever worried about was makeup and boys, definitely not about fighting in a potential war.

Cathy stirred in her sleep and opened one eye. She always did that, as if she was testing whether it was worth fully waking up for. She saw Emily staring at her and smiled sleepily.

"Hey," Cathy said, stretching out and yawning.

"Morning," Emily replied. "Good sleep?"

Cathy nodded. "You? Or silly question?"

Emily smiled. "What do you think?"

"Sorry Ems–hey, what happened to that weirdo that tried to attack you during your match?"

"Oh, Gary Coles?" Emily said. "He got excluded and sent to the Special Unit for Dangerous Warriors, so he won't be out for a long time."

"Osaki really sucks," Cathy said. "Don't you lot do anything fun? Is it always fight here, fight there?"

Emily laughed. "The Revolution Night party is coming up. That should be fun."

Cathy looked at her in disbelief. "The same party where Lox tried to kill you! Fun?"

"Hopefully it won't happen this year," Emily said, half-joking and Cathy shuddered.

"How's the whole Gabriel issue going?"

Emily shook her head. "He's avoiding me."

Cathy tutted and sat up, so she was resting against the headboard. "I think you should stay clear. You have your own crap to think about."

"Trust me, if I could, I would but if Neci's warriors are blackmailing Gabriel, it's a big problem for everyone. We have no idea what they're up to and if it's anything to do with this missing warrior, then we're screwed."

Cathy huffed, clearly annoyed with Emily's observation. "Well, what about Lox?" she asked, after a moment of silence.

"What about him?"

"Whose side is he fighting for?"

Emily put her head in her hands. "I don't know."

"Come to think of it, shouldn't you all be looking for him as well?" Cathy said accusingly. "Your dad hasn't managed to find him yet. I mean isn't *he* the missing warrior Neci's banging on about?"

"I don't think so," Emily said slowly, lifting her head up. "I think it's another strong warrior with a unique power, but I don't have a clue who it could be."

Cathy ran her fingers through her curls, tying it up into a messy bun at the top of her head. "I think it's a trick. I bet Neci wants you to think it's another warrior, so that you focus all of your energy on finding this person that doesn't exist, but all along it's Lox."

"Do you think so?" Emily asked.

Cathy rolled her eyes. "Well really, Emily, who else could it be?"

James, Yvonne and Rosy were eating pancakes and strawberries at the dining table when Emily and Cathy walked in. Yvonne and Rosy were only seven and six and eating for them resulted in another change of clothes. This morning, the girls were dressed in their fancy clothes, so Sally had put a cloth tucked under their necks and on their laps.

"Morning, guys," Emily said, sitting in front of her plate of food.

"Morning, Emily," they chorused.

"Emily, can you take me out today?" James asked excitedly.

Emily needed to remind Sally and Michael to cut his fringe, which he kept flicking out of his eyes.

"No, we all have school."

"We don't!" the kids chorused.

"It's bank holiday, babe," Cathy said, dipping a strawberry in fresh cream. She opened up a newspaper that was on the table and flicked through the pages.

"Oh," Emily replied. At Osaki they didn't get any holidays apart from Christmas and summer.

"Mummy said one of you have to drop us off at Lauren's house for her party," Yvonne said, grinning and showing her missing front tooth.

"Where is Sally?" Emily asked. She never missed breakfast with the family. The only one who did was Michael because of his work schedule.

"She's at Aunt Roberta's," James said, rolling his pancake in one and stuffing it in to his mouth, to the delight of his younger sisters, who giggled.

"Quit it, James before you choke," Cathy said sharply. "Isn't it a bit early for a party?"

"Lauren said if we come early, we can play on the bouncy castle before the other kids arrive. Please," Rosy pleaded, looking at Emily with her huge blue eyes.

"Okay," she said and the girls cheered. "I can drop you before I go to school. James, are you coming?"

"No way," James protested. "That's a baby party. Cath, can you take me somewhere today?"

"Not if you keep stuffing whole pancakes in your mouth. Emily—look!" Cathy passed over the newspaper and pointed to page six.

"Fireball attacks in New York," Emily whispered. She picked up the paper and quickly read the article.

"Can we go?" Yvonne moaned, tapping on the newspaper, making Emily jump.

"Yes, let me put on my uniform." She caught Cathy's eye and she mirrored her pained expression.

Neci and her team had blocked the Brooklyn Bridge and were only letting people pass if they accepted the chip in to their arms. Those that resisted were punished. *What exactly did the chips do?* Emily wondered. Her stomach was in knots when she thought of Lox. If he was involved in the attacks, she didn't know how she could ever defend him again.

When she came back downstairs, Sally still wasn't back, so Emily placed her school bag in the corridor and inspected the girls' dresses which were in perfect condition.

Emily opened the door and was instantly swamped by the paparazzi, which had stopped fazing her. Whether she was at school, or not, they were camped at Legends Village. She had no idea how they got past the gates. The paparazzi followed behind them, snapping pictures and shouting out questions about Neci, Lox and Thomas. Emily was impressed with Rosy and Yvonne who conducted themselves maturely—the only way Emily guessed they were scared was because they gripped her hand a bit tighter.

Lauren Babel's house was a five-minute walk, on a street that was very prestigious, but not as exclusive as Legends Village. They were what Michael called 'old money.'

The Babels lived in an elegant cream mansion with large windows, so that you could see into their grand living room, which the maid was currently hoovering. Emily, Rosy and Yvonne climbed the steps that led to the front door with the press waiting at the bottom. Emily rang the bell and a harassed-looking Mrs Babel answered the door. She was a skinny, white woman with shoulder length brown hair and tired brown eyes. Her mouth dropped and her eyes bulged when she saw Emily, but she swiftly replaced it with a false smile. The last time Emily had seen her, she had had so much Botox that her face was frozen. Yvonne and Rosy immediately ran into the house, hollering Lauren's name.

"Sorry about them, they're very excited," Emily explained.

Mrs Babel looked past her and was staring at the press, who were taking pictures of her. She stood up a little straighter and flicked her hair. "Emily dear, so sorry, I was expecting Sally to bring the girls."

"Oh yeah, she went to see someone. What time should they get picked up?"

"No, Cathy? She couldn't have brought them?" Mrs Babel asked, as if Emily hadn't spoken.

Emily frowned. "No, is there a problem?"

Mrs Babel leaned closer to her and whispered, "Oh no dear, not with me anyway, but my husband . . . his feelings towards Thomas Knight aren't the most popular if you get my drift."

Emily stared at Mrs Babel and suddenly all the anger she had been feeling recently began to bubble to the service. "No, I don't. Why don't you tell me?" she asked in a loud voice.

Mrs Babel winced. "I'm sure you read the paper this morning about Neci in New York? It's absolutely dreadful what these warriors are doing to innocent people. This has nothing to do with non-warriors. This isn't our fight."

"You think that Neci won't kill you, or burn your house, or kidnap members of your family because you're not a warrior? Do you really think she cares?"

"Let's just leave it there, Emily," Mrs Babel stressed. "One doesn't want to make a scene."

"A scene? You listen to me, when Neci personally blows up your house, don't be surprised when I slam my door in your face!"

Mrs Babel turned an ugly shade of red. "Well, I never!"

"Your biggest problem is you think everything that's been happening doesn't affect you, but what are you going to do when Neci and her team force you to get a chip in your arm? We don't even know what the chip does. But I can guarantee that you'll wish that a good warrior would help you. Don't you dare turn to me for help."

Emily stomped down the steps and Mrs Babel called out after her, "You warriors want respect but you all act like brutes!" She slammed the front door, which echoed through the empty streets.

"Wasn't that fun?" Emily said to the nearest reporter, who seemed to have lost the ability to speak as she personally addressed him and before he could answer, Emily bent her knees and soared into the air.

Later that morning, when Sally dropped Emily at Osaki, Emily was surprised to see Sally get out of the car and follow her up the slope towards the school. Emily frowned at her and accusingly asked, "Where are you going?"

"Oh, I have a meeting with Mr Davon, didn't I say?" Sally asked, deliberately avoiding Emily's gaze.

"A meeting? About what?" Emily asked, now noticing the smart shirt Sally was wearing over tight black trousers.

"You'll find out later. Come on, give me a tour of the famous Osaki Training School," Sally said, linking arms with Emily.

Although displeased, she led Sally towards the building.

They walked up the slope in silence. Sally was staring at the white building in awe.

"What was your conversation with Aunt Roberta about?" Emily asked. Sally blushed but she didn't respond. Not even when Emily stopped walking.

Sally turned to her and looked around bewildered to see Emily behind her, scowling. "Emily, come on." When Emily didn't move, Sally sighed. "I promise you'll find out soon. Please, let's go."

Emily huffed and caught up with Sally but she refused to link arms with her. They walked into the hallway when Sally stopped. Her eyes immediately caught on to the quotes on the wall.

"Dad's on there," Emily said. "And they have an Osaki Wall of Fame upstairs."

Sally raised an eyebrow. "Is Lox on there?"

"Yes, for winning the World Warrior Championship and Warrior Tournament."

Sally stayed silent.

"Mrs Meran?" The deputy headmaster, Laton Chin approached Sally. He bowed his head slightly to her. Sally looked at Emily confused and Emily gestured for her to copy, which Sally did. "Thank you for coming. The headmaster is ready to see you now. Miss Knight, breakfast is being served."

Emily took that as her dismissal. She bowed to Laton Chin and made her way to the hall, watching Sally over her shoulder until she disappeared. Emily sat down next to Wesley. Jason was talking in a low voice to Michella and Michella shifted away from him when she saw Emily.

"Hey, Roberta was looking for you," Wesley said, whilst eating his toast.

Emily looked around the noisy hall, but couldn't spot her. She began to pile sausages on to her plate when the hall fell silent. Emily looked up and saw Roberta marching down the hall, dragging Alice Archinia along side her in a claw-like grip. Emily was even more taken aback to see a genuine fear in Alice's eyes.

"Up," Roberta hissed to Emily and Emily stood and followed Roberta and Alice out of the silent dining room.

Roberta stormed up the stairs in silence. Emily tried to catch Alice's eye, but didn't manage to. Roberta opened a door on the very top floor to reveal a small, dark, dingy office which she flung Emily and Alice into. Alice fell on to a chair and Emily buckled backwards as she tried to avoid it. Roberta's livid face looked from Emily to Alice.

"Well?" she demanded. The girls stayed silent. "Anything either of you want to confess?"

Emily and Alice exchanged worried glances.

"Shall we start with, Alice? Who's got millions of views on an online video of her brutally honest opinions on her team members, who don't seem to measure up to her expectations? Even though we specifically said to keep the training a secret! It's been shared all over the internet!"

Alice turned red and hung her head.

"Or Emily? Whose tactless words are going to be on every front-page newspaper tomorrow, that you threatened to blow up someone. Now, the big news that our team are finding warriors who are working for Neci and sending them to S.U.D.W will be shoved into a little corner."

"But I didn't say I would blow up—"

"WHO CARES?" Roberta screamed and Emily fell silent. "How many people are going to trust and support us after what you two just did? We have already removed the video, but the damage is done. Are you both forgetting that we're on the hunt for a warrior whose identity we don't know, with a war just around the corner? You both need to shut up, smile, and make people trust you if you want to survive this!"

Roberta glared at them one last time and muttered, "Ragazze stupide," before she marched out of the room and slammed the door so hard that it broke off its hinges.

When Emily walked into the Foughtgon room, the Ogragon and Berbinin students were talking loudly to each other. She received curious glances from the students when she walked across the wooden floor. Master Zen wasn't in the classroom yet, so Michella, Wesley and Jason drew her into a corner.

"Well?" Jason demanded.

Emily sighed. "We kind of did something stupid . . ."

She told them about her encounter with Mrs Babel and Alice's video rant. Michella stared at her with a stony expression and Jason looked at her in shock. Only Wesley seemed to look impressed with Emily's audacity.

"When you both left the room, I heard Tanya and a few other Linkties talking about Alice's video. What an idiot!" Jason said.

"Do you think I'm an idiot?" Emily asked in a small voice.

"Yes," Jason said at the same time Wesley said, "No."

The boys looked at each other. Emily felt uncomfortable under Michella's glare.

"I don't think you get it," Michella said harshly. "You don't understand how important you are and how your actions affect everyone."

"I wasn't really thinking—" Emily began defensively.

"You never do!" Michella snapped and Emily recoiled.

Master Zen appeared in the room, holding a bottle of Reviving Water and beckoned them over. Emily and Michella held each other's gaze before Michella walked away.

"Come on," Jason said, gently pushing Emily forward. "She'll calm down."

Emily hugged herself and sat with the rest of the class, aware that everyone kept looking at her.

"Today we're going to learn about different powered fireballs. You may have noticed that everyone's fireball comes in different colours. There isn't a scientific reason for it, it's just how your energy manifests, but there are certain colours that represent the power within the fireball."

Master Zen put down his bottle by his feet and created a black fireball in one hand and a white one in the other. They both had sparks flying out of them. Emily leaned forward to get a closer look.

"These are killing fireballs. Any fireball can harm you, but it will take one like the black and white fireballs, that have a huge energy power, to kill someone immediately, but only a very powerful warrior can produce one. The downside is, it takes up most of your energy to create one. For those who are unaware, Neci used the black fireball to murder, Cecil Archinia."

A few people gasped. Emily wondered how it felt to hold a killing fireball. If she could learn to create one, maybe she could stand a chance against Neci. The fireballs disappeared and Master Zen swayed on his feet. A white boy with black spiky hair named Todd Waters handed Master Zen his bottle of Reviving Water, which he drank in one go.

"Thank you," Master Zen said, when he was steady on his feet. "You must also have the intention to kill to produce one. The other killing fireball is Sino. Everyone stand back."

The students hurried behind Master Zen as he faced the Masonka wall. He held out his hands in a 'V' shape and a white, wispy light shot out at lightning speed and the Masonka wall heaved forward to absorb it before it stood still again.

"Master Zen, it was too quick to see!" Lisa Fowler moaned.

"That's the whole point. Sino is a beam that will go inside of you and a few seconds later you'll die." Emily raised her hand. "Yes, Miss Knight?"

"With Sino, can you see the light trapped inside of you?"

Master Zen nodded again. "The white beam stays trapped and the frightening part is you watch it growing brighter and brighter and there's nothing you can do stop it, then you explode." He paused and looked at her stricken face. "Are you okay, Miss Knight?"

Emily clutched her chest and leaned forward. Scarlett would do that to her, she knew it.

"Emily?" Wesley said softly, rubbing her back.

She jumped at his touch and saw that everyone was watching her curiously. "Sorry, sir, yes I'm fine."

"Are we going to learn how to create the killing fireballs?" Wesley asked.

Master Zen smiled. "Not today, Mr Parker. That is too advanced for second years."

The class groaned.

"So we can't learn killing fireballs, we can't teleport–it's like we're being set up to fail," Wesley said and the class shouted their agreement.

"Why can't we learn them all?" Jason asked. "Don't you think we should, considering Neci's back?"

"You will have to talk to Mr Davon about that," Master Zen said. "But if it was up to me, everyone would learn how to teleport. Killing fireballs however, at the level you're at, will drain all of your energy. It wouldn't be safe. Now, there are also spoken fireballs, which are stronger than the unspoken fireballs we usually do in class. The one we will learn today is called Anyosingh. Repeat it together–An-yo-singh."

"Anyosingh," the class repeated.

"Again," Master Zen said.

"Anyosingh," the class chanted.

Master Zen made the class repeat themselves until everyone was pronouncing it properly. He held his hand up to silence them before he instructed the class to go into a line. Emily was near the end of the line, but Master Zen beckoned her to come forward to Emily's dismay.

"Everyone place you hands on your forehead, on top of each other with your palms facing me. Miss Knight, focus on the Masonka wall and chant Anyosingh until the fireball forms and then shoot it."

"Anyosingh, Anyosingh," Emily said.

"Louder!" Master Zen said.

"ANYOSINGH! ANYOSINGH!"

A huge, blood red fireball appeared out of Emily's hand and shot at a rapid speed to the Masonka wall. Emily rebounded back and fell painfully on to the floor. Master Zen offered her a hand and pulled her up. The class applauded, looking at Emily in awe.

"Good job," Master Zen said, looking impressed and Emily smiled. She remembered last year, how embarrassed she was because she couldn't produce a Baby Ball. "If you don't rebound back off the fireball, it means it wasn't as strong as it could be. With practice, you will be able to withstand the power," he said to the class.

Master Zen bowed to Emily who bowed back, before she walked to the nearest bucket of Reviving Water and drank from it.

She watched as the rest of the class had their turn. Wesley had a deep frown as he focused hard on producing his fireball. She could see the outline of his strong back through his thin, white training kit and Emily watched him guiltily. Jason was behind Michella in the queue and he was whispering something into her ear. Michella was trying hard not to laugh and she covered her mouth to stop herself. Emily almost chocked on her water when she saw Jason reach for Michella's hand and hold it briefly before Michella moved her hand away. Emily studied Jason's reaction carefully; his jaw was tense.

"Hey, pass us some," Wesley said. Emily handed him the bucket and he drank down the Reviving Water, finishing by smacking his lips. "That fireball is something else. I almost broke my neck from that fall."

"Tell me about it. Random question, but have you noticed anything between Michella and Jason?"

Wesley shook his head. "What do you mean?"

Emily explained the intimate gesture between the two. Wesley raised his eyebrows and glanced at them. They were now standing in silence.

"I guess we've got to keep an eye on them. Speaking of Michella, what is going on with you two?"

Emily shrugged. "She just doesn't understand. Not everything is black and white."

Wesley nodded. "Michella's never been one to see the grey areas. She's just worried for you. It will work out."

They both turned at the same time to see Michella shoot her fireball into the Masonka wall and fall back on to the floor. Master Zen helped her up and she walked over to them smiling broadly, but when she caught Emily's eye, she looked away.

"That looked good, Mich," Wesley said.

"Thanks, that's one tough fireball." She drank down the Reviving Water from the bucket and turned to Emily. "I shouldn't have snapped at you. Can we have a night away from all this war stuff?"

A part of Emily wanted to tell Michella to go away, but the sincerity in her voice made her think otherwise. "Sounds like a plan."

"I think we need a sleepover. Maybe you could stay tonight after the Revolution Night party?"

"Yeah," Emily said, feeling excited. "I'll ask Ms Macay if it's alright. I know Sally will be fine about it."

"And the universe is balanced once again," Wesley declared.

Flying class was miserable and wet and the thin fabric of Emily's training kit was stuck to her body. Ms Macay had to shout over the howling wind and her red hair was matted to her scalp.

"This is a perfect opportunity to practice flying in different conditions. Weather is unpredictable in a battle and especially with this wind, if you don't have enough control, it can make flying dangerous. Ogragon against Linktie flying match and the winners will get to sit in the stands and get dry, whilst the losers will have to do laps around the stands for the whole lesson." The class groaned. "You better win then! Okay, two lines, Ogragons over here, Linkties over there and please control your flying."

Violet Hijen from Ogragon and Isaac Gohan from Linktie were the first to fly. The pair were tied when they reached the other end of the stadium, but when they flew back, the wind blew Violet's black hair into her face, blinding her for a second, but that was all Isaac needed to win.

"That's not fair!" Violet protested.

"You left your hair out, Hijen." Ms Macay shrugged.

Violet stood with her arms crossed, glaring at Ms Macay. "Okay, next."

Emily looked to see her opponent was Tanya Frank. Emily smirked. She'd been waiting for an opportunity to get back at Tanya since the Survival Training.

Ms Macay blew her whistle and the pair shot off. Tanya was a fast flyer and was just behind Emily. They were both used to flying in bad weather because of the Dojo matches. When they reached the other side of the stadium and everyone else looked like dots, Emily glanced back to see Tanya a second away from her and she spun around and punched Tanya hard in her stomach.

"Oof," Tanya moaned, as she dropped several feet.

"That was well overdue!" Emily hollered before she flew back, leaving an agonised Tanya behind.

When Emily returned to the class, Ola Ade looked past her, squinting her eyes to see through the rain. "Where's Tanya?" she asked.

Emily shrugged. "She said something about her belly."

Emily landed and smiled to herself. She joined Isaac in the stands and watched Tanya flying very slowly, with one of her hands on her stomach. When she landed, Emily could hear the other students asking what had happened, but just like she thought, Tanya shrugged it off. She would never admit that Emily had hurt her. Ms Macay looked unbothered with Tanya's injury and made her fly in the ferocious rain, lap after lap for the rest of the lesson.

That evening, the Ogragon girls were in their bedroom, with makeup and clothes scattered over the floor. Sarah John had just finished curling the last bit of Emily's hair, so that it was now hanging over her shoulders in big, bouncy curls.

"Can I look?" Emily asked and when Sarah nodded, she ran to the mirror and smiled at her reflection. She was wearing a fitted black dress that emphasised her toned body and black kitten heels (both borrowed from Michella). Emily grabbed the black eyeliner on the dresser besides Lisa Fowler's bed and placed a neat beauty spot just above her lip.

Emily was hoping Roberta would be impressed with their tribute to her. All of the Ogragon girls were dressed up as different versions of Roberta Taniana. Nicky Johansen even went as far as to put in green contacts.

"We look so hot," Violet Hijen said, fluffing out her hair. "Jason will definitely notice you tonight, Lisa."

Emily glanced at Michella, who was staring at Lisa through the reflection from the mirror. Michella was wearing a red dress with gold high heels. Her braids were swept up in an elaborate bun. She had taken inspiration from Roberta at the Warriors for Peace Awards and Emily had never seen Michella look so beautiful.

"I hope so," Lisa said, breathing out deeply. She was the complete opposite of Roberta. Light when Roberta was dark, straight bodied instead of curvy, but everyone was determined to dress up the same.

"Do you know who's looking really hot?" Sydney John said, sitting on her sister, Sarah's bed. "Like so hot I can't stop staring at him—Wesley Parker. Those eyes are so hypnotising."

"You like Wesley?" Emily asked casually.

"Duh! So many girls do. I overheard Harmony Loving-Dale talking about how good he smells. Lucky cow gets to sit so close to him at every Dojo match." Sydney sighed. "He could have been my Jenkins tonight."

The girls laughed. Emily laughed with them, but her heart was thumping so loud, she was shocked no one had noticed. *Harmony liked Wesley?*

"Come on—before the food's all gone," Daisy Atam said, looking completely out of character with her blonde pigtails replaced with big, wavy hair.

The girls trooped down towards the Foughtgon room and Emily felt anxious. Memories of last year flashed though her mind—Lox holding her up by her the throat in the middle of the party until Mr Davon scared him away. Emily shuddered. She prayed nothing crazy would happen tonight.

The room was once again covered with white curtains and the disco ball in the centre was spinning, so that bright lights splashed across the room. Daisy immediately went to the far end of the hall, where the food was piled high on the long table.

Emily scanned the costumes, looking for Wesley and Jason. She spotted them dressed up as secret agents again, with the same dark sunglasses and black suits. Emily hadn't noticed last year, but Wesley looked good in a suit. He raised his eyebrows when he saw her. He tapped Jason, who looked over to the girls and they walked towards them.

"Oh my gosh, oh my gosh, he's coming," Lisa said, flapping about. "How's my hair?"

"Not big enough," Nicky scowled. "You should have let me curl it for you."

Jason let out an appreciative wolf whistle as he looked them over. Lisa went as red as Michella's dress.

"You ladies look beautiful," Wesley said.

Sydney John took a bold step forward, but scowled when she saw Wesley's eyes stop at Emily. He slowly looked at her up and down, which made Emily blush. He held out his arm and Emily linked it with her own.

Wesley bent his head, so his lips brushed against her ear, sending a shiver up her spine as he whispered, "I think we look good together."

Emily smiled. "We would if you were meant to be Jenkins."

"No problem," Wesley said, taking off his sunglasses and pocketing them. "Perfect fit."

Wesley led her to the middle of the dance floor, pulling her close. Emily's arms flopped to her side until she realised how stupid it looked and placed them around his neck. She was glad they weren't grinding like most of the students, but instead he was guiding her around the dance floor.

"So was there a point to you all dressing up as Roberta?"

Emily nodded. "Trying to get in her good books."

"With a butt like that, who wouldn't put you in their good books?"

"Wesley!" Emily squealed, secretly delighted, as she playfully hit him.

He laughed. "I promise to behave."

They danced together all night. Emily was enjoying herself for what felt like the first time in ages. She could see Ambria and Julian talking in the corner, but she noticed there was nothing flirtatious in Julian's body language, unlike Ambria, who was constantly touching him. Tanya was dressed as a witch, which Emily thought was more than accurate and she was standing with some students from Linktie. Alice Archinia was dressed as Alice Archinia. She looked how she did on TV with her overly made up face, long tousled hair and expensive clothes, lapping up the attention everyone was giving her. It was like she had to remind everyone that she had been the star of the most watched reality television show.

Emily scanned the crowd to find Gabriel Thompson, but she couldn't recognise him in any costume. Wesley pulled her closer and Emily embraced him, enjoying the envious glances she was getting from the girls walking past. Emily caught Harmony Loving-Dale's eye as she walked past them dressed in a long floral dress, with a giant peace sign necklace and a daisy headband. She smiled innocently at Emily, which made her question whether Sydney was right about Harmony liking Wesley.

"Hey look," Wesley suddenly said. He spun Emily around and she watched Jason and Michella dance by looking only at each other.

"They look so cute," Emily said, watching Jason's handsome face, completely alive as he danced with Michella.

"Yeah, they do," Wesley said, spinning her back around. "At least they're not the only ones."

Emily let out a contented sigh. In that moment, she didn't care if Neci herself came to mess up this year's party. Nothing could ruin this night for her.

It was past midnight when the DJ played his last song and Emily told Wesley she was going to head up to bed. He offered to walk her back to Michella's bedroom. It was only a few doors from his, but she was thrilled that he'd offered.

They walked up the stairs, passing students talking on the steps, or kissing in the shadows of the corridors. Wesley whistled to himself and Emily stole a glance at him when he wasn't looking, taking in how effortlessly handsome he looked.

"Emily!"

Emily stopped as Julian Kena walked towards her. He was dressed like a pirate this year, with a fake eye patch covering his eye, a stuffed parrot on his shoulder and a toy sword hanging from his belt. Somehow Julian made the costume look sexy.

"Hey," Emily said. The atmosphere between the three immediately became tense.

"Hi, Wesley," Julian said.

"Hey," Wesley said off-handedly.

"Sorry, I was trying to catch you tonight, but I didn't want to disturb you both," Julian said, which made Emily feel guilty, even though she didn't know why. "I just wanted to tell you that me and my mum are moving to Legends Village next week and I was wondering if you wanted to give me the grand tour?"

"You're moving to the Village?" Emily frowned, unsure if she had heard right.

"Yeah, my grandfather doesn't use his place anymore, so he said we should stay there and my mum kind of wants a new start somewhere else."

"Well sure, I know where Tainwo's house is, so I'll come knock for you and show you around."

"Great." Julian smiled. His deep brown eyes locked on to Emily like she was the only person in the corridor, which only made Emily more aware that Wesley was next to her.

"I'll see you later," Julian said, waving and Emily watched him go.

Wesley walked Emily up in silence. They stood outside of Michella's room and Emily looked nervously at her shoes.

"I had fun tonight," he said after a while.

"Me too." Emily felt like she was glowing. "Thank you for the many dances."

Wesley grinned. "You're welcome." He scratched the side of his neck and looked down at the floor, looking nervous. "Emily . . . I—"

"You are such a cow!" Lisa screeched from behind the door, making Emily and Wesley jump. Emily opened the door at the same time Lisa ran out with tears streaming down her face.

"Lisa, what's wrong?" Emily called, but Lisa ignored her as she ran past.

"I should—" Emily began.

"Yeah go," Wesley said, the disappointment written all over his face. "See you tomorrow."

He walked off, leaving Emily feeling deflated. Emily entered the bedroom and was surprised to see only Michella inside, changing out of her red dress and unravelling her perfect bun.

"What happened with Lisa?"

"She's angry I was dancing with Jason. She said I was selfish, delusional and loads of other names." Michella tried to say it as if she didn't care, but Emily could hear the hurt in her voice. She pulled on her pyjamas, leaving on her makeup and crawled into bed. Emily watched her silently. Michella was lying on her back and was looking up at the ceiling.

"I thought you looked really beautiful tonight," Emily said softly. She wasn't sure if Michella had heard, so she began to wipe the makeup off her own face in the mirror.

"Everyone always tells my sister, Madison, how beautiful she is and how she's going to grow up to be a knockout. I always feel like I can never compete," Michella said, sitting up on her bed. Emily froze and watched Michella in the mirror. "I'm used to *her* being the beautiful one, but tonight I felt amazing and it was perfect." A tear fell down her perfectly made up face.

"Oh, Michella," Emily said. She walked over to her and climbed on to the bed. "You are beautiful."

"I'm not." Michella sniffed.

Emily held her hand and squeezed it tight. "Yes, you are and I don't want to hear otherwise, okay?"

Michella leaned her head on Emily's shoulder. "Thank you," she whispered.

It was dark and silent. The only dull light came from the moon's glow outside the window. The shadow Emily could see was of the person in front of her. The one walking fast and dragging her by the arm. Something rough was tied around her mouth, so when she cried out, it sounded muffled. Emily tried to fight them off, but the person grabbed her tighter. All Emily could make out was that they were taller than her. For a second, she thought it was Lox but then remembered that Lox had a bigger build.

They were climbing down a flight of stairs and the cold, wooden floor under Emily's bare feet made her flinch. They walked down the long corridor that some of the students referred to as Knights Row. It had a line of knights dressed in suits of armour and it was to remind everyone of a historic battle from the medieval times between the warriors and the knights. The warriors won. The person stopped in front of a suit of armour, knocking quietly on the knights hand. They waited. Slowly and silently, the suit of armour slid to the left and Emily could see a tunnel of darkness.

The person pulled her again, more rough this time, and she climbed down more steps. Emily's breathing became louder and harsher and she could see her breath. Every step made her groan as the temperature dropped dramatically.

Suddenly, they stopped and Emily could make out a door. The person opened it and she gasped. Every inch of the room was covered in ice. The cold air hit Emily hard and she tried desperately to turn back, but the person pulled her and she fell, hitting her elbow painfully on the ice and ripping the sleeve of her nightie.

She heard the person sigh and mutter something before helping her to her feet and pulling her across the ice. She hung on to the person for safety, almost crying from the sharp cold, but she couldn't help but marvel on how beautiful and majestic the room looked.

They stopped in the centre of the room, in front of a slab of ice. Emily looked carefully at the inscriptions on it. They were written in Hariem, a language Emily didn't know. The person, in a deep male voice, began to whisper the words written on the ice. Emily panicked and looked from the man, to the ice and back to the man. The inscriptions began to glow a bright blue.

I want to wake up, I want to wake up, Emily chanted in her head. She closed her eyes, praying that when she opened them she would be back in the girls' bedroom. The ground began to rumble. Emily opened her eyes and the ice was glowing an unnatural bright blue. Emily gasped and pulled her arm out of the man's grasp. He had stopped chanting when he realised that Emily was halfway across the room and the ice faded back to its natural white shine. Emily half-ran, half-skidded across the ice towards the exit. She ripped of the material covering her mouth and threw it over her shoulder. The man lunged at her and grabbed her foot.

She woke up.

Emily sat up breathing rapidly looking around the room with sweat dripping off her body. She was back in her bed in the Ogragon girls' room. Emily pulled the duvet tight around her. Her body was shaking. She couldn't feel her feet. Emily looked at the other girls who were all sound asleep. She wiped her brow, closed her eyes and attempted to slow down her breathing. Once her heart had stopped racing, she looked down at the floor to double check it was carpet and not ice before getting out of the bed. She gritted her teeth, when she felt a sharp pain in her left elbow. She walked to the bathroom and turned on the light. Emily stared at her reflection in disbelief. She walked slowly to the mirror and touched her bare arm, where her sleeve had ripped. She twisted her arm and noticed that her left elbow was bleeding.

CHAPTER SEVEN

The Speech

Emily couldn't clear her mind of the ice room. She had confided in Michella about it as soon as she had woken up, but Michella had instantly dismissed it as being ridiculous.

"So you think I'm lying?" Emily had asked, looking at Michella in disbelief.

"No, but I know the difference between dreams and reality." Emily scoffed and Michella shook her head. "I'm sorry, I didn't mean it like that. Just . . . okay, how did you leave the room without any of us not hearing you? Especially if someone was dragging you out?"

"How do you explain this?" Emily said, pointing at her ripped nightie and the red wound on her elbow.

"You could have done it yourself. I mean your dreams do get pretty intense."

Emily's eyes widened. "Are you serious?"

"Someone would have heard you, Emily. I know it was a scary dream, but it was just a dream," Michella said with a finality in her voice.

"Whatever," Emily said, storming into the bathroom and locking the door.

For the rest of the day, Emily avoided Michella. It wasn't easy seeing as they were in every class together, but anytime Michella spoke, Emily made a point of turning the other way. It didn't take long for her to realise that Emily was mad at her. Emily caught Wesley and Jason exchanging looks with each other.

"I thought you two were okay?" Wesley asked her, when they walked towards Water Studies together.

"Not any more," Emily said. "I think a break from Michella is perfect right now and no, I don't want to talk about it," she added when Wesley tried to interrupt.

He nodded and didn't question her further.

Once Water Studies was over, Emily didn't go to dinner. Instead, she waited outside Osaki for Sally and was surprised to see her counsellor, Jenny Li. It started to rain and Emily ran into the car, with her head bent.

"Hey, what are you doing here?"

"Sally said she would see you at home," Jenny explained. There was a hardness in her voice that Emily wasn't used to.

"Are you okay?"

Jenny nodded her head towards the back of the car. "There's something you need to see."

Emily noticed the newspaper on the back seat. She picked it up and gasped. The headline read, 'I'LL BLOW YOU UP' and the front page had an unflattering picture of Emily looking menacing. The type of person who *would* blow up someone.

"I didn't say I would blow her up," Emily said hurriedly. Jenny didn't react as she continued to drive the car. "You believe me, right?"

"We'll talk about it later," Jenny said and she leaned forward and put the radio on.

Emily opened her mouth and then closed it again. She slumped in her seat and stared out of the window miserably.

Jenny didn't speak to Emily for the entire journey and when they drove through Legends Village, Jenny turned the radio off. She parked in the Knights' driveway and stared out of the window. The rain was pounding on the car. Emily glanced nervously at her.

"You do know you need a better explanation than 'I didn't say that'?"

"But I didn't," Emily protested. "What I said was Neci was going to blow up her house."

"Oh, so that's better, isn't it?" Jenny said, raising her voice. "Telling her Neci is going to kill her?"

"It was in the heat of the moment. She was rude to me because I'm a warrior, like that's my fault," Emily said, looking at the floor.

"Look at me," Jenny said, lifting Emily's head up by her chin. "You were wrong for what you said, but so was she. Sometimes in life, you have to be the bigger person, okay?"

Emily nodded. "Are they really mad?"

"Let's just say, I wouldn't want to be you, kid. Go on."

Emily opened the car door and ran towards the house. She looked back at Jenny, who waved at her before driving off.

The house was silent. Emily walked to the dining hall, dripping on the wet floor. Sally and Michael were seated at the table with stony expressions.

"I'm sorry," Emily said quietly.

"Sorry!" Sally roared, jumping to her feet. "Do you know how bad this looks? What would your dad think if he saw that? Do you know how hard everyone is working to make sure Neci doesn't cause anymore damage and you and that other silly girl go and do this!"

Michael took of his glasses and rubbed his forehead. He looked at Emily and said, "I expected more of you."

"I'll fix it," Emily cried. "I'll fix it right now."

She hurried out off the room ignoring Sally's calls. She ran back into the rain to Roberta and Jenkins mansion and raised her hand to knock on the front door, but before she could knock, Jenkins answered it.

"I'm sorry. How can I make this better? I'll do anything," Emily said desperately.

"Roberta said you would come," Jenkins replied casually and Emily realised that he didn't look the least bit surprised to see her outside his house in such a state. "We need to go through this speech and you're the perfect person for the job."

"Speech?" Emily frowned. "What are you—"

"Anything, right?" Jenkins cut in before he stepped aside and a baffled Emily entered the house.

Two days later, Lenny Kinkle had arranged an early Dojo practice. The day before, Mr Davon had announced that

Ogragon were going to battle Linktie in a few days. Berbinin was disqualified from the running and if Ogragon beat Linktie, they would finally face Pentwon for the cup and hopefully win before Lenny graduated. That was only if they could knock out the powerful, Alan Fair.

The school was quiet when Emily walked in, rubbing the sleep out of her eyes. She went to the dining hall, craving something hot, but it was locked. Frustrated, she stomped towards the pitch. The air was cold and frosty, but the sky was a pretty mix of pink, blue and yellow. The cold weather was slowly waking her up.

Since that night, Emily hadn't laid eyes on the ice room and she was starting to doubt if it was real. She questioned how nobody had heard, or seen her being dragged out. She sighed. Maybe Michella was right, but it didn't make falling asleep any easier.

She could hear the laughter and talking from her Dojo teammates. Emily entered the brightly lit stadium and was surprised to see Gabriel Thompson sitting in the stands, alert and watching them. She had not spoken to Gabriel since their last training session. Lenny Kinkle was studying a piece of paper with Summer Wind, who was pointing out various things on it. Warren Kinkle and Jessie Kendaschi were having an arm wrestling match that everyone was cheering on.

"Morning," Emily said.

"Morning, Emily," they choroused.

"What's Gabriel doing here?" Emily asked Rosa Martin.

Rosa, the smallest one on the team, swept up her hair into a messy bun and said, "Dunno."

"But he's in Mentorawth," Emily said, staring at him suspiciously. "Is he even allowed to be here?"

"Well . . . no, but it's Gabriel Thompson! I'm kind of flattered that he wants to watch us train."

"Okay, let's not waste anytime. Guys, can you cut it out?" Lenny said.

Jessie looked up and Warren slammed Jessie's hand down.

"Yes!" Warren yelled, punching the air.

"Not fair, Lenny was talking," Jessie protested.

"SHUT UP!" Lenny yelled over the both of them and they instantly fell quiet. Lenny took a deep breath and forced a smile on his face. "Let's have a quick spar to warm up. Seeing as Warren and Jessie have so much energy this morning, they can go first. Summer, Rosa and Raquel, you guys distract them, the rest of you can fly around to get warm."

Emily shot up in the air above the stands and floated in a circle around the stadium. She kept glancing at Gabriel, who was staring at her and not watching the battle. Emily felt uneasy with his presence.

"Emily, watch out!"

She spun around and the fireball hit her hard and fast on her shoulder before it soared up into the air and exploded. Sharp pains shot up her arm and she flew back down to the sandy floor, holding her sore shoulder.

"Are you alright?" Lenny asked, running up to her. "I didn't even see where it came from."

"I'll be fine," Emily said, walking towards the stands with Lenny on her heels.

She sat down a few seats away from Gabriel, who was now looking at the pitch.

Lenny sat beside her. "It's not like you not to sense a fireball coming. What's up?"

"Nothing," Emily muttered.

Lenny chuckled. "It's that the best you can do?"

Emily hesitated. She wasn't sure if Lenny was the best person to talk to, but she knew he wouldn't leave her alone until she told him. "Michella and I had an argument the other day."

Lenny frowned. "You and Michella? About what?"

"Well, I told her something and she didn't believe me. But it wasn't something small, it was a huge, scary thing, but now I don't know if what I saw was true. As my best friend, she should have my back though, right?"

Lenny didn't respond. Emily brushed her hair out of her face and watched the Ogragons shooting fireballs at each other.

"Michella's a very suspicious person. She gets it from our mum, but also being related to Warren and Pete doesn't help," Lenny said, as he scratched the hair in between his cornrows. "Is there anyway to prove that what you saw was real?"

Emily shuddered at the thought of ever going back to the ice room. "I don't think so."

"Well, I think it's a good idea to talk to her. She would never mean to hurt your feelings."

"I know," Emily agreed. "I'll try and chat to her later."

"Good. How's your shoulder?"

Emily rolled it back. It hurt a bit but was manageable. "It's okay."

Lenny stood up. "Then let's go train."

And for once Emily didn't complain.

Training went on longer than planned, so they all missed

breakfast. Hungry, tired and sore, Emily hurried to Foughtgon class and arrived ten minutes after the lesson had started. Everyone stared at her when she entered the room.

"Miss Knight, why are you late?" Master Zen asked, crossing his arms over his chest.

Emily bowed to him. "I'm sorry, sir. I was training with my team for the Linktie match. I can get a note from my captain, Lenny Kinkle?"

"I see," Master Zen said, sounding nicer than before. He found it difficult to be angry with a student who had been training all morning. "That's fine, please grab a partner. We're working with wood today."

"Fun," Emily mumbled to herself.

She searched the room, but everyone was already in pairs. She was about to point this out to Master Zen, when she saw Michella sitting on a blue mat near the back of the room, massaging her ankle. Emily walked towards her and sat down.

"Hey," Michella whispered.

"What's wrong?" Emily asked, keeping her eyes to the front of the room, where Master Zen was demonstrating something with the wood.

"I sprained it this morning," she said, rubbing her ankle and wincing. "Daisy had to help me down here."

"How did you do that?"

"I tripped over Violet's shoes. She's always leaving them in the middle of the room. Emily, I think we should talk about—"

"No, we don't. Maybe you were right about me imagining it," Emily said.

Michella stared at her surprised. "But you seemed really convinced?"

"I know I did because it felt real, but I do have crazy dreams where I fight in my sleep, so maybe I did hurt myself? And you're right, how did I get in and out of the room and no one noticed? Plus the person spoke in Hariem."

"Exactly," Michella said, looking relieved. "Master Zen said last year that no one at Osaki knows how to speak in Hariem. If you were being dragged out, you would have screamed, or something."

"Well, I had something over my mouth, so I couldn't."

Michella frowned. "You didn't mention that. Have you told anyone else? Like Roberta?"

Emily shook her head. "I figured she would want more proof, like where exactly the ice room is and all I know is that it's at the end of a tunnel that is hidden behind a suit of armour."

There was a moment of silence before Michella said, "Maybe we should see if we can find it."

"What?" Emily asked baffled. "You said it wasn't real."

"It's not . . . I mean . . . I think it would be good to double check, for peace of mind. If it's not there, we forget about it, but if it is, and it's a massive 'if', then we need to tell an adult."

"Okay," Emily agreed. "Let me get the Linktie match out of the way first."

"Deal. Are you excited for Visiting Day tomorrow?"

Emily hesitated. Visiting Day was when Roberta and Jenkins wanted her to do a live televised speech, in front of the entire school, parents and the media. They stressed to Emily that she was not allowed to mess this up. Only her family, Roberta, Jenkins and Mr Davon knew about the speech.

"Can't wait," she replied weakly.

"Miss Knight!" Master Zen hollered, making Emily and Michella jump. "Ten minutes late to my lesson and you're talking to Miss Kinkle? Come here."

"Actually, sir, I spoke to her first," Michella piped in but Master Zen held up his hand to silence her.

Emily stood up, groaning at the aching muscles all over her body. Master Zen walked over to her, kindly offering out his arm which she held on to and he helped her walk to the front of the room. He led her to the wood that he was demonstrating with. Emily could have sworn it was a tree trunk.

Emily gulped. "What do I do?"

"You break it . . . with your head."

Emily looked at him alarmed. "What? Can you show me?"

Master Zen crossed his arms and shook his head. "Ladies first."

Emily placed her arms beneath her head, with her eyes closed, feeling a mixture of emotions. She was anxious, frightened and a bit excited. If today went as planned, it could change everything.

"Em, you awake?" Cathy asked.

"Yeah," Emily said, turning to look at her.

Cathy had a huge smile on her face and she clapped her hands excitedly. "Today's the big day!" She hopped out of the bed and drew open the curtains, revealing a miserable grey sky. "Come on, we're going to leave soon."

She left the room and Emily sat up in her bed. Today was Visiting Day and Sally, Michael, Jenny and her foster brother and sisters would be coming to the school. This was also the day where she would be giving her live speech.

Mr Davon thought it would up morale if someone could encourage all of the warriors that they stood a good chance against Neci, as long as everyone stayed united. Roberta had told Sally the idea and suggested that Emily should do it. Mr Davon had had a meeting with Sally to discuss how it would work and Sally had agreed. Emily strongly disagreed and she even suggested that Alice would be best suited because she had a huge following from her show, but the idea was shot down. They all wanted it to be Emily because she was Thomas Knight's daughter and they felt hearing it from her would make people feel safe. Also, Roberta wanted her to communicate a message to someone and only Emily could do that.

Emily was quiet the entire journey to school, whilst the rest of her family and Jenny were talking excitedly about finally visiting Osaki. Cathy kept pulling down her skirt, which barely covered her bottom. Emily had advised her not to wear it, but Cathy had ignored her.

Jenny squeezed Emily's hand. "How are you feeling?"

"I'm just a bit nervous."

"Did you practice the speech Roberta gave you?"

Emily nodded. "Every day and I know it off by heart. Plus, I have the notes in my bag."

"Then you're going to be fine," Jenny said reassuringly.

As soon as they reached Osaki, everyone looked in wonder at the elaborate Christmas decorations around the school. At the doorway was a ten-foot tall Christmas tree, and students were up in the air placing decorations on it.

Emily had to go and have a training session with Roberta,

Jenkins and the rest of the team whilst her family and Jenny went into the dining hall with the other families. She was disappointed that she couldn't give them the grand tour of Osaki herself and being stuck with Gabriel and Alice made her day even worse.

On the way to training, she heard her name being called out and she yelped when she felt something cold float past her.

"Sorry, sorry," Niles gushed.

"For goodness sake, Niles! Jeez!" Emily cried.

"Sorry," Niles repeated looking sheepish. "I just wanted to know if you found out what was going on with, Gabriel?"

"Not yet. We're not exactly on best terms at the moment."

"He said he went to watch you during Dojo practice and you fought really good."

"He said that?" Emily asked surprised. "I didn't get to talk to him."

"Can you try today at training?" Niles asked eagerly.

"Yeah . . . I mean I can try."

"Okay thanks and good luck with the speech!" he said before he floated off.

Training was in the Foughtgon room. Emily's stomach rumbled loudly. She was starving, but they were going to eat after their session. She opened the door and saw the rest of the team were already sparring and warming up. Emily dropped her bag at the door and was surprised to see Jason talking to Julian on the other side of the room.

"Jason," Emily called, running over and embracing him. "What are you doing here?"

"Jenkins wants to do one-on-one sessions with me because of my telekinesis. He asked me to train with you guys, so I can grow this new power. I'm a bit nervous though," he confessed.

"Wow, that's amazing. Don't worry, you'll be fine."

"Okay, everyone over here," Roberta called from the front of the room, holding Antonio's hand.

Gabriel was looking down at the floor, dragging his feet. His face looked paler than usual. In contrast, Xavier sprinted towards his mum, clearly eager for the training to start.

"First of all, I want to introduce Jason Notting," Roberta announced. Everyone clapped for him. Emily noticed Alice eyeing him up. "Jason here is a telekinetic. That means he can move things with his mind."

"Cool," Xavier said, looking at Jason in awe.

"It's an amazing gift and it's very rare in such a young person. I know Jason's not related to the Five Warriors or any legends, but his gift will give us a great advantage against Neci. Jenkins is training him and he will join in with our training sessions.

"Right, before we get into our lesson, I just want to tell you that Emily will be giving a speech and we will *all* be standing behind her showing a united front." She looked at Alice, who rolled her eyes. "And if anyone has a problem with that, then please leave."

Emily looked around. Everyone was looking at Roberta, although Gabriel did glance wistfully at the door. He caught Emily's eye and immediately looked down at the floor again. His black fringe fell over his glasses.

"Please be vigilant today," Jenkins announced. "There will be many guests here and we're hoping that they are all on our side, or at least we can persuade them to be. We still need to find this missing warrior. We don't have a figure of how many people are fighting for Neci, but we know that she has microchipped hundreds of people. We are still not sure exactly what it means, but we have a theory that she may have a device that will be able to control them. It's just a theory. We haven't seen or heard of a device, but I can't think what else they would be microchipped for."

"What?" Emily exclaimed. "But she forced those microchips into people and now she's going to make them hurt others?"

"Do you have any clue who the missing warrior is yet?" Gabriel interrupted.

Everyone looked at him. He usually never spoke in sessions. Even Jenkins looked surprised, but recovered quickly. "No, not yet," he said regretfully.

"So the plan for today's lesson is one-on-one battles," Roberta explained. "Julian vs. Gabriel, Jason vs. Antonio and Xavier—sorry, Jason, but we've got to throw you in the deep end—and Emily vs. Alice."

"Yes!" Emily said to herself, punching her fist into her open hand.

"So if everyone can wait outside except for Emily and Alice."

Jason squeezed Emily's arm as he left the room. Emily and Alice stood opposite each other, with Jenkins in the middle.

"There's a lot of tension between you two and hopefully this battle should clear the air."

Alice cracked her knuckles. "I'm ready."

Jenkins closed his eyes and the room began to change. The wooden floor transformed into a sandy ground. Emily bent down and touched it, amazed at how real it felt. The ceiling turned into a blue sky and in the middle of the ceiling was a blazing sun that Emily could feel burning her shoulders.

"It's a desert," Alice said looking around, turning her head sharply when she heard a bird cry in the distance.

"Just try not to kill each other," Jenkins said half-joking as he left the room.

Emily and Alice faced each other. Alice peeled off her training kit top, so she was in a black sports bra, so Emily did the same, feeling instantly relived with the faint breeze that touched her skin.

"You won't beat me," Alice declared.

Emily smirked. "We'll see."

Alice charged towards her. She formed a yellow fireball in her hands, that she shot at Emily, who jumped up into the air and soared above Alice. The fireball exploded at the far side of the room and Emily locked her legs together and kept her arms by her side and shot down like a rocket towards, Alice. She head-butted her shoulder and Alice cried out and covered her shoulder protectively. Emily spun around, aiming a kick at Alice's head, but Alice caught her leg and swung Emily in a circle with both hands, throwing her to the end of the room, where Emily fell painfully on to her back.

Emily sat up and spat out the sand in her mouth as Alice teleported in front of her. Alice swung a punch, but Emily dodged it and went to punch back at Alice, who blocked it and the two of them began to spar, dodging each other's blows whilst flying over the desert.

Alice dug her fist into Emily's stomach, making her double over and then pushed her hard, so that Emily fell backwards. She landed with a heavy thud on the sand and a sharp pain shot through her torso. Multiple fireballs flew at Emily and she found herself sinking into the sand. Emily hunched her body into a ball and felt the pain and the strong heat of the fireballs hitting her arms.

Very slowly, Emily moved one arm away from her face and placed it out in front of her and caught one of Alice's fireballs. There was so much smoke surrounding her that Alice couldn't see what Emily was doing. Emily heard Alice laugh and she stopped firing, for a split second, so Emily quickly formed a fireball in her other hand, merged the two together and shot a huge fireball back at Alice. There was a deafening boom and Emily heard Alice fall to the floor.

Emily groaned and slowly sat up. Her torso was on fire and she wobbled as she got to her feet. She dragged herself towards an exhausted Alice and swung her foot, kicking Alice hard in the stomach. Alice kneeled over and Emily painfully bent down, grabbed Alice's blonde hair and sat her up. Alice yelled and scratched at Emily's hands, trying to get her off and Emily kneed her in her chin. Blood poured out of Alice's mouth and Emily, still holding her hair, punched Alice hard in the jaw, so her blood scattered over Emily's stomach.

Alice fell to the floor groaning. Emily walked off balance towards the other side of the desert. The searing heat was making her light-headed. Sweat was dripping down her forehead into her eyes and it stung. She positioned herself opposite Alice, with her hands on her forehead, chanting softly to herself and waited.

Alice was coughing and spitting out blood that was staining the sand. She was on her hands and knees with her body facing away from Emily.

Alice wiped her mouth with the back of her hand. She suddenly spun around and screamed, "MAYOWA!" at the same time Emily screamed, "ANYOSINGH."

Emily's red fireball and Alice's purple fireball met in the

middle of the desert with a big bang. The sand soared into Emily's face, blowing her hair wildly, so for a few seconds, Emily was blinded. Emily walked slowly towards Alice, with her fireball dominating hers.

Alice increased her energy and her fireball grew bigger, making Emily stumble back. Emily gritted her teeth and kept on walking towards Alice, pushing her fireball forward. The red was overtaking the purple and the fireballs had backed Alice into a corner. Alice dropped her arms in defeat and Emily's fireball hit Alice in the chest, with a deafening boom. The room was devoured in a white light and Emily shielded her eyes. Once the light was gone, Alice was face down on the floor, completely still.

Breathing heavily, Emily painfully walked toward the exit. The sandy ground turned back into the wooden floor and the walls with the Hariem inscriptions reappeared. Emily took one last look back at Alice, sprawled out on the floor and left the room.

"Are you ready?"

Emily looked over her shoulder and Wesley was closing the door behind him.

"Hey," Emily said, hugging him tight. "You're not meant to be in here."

"I know, but I wanted to wish you luck."

Emily beamed. She was in an empty room behind the dining hall, where all of the students, parents and media were sitting. She could faintly hear Mr Davon speaking to them and Roberta, Jenkins and the team were positioned at the front of the hall, standing beside him.

After the battles, they got dressed in their Osaki uniform and Emily and Alice were covered in heavy makeup. Alice had a faint bruise under her mouth and before they were dismissed to grab some food, she had said, "You don't fight too bad." She assumed that was Alice's way of showing her a bit more respect.

"You look really nice," Wesley commented.

Emily had her makeup done professionally for the speech and she didn't even recognise the beautiful girl, with the strong cheekbones and piercing eyes that stared back at her.

"Thank you. Is the hall full?"

Wesley laughed. "That's an understatement. I better get back, but you'll do great today." He kissed her softly, purposely catching the corner of her mouth, surprising Emily. They locked eyes. Emily moved forward and Wesley responded. She closed her eyes and heard Wesley whisper, "You have to go."

"What?" Emily said. Her eyes were still closed, waiting for his kiss.

"They just called your name. You have to go."

"Crap!" Emily said, snapping out of it.

She grabbed her notes from the floor and hurried out of the door to a thunderous round of applause and bright lights. Emily caught her breath, as she saw the magnitude of people in the hall and all their eyes on her. She walked to the podium, clutching her notes tight in her hand. She stepped in front of the microphone and leaned forward into it.

"Hi."

Hundreds of eyes stared back at her. Reporters were already

scribbling away on their notes, exaggerating Emily's entrance and the photographers flashes were blinding her. Emily stared into the main camera lens, knowing that millions of people were watching her live from their homes. She was certain Neci would be watching. She was hoping her dad and Lox would be as well.

"My name is Emily Knight. I want to thank everyone for being here today. First of all, I want to apologise for my recent actions. It was taken out of context," she said, with a hard edge to her voice. She caught Jenkins eye and he subtly shook his head.

"But that isn't an excuse," Emily hurriedly added. "I am truly sorry. I also want to apologise on behalf of Alice Archinia, for her rant on the internet. It was also a very stupid thing to do. I am speaking on behalf of every warrior that wants peace. Neci will not destroy the harmony that my father fought for, that we have all fought for. We will not take it lying down!"

The hall erupted into cheers and applause. Emily exhaled and allowed herself to smile properly. Feeling more encouraged, Emily grabbed the microphone off the stand. "Thomas Knight will not abandon us. He will fight with us and for us!"

"Go, Emily!" Cathy cheered over the applause.

"My brother, Lox Knight, will make the right decision. He will fight with his family. He will defend me. He will defend all off us. Lox always comes whenever I need him and he knows that right now, I desperately need him." Emily dramatically paused like Roberta told her to. She counted up to five in her head before she carried on. "I know some of you look at us and think, they're just kids. Antonio and Xavier Jenkins are only little boys. Yes, we are children, but trust us. Neci has targeted *us* and we will not give up without a fight. Are we going to allow Neci to intimidate us?"

"No!" the hall chanted.

"Are we going to allow her to hurt innocent people?"

"No!"

"Are we meant to sit back as she destroys Gabriel Thompson's house?"

"No!"

"We will do everything in our power to prevent this war, but if we have to fight, we will get ruthless, we will get wild, we will do whatever needs to be done. And Neci, if it comes down to a war, do not underestimate us. We will win."

The hall exploded with loud cheers. Roberta came up beside her, grabbed her hand and held it up. The audience stood, clapping hard and stared at her in admiration and Emily smiled, desperately wanting to believe her own words.

"I'm so proud of you, baby," Sally said, hugging her as soon as she came down from the podium.

"You did an amazing job, Emily," Michael said, hugging her next. "Look how much hope you have given to everyone."

It seemed like the entire hall had approached Emily to congratulate her on her speech. She had signed countless autographs, taken pictures and given numerous interviews. The hall was buzzing with excitement and promise. She could see Alice, Gabriel, Roberta, Jenkins and Mr Davon being interviewed also.

"You did great," Cathy said, hugging her tightly.

"Can we see the stadium now?" Yvonne asked, grabbing on to Emily's hand.

"Of course," Emily said, kissing her forehead.

"Emily! Emily!" Harmony Loving-Dale was running towards her with her family. Her blonde hair was plaited into a fishtail, with a pink ribbon woven through it, which was swinging from side to side with her footsteps.

"Hi, Harmony."

"Hey, my family really wanted to meet you. Your speech was epic!" She pointed to a young boy, who looked the same age as Mike and Madison Kinkle. He had brown hair pulled back into a ponytail and he had Harmony's blue eyes. He was wearing a bright tie dyed t-shirt over red jeans and he wore a small, cream coloured shell around his neck. Two young blonde girls came and stood beside him, looking up at Emily in amazement. "This is my brother, Memphis and my sisters, Season and Skye."

Season looked a bit older than Memphis, whilst Skye was a gorgeous little girl. They were miniature versions of Harmony, with the same hair and eyes.

"Can we have your autograph?" Season asked, holding out a piece of paper.

"Of course," Emily said, signing it.

"So cool," Memphis said, as Emily signed his.

"And these are my parents," Harmony said.

"Wow," Emily said surprised.

Harmony's father was a tall, lean man with shaggy, brown hair and small, emerald coloured eyes. His arms and neck were covered with colourful tattoos that would make Janette Kinkle envious. Like Memphis, he wore a shell (although bigger) around his neck, over a turquoise t-shirt with a green dragon, blue ripped jeans and muddy, black boots. Harmony's mother looked like a model and more like Harmony's older sister. She had the same long, blonde hair and big blue eyes, with the highest cheekbones Emily had ever seen. She had silver rings that covered every finger and her nails were painted black. She was wearing a skull t-shirt over black ripped jeans and spiked heels.

"This is Kevin and Susan Loving-Dale," Harmony said, smiling at her parents.

"Seriously?" Cathy murmured and Emily shot her a sharp look.

"Nice to meet you," Emily said, shaking their hands. "These are my godparents, Sally and Michael Meran."

"Great to meet you both, and what an amazing speech that was Emily," Susan said, in a melodic voice. "So inspiring and uplifting. I can see why Harmony speaks so highly of you. She says you're an amazing fighter."

"Oh thanks," Emily said, surprised.

"Your energy must be huge being the daughter of Thomas Knight," Kevin continued. "It's a shame your match isn't today, I would have loved to have seen you battle."

Emily blushed.

"I wish I was a warrior," James said, looking around wistfully.

"You might be. Oh, I hope I am! I want to be in Ogragon," Memphis said.

"Ooh me too!" Season declared.

"And me!" Skye chipped in.

"Traitors!" Harmony said, ruffling Memphis head, who laughed. "What about Jenkint? We've got Jenkins."

"He's so cute," Season sighed.

Memphis shrugged. "Jenkins is great . . . but he's not

Thomas." Memphis looked past Emily and pointed. "Shut up . . . that's Cecil and Niles! Season, come on."

Memphis ran over to them with Season following and Skye waddling after.

"Emily, have you seen Wesley?" Emily's head jerked back to look at Harmony, who was smiling innocently at her.

"Err, Wesley, why?"

Over Harmony's shoulder, Emily saw Wesley leave the dining hall with his sister, Cammie, their grandmother and Jason and his parents. Emily raised her eyebrows when she noticed Harmony's cheeks redden.

"I just wanted to introduce them to my co-commenter."

"Yeah right," Cathy hissed. "Hey, Roberta's waving at you."

Emily followed Cathy's gaze and Roberta was tapping on her wrist. Emily had almost forgotten. "I'm so sorry guys. I have to do something."

"Oh, Emily," Sally moaned. "Are you ever going to show us around? We only have a few hours left."

"Sorry," Emily said, feeling guilty. "But maybe you should join Jenny in Ruth Walker's office to hear about my progress? Or lack of it. Sorry, I have to go."

Emily sprinted out of the hall before anyone could object. She ran past the press, students and parents who were calling out to her, but Emily ignored everyone. She ran towards the forest at the back of the school, dodging through trees and ducking under branches. She could feel the pain in her torso, but Emily didn't stop running until she reached the place where she first saw him. Just like Roberta saw in her vision, standing tall and strong, with his thick, knotty, dark hair and tattered clothing was her brother, Lox and he was waiting for her.

CHAPTER EIGHT

Warren and Pete's Secret

Emily couldn't take her eyes off him. A part of her was surprised that he turned up, even though Roberta's visions were always accurate. She could remember their last encounters clearly. Lox appearing at his bedroom window, warning her not to go to Osaki, then Lox telling her that Neci was coming to get her. Emily shuddered. She hated to think about what would have happened if she hadn't teleported them both to safety.

Emily studied his frame. He was still muscular, with a gaunt yet handsome face and defined cheekbones. His leather jacket was ripped in random places, so she could see parts of his tattooed arms and his jeans were dirty and battered. His eyes kept shifting from left to right as if he was paranoid that someone would catch them.

"Thank you for coming," Emily said, breaking the silence.

Lox scuffed his worn out trainers into the ground. "It's not every day you hear your sister on live television saying that she needs you."

Emily wasn't seeing Lox in front of her. She was seeing him lying on the floor unconscious and Neci dressed in her trademark black cloak and white mask; her strong power surrounding them, giving Emily goosebumps.

"You could have called, or wrote to me to tell me that you were safe," Emily said, shaking her head to get rid of the image.

Lox scoffed. "That's not the usual manner when you're on the run."

"I thought . . . I thought that Neci maybe—" but Emily was cut off by Lox laughing. She stared at him surprised.

"Oh you thought—you thought," Lox said in between laughter. "You thought Neci killed me? Please, she's like family."

Emily felt as if he had slapped her across the face. "I'm your family." She wanted it to sound strong and certain, instead she choked on every word.

He had the decency to look embarrassed. "Sorry, I didn't mean it like . . . look I'm here for *you*," he said desperately.

Emily crossed her arms, wanting to shield herself from Lox and his harsh words. "Why did you run away again if Neci is your new mum?" she demanded. "Mr Davon said you had to go into hiding."

"Of course I did. She would have been mad that I didn't complete my mission, but we're cool now."

"You've seen Neci? You're on her side?"

Lox stared at her coldly. "It's complicated."

"Isn't it always? Who's behind this whole Gabriel thing?" she asked.

Lox frowned. "What Gabriel thing?"

"The fire at his house in the summer and someone has been threatening him. It's a lady."

Lox shook his head. "I don't know, but it's definitely not Neci."

"How do you know?"

"She's scared of fire, something to do with her childhood." Lox shrugged.

Emily raised her eyebrows. "I didn't think Neci was scared of anything."

Lox chuckled. "Yeah well, everyone's scared of something. My guess is Scarlett. The pretty redhead. She can create fire, so she must have burnt down the house."

"I know who she is. She tried to attack Sally and I on our way to Osaki."

Lox's mouth dropped. "Are you kidding me?" Emily shook her head and Lox clenched his fists. "How did you get away?"

"Roberta came and teleported us. To be honest, I don't know if we would have escaped without her."

"Emily, I'm sorry. I didn't know about that. I had nothing to do with it," Lox explained.

"I didn't think you did," Emily confessed. "So how come Neci isn't scared of Scarlett and her powers?"

"Would you be scared of something that you can control?"

"I guess not," Emily said. "So, you can't be the missing warrior Neci is talking about."

"It's not me."

"Can you tell me who it is?"

Lox hesitated, then shook his head. "Emily, if this war happens, you won't win, so please don't fight it. Neci has Scarlett, Maggie, Dion and this missing warrior, plus thousands of people that are supporting her. The only warriors you lot have that can even stand a chance against Neci are

Dad, Roberta and Jenkins and let's not forget that Neci took on all of the Five Warriors and she was winning."

"But Dad beat her," Emily argued.

"Yes, but Dad's power only soared when she murdered Cecil and Niles, that was like a trigger for him. I don't know if he can beat her again. Neci is building an army. You've heard about New York, right? She's been micro-chipping people."

"Doesn't it just prove that they support her?"

"No, it means—" Lox stopped abruptly. "I can't say any more about it."

"You didn't say your name for either side," Emily said and Lox turned away from her. "You should be on our side. He's our dad. We have to stand by him."

"Like he stood by us?" Lox shouted. His face was contorted into an ugly sneer. "Like he stood by Mum when she got sick? But he had time to see other women and play the hero."

"There were no other women!" Emily yelled. "He cares about us, he loves us. Why do you think he has been gone for so long, trying to find you?"

Lox laughed. "All he cared about was creating a legacy and making me his protégé. He's a fraud. Everyone thinks he's this great, selfless man, but Mum was dying, we were only kids and he wasn't here."

They fell silent. Lox was breathing heavily, like he had just run a marathon.

"Neci said if I don't fight, then you won't fight and she wouldn't harm us," Emily said softly.

Lox nodded. "She told me."

"And what did you say? Are you still going to fight?"

Lox hesitated and nodded.

"Lox," Emily said, moving closer to him. "Who *are* you fighting with?" Lox opened his mouth, then closed it as if he was stumped. "I didn't want to fight. I wanted us to be free from all of this, but I will fight her and anyone else who supports her, but what I don't understand is, what have I ever done to you that would make you consider fighting against me?"

Lox sighed. "Emily . . . it's not about what *you've* done." He went to kick at the stone by his foot, but jumped back when the rock disappeared. "What the . . ."

The forest was changing. The trees and the branches that surrounded them was transforming into large armchairs and a long staircase. The dirty floor once covered with stones and leaves was now a clean, sparkling, marble floor. Lox looked around in disbelief as pictures of him as a young boy materialised out of thin air. Lox winning his first Dojo match, Lox's fifth birthday, Lox as a baby.

"This is our home," Lox said, exploring the living room, they were now standing in. "I don't understand. How did you get us here?"

"I didn't do anything," Emily said, watching her brother closely.

He was slowly walking around the house that he ran away from. Lox picked up various items, studying them like he had never seen them before and he was looking around in a state of shock. They heard footsteps above them. Lox put down the vase he was holding and looked up. Emily followed his gaze and they watched a lady with long, wavy hair walk gracefully down the stairs.

Lox let out a small cry and slumped on his knees to the

floor. He was visibly shaking as he stared at his mother. Leah Knight was standing on the bottom step, wearing the same pink jumper and blue jeans that she wore on Mount Gregory. Her light brown eyes, lit up as she stared at her son.

"Hello, baby," Leah said, smiling at Lox. "It's been too long."

Lox was transfixed. He squinted his eyes as if he couldn't see properly and whispered, "Mum, is that really you?"

Emily closed her eyes. The pain of seeing her mother again hurt too much, knowing that she was only here for a few more seconds.

"What was the one thing I told you to do?" Leah asked Lox.

"I'm so sorry, I'm so sorry," Emily heard Lox whimper.

"What was the one thing, Lox?" Leah demanded.

"To look after Emily," Lox replied in a defeated voice.

Emily surprised by the response, opened her eyes and looked at her brother.

"I am trusting you to uphold that promise," Leah said.

Lox let out a long, heavy sigh. "Mum . . . it's so complicated."

"The one thing, Lox!" Leah said with a raised voice.

Lox bowed his head. His hands clenched by his side. "Stop it," he said quietly.

"What?" Emily asked baffled because she wasn't doing anything.

"Stop it!" Lox said, looking at her sharply. "Whatever you're doing, stop it. I get it, okay. Just stop."

"It's not me," Emily said, holding up her hands.

Lox looked around frantically. Emily noticed that his eyes were wet and he was avoiding staring at their mother. "I don't believe this," he muttered. Lox stood up, brushing his jeans. "Uncle Jenkins, you made your point and that's enough."

And just like that, the room slowly turned back into the forest surroundings. The illusion of Leah Knight began to disappear. Emily caught one last glance of her mother before she was gone again. The same pain in her heart returned and Emily bit down on her lip hard to stop herself from crying out to her.

Jenkins stepped out from behind a large tree, still wearing his dark blue Dojo kit from the speech. "Hello, Lox, I thought you needed some reminding," he said, with his arms folded.

"Very cute," Lox replied. He looked at Emily in admiration and surprise. "You set me up."

Emily smiled. "I can't take all the credit."

"We just know how to get your attention," said a husky voice from the bushes. Lox stared with his body tense looking from Emily to Roberta to Jenkins. "You've seen better days, Lox," Roberta said, in a teasing voice.

Lox laughed, but still looked guarded which hurt Emily's feelings. "Running isn't a clean job. Look, you can't beat Neci and her team."

"Oh, we know," Jenkins said simply. "We know we need more strong, experienced warriors on our side. We need you and we need Thomas."

"So we'd appreciate if you would stop running, so Thomas can come home," Roberta said.

"I don't think she will appreciate that," Lox replied swiftly. "If he was quick enough he would be able to catch me. He seems to always be one step behind."

"What do you mean?" Emily asked confused.

"When you are at one with your powers, you are able to sense a specific person's energy. Thomas can sense Lox and then is able to track him down, but Lox knows how to hide his energy well, which is why Thomas loses track of him," Jenkins explained. "Did Neci teach you how to do that?"

"Yeah, she did and with a good disguise, I can blend in anywhere." Lox turned to Roberta and tapped his forehead. "I know you told him I would be here and by the time he comes, I'll be gone."

Emily stared at them all bouncing off one another until it clicked. "Another game?" she shouted, pointing accusingly at Lox. "You've deliberately kept Dad away, so he wouldn't be here to fight with us? What the hell is wrong with you?"

"Emily, cool it," Roberta said, restraining her before she lunged for Lox.

"No!" Emily said, pushing her off. "Bring Dad here, right now!"

"No," Roberta said sternly. "Lox will do the right thing."

"No, he won't!" Emily said outraged. "He's such a selfish git and I'm sick of it. Did he even tell you that Neci is scared of fire? Of course not! Because then we would have an advantage. You two have been telling everyone that we can win, when you know we don't have enough warriors that are strong enough to face her. He needs to get over this stupid vendetta against Dad and he needs to help us!"

"Oh, we can win. We will have the best warriors fighting for us, including this one," Jenkins said, putting a hand on Lox's shoulder. "Because the one thing Lox always did was listen to his mother, isn't that right?"

Lox bit his lip. Everyone watched him, waiting.

"I can't just stop," he eventually said.

"You better," Emily said fiercely before anyone else could

speak. "Or I swear on Mum's grave that I will kill you myself. Do you understand?" Emily dug him hard in his chest with her finger. "I will kill you."

"Noted," Lox said before he teleported.

"Emily—" Roberta began.

"Don't," Emily said harshly before she stormed back towards Osaki.

Snow was lightly falling in Legends Village that was lit up with fairy lights. Emily walked past the huge Christmas tree in the centre of the Village which was beautifully decorated as she walked over to Tainwo Kena's mansion. She was heavily wrapped up, but was still freezing. She rubbed her hands together and formed a small Baby Ball. The heat made her sigh with pleasure.

Tainwo's mansion was one of the oldest and nicest ones in Legends Village. It was a huge, white building with apartments connected to the main house, which the maids lived in. It also had a grand, circular driveway that went around the mansion and in the middle of it was a little flower bed with white roses. Tainwo hadn't lived there for years and now Julian was going to live there with his mother, Tahama, Tainwo's only child.

"Emily?" a voice called from afar.

She could spot Julian in the distance and he pointed his gloved hand towards the children's park, opposite Tainwo's mansion and Emily made her way over to him.

"Sorry, I already went exploring," Julian confessed.

"No problem." Emily smiled. "What do you think of the place?"

Julian's eyes widened. "Amazing! I can't believe you've lived here your whole life. You're so lucky."

"Yeah, I guess I forget how cool it is here. Usually the paparazzi are roaming around, but they've hired better security for the gates now, thank God."

They walked into the children's park and sat on the snow-covered swings.

"How are you finding training?" Julian asked as he swung lazily, barely leaving the ground.

"Not the best experience," Emily confessed.

"How come?" Julian asked innocently.

Emily raised her eyebrows at him, surprised he hadn't noticed. She told him about Alice's obvious dislike for her and Gabriel and his weirdness. Julian nodded earnestly to everything she said, not interrupting her once. Emily was surprised how comfortable she felt talking to him. Usually when she was around him, she felt nervous and awkward. So she took a chance and told him about the ice room.

"Whoa wait," Julian said, jumping off the swing. "Someone dragged you to a room full of ice and it's in Osaki?"

"It might have been a dream, but deep down I don't think it was. I felt the ice. I felt this person dragging me around and the cold all over my body. It was too real. I haven't seen the ice room since. Michella and I were going to go look for it once the Linktie game was over."

"But that's crazy!"

Emily's spirits fell. "You think I was dreaming?"

Julian shook his head. "That's not what I meant. It's crazy

that there could be an ice room in Osaki and no one's seen it. Have you told Mr Davon, or Jenkins and Roberta?"

"No," Emily said, looking to the floor. "I need to see for myself if it exists. If I tell them there's an ice room and there isn't, I'm going to look stupid."

"They might also think that you're cracking under the pressure and take you out of the training group."

"I didn't think of that," Emily said, looking worried. "I'm not cracking. I know I'm not."

Julian sat back on the swing. He was watching the snow-flakes fall on to his trainers. "Did Michella think it was real?"

"No, she thought I dreamt it."

Julian fell silent again. Emily wished she knew what he was thinking. "Would you show it to me?" he asked, after a while.

Emily stared at him surprised. "You *want* to see the ice room?"

"Yeah," Julian said, as if it was the most obvious thing. "And if the person who dragged you there appears then he or she won't have much of a chance with us both there, will they? Do you know where it is?"

"It was behind one of the suits of armour. To be honest, I would rather you came with me than Michella. I know she thinks it's all in my head."

Julian smiled cheekily. "So it's a date?"

Emily laughed. "Err, that's the worst date ever."

"Okay, it can be the pre-date. After we look for the ice room, we can have a proper date." Emily blushed and looked at the floor. She couldn't believe Julian Kena was asking her out. "Unless there's something with you and Wesley?"

Emily looked up sharply. She thought of Wesley's kiss before her speech and how it had made her heart race. Nothing had happened since then and they hadn't spoken about it. In fact, he was acting like nothing had happened at all.

"We're not together," Emily said truthfully and Julian punched the air, which made her laugh again. "Where would we go on our real date?"

"Well . . . I would take you over to my house where Charlotte—she's the cook—would make us a meal. Then after we would go to the cinema suite and watch a movie and I would introduce you to my mum, who would love you."

"How do you know that she'd love me?" Emily asked intrigued.

Julian scoffed. "Well because you're pretty, brave, talented—"

"You think I'm pretty?" Emily asked surprised.

Julian nodded.

Emily was floored. Julian Kena thought *she* was pretty!

Julian exhaled deeply; he opened his mouth, as if he was going to say something and then they heard a shrill voice shout, "Julian!"

A petite Korean lady was standing at the entrance of the park, wrapped up in an oversized cardigan with her dark hair knotted in a bun at the top of her head.

Julian cupped his mouth. "Mum, this is my friend Emily, Thomas Knight's daughter."

Tahama waved at Emily, who waved back. She pointed at her watch and Julian sighed.

"I've got to go," he said standing up.

He stood in front of Emily and swiped her hair out of her face. Leaning close to her, so that his lips were next to her ear, he whispered, "Merry Christmas, beautiful."

Emily watched him run over to his mother, who only came up to his chest. They linked arms as they trudged through the snow together. Julian looked back at Emily and waved. Emily waved back before she walked home, embracing the peacefulness and beauty of the Village, which she hadn't done in years.

As soon as she got home, Emily walked into the kitchen where Cathy and Sally were covered in flour. Stuck on the fridge was the front page of the Daily Steward, with Emily behind the podium and the slogan, 'Our Knight Has Come.'

She leaned against the marble counter and sighed. "I think I'm in love."

"No way," Cathy squealed. "Is it Julian? Tell me everything."

Emily nodded. The smile wouldn't leave her face.

"That's great, Em," Sally said, but her eyes didn't leave the cookbook. "Can you help the kids decorate the tree?"

"Mum, what is wrong with you?" Cathy asked baffled. "Emily's in love. This is massive news."

"I would appreciate this, love, if she could get the tree ready. It's the least she could do for abandoning us on Visiting Day."

"You're so mean," Cathy responded, with her dough covered hands on her hips "You know that wasn't her fault."

The two argued back and forth as Emily hugged herself tight, not listening to a word. She was only thinking of the one word Julian had said to her. Beautiful.

On Christmas Day, the catering company that Michael had secretly ordered came early in the morning. They threw away the inedible cookies Sally and Cathy had made the night before, so by the time lunchtime came around, the dining table was heaving with a giant golden turkey, apple and chestnut stuffing, roast potatoes, sweet potato pie, corn on the cob, glazed carrots, a massive red velvet cake, dozens of minced pies and a fresh batch of edible chocolate chip cookies. Emily made sure she ate a piece of everything until her stomach felt like it was going to explode and she had to unzip her jeans.

Emily watched her family with a smile on her face. They were talking, teasing and laughing with each other, a big difference from last year when she, Sally and Michael wore forced smiles, as they attempted to keep Lox's break-in at the Kinkles under wraps. At the time, they didn't know it was Lox, but he had come to the house to take Emily to Neci. He hadn't counted on there being so many strong warriors present in the house.

Thinking about Lox made her stomach feel tight and for a moment, Emily's smile slipped. She hadn't heard a word from him since. Even Neci's antics had quietened down. She hadn't retaliated to the speech and it made her feel nervous. She had a feeling that Neci was staying deliberately quiet. She wished her dad had come to the forest. Even if it was for a minute, she just wanted to see his face.

"More mulled wine?" Cathy said, offering her the bottle.

"Yes, please," Emily said, smiling again. At least Julian had believed her about the ice room. With him by her side, she didn't feel as afraid to see it again.

In the evening, they sat down and argued about what Christmas movie to watch. Emily stood her ground, saying that she wanted to watch The London Flyaways vs. The Birmingham Warriors Dojo match.

"I'd quite like to see that," Michael chipped in, making the girls apart from Emily groan.

"Yeah, yeah put it on!" James said excitedly.

And it was the best Dojo match Emily had ever seen. She explained to them the rules of Dojo and was surprised how much Cathy got into it. She was cheering at the screen at Janette Kinkle, who was possibly the best Distracter ever, but what impressed Emily the most was their tactics. Both teams knew how to maximise their players successfully, especially Janette, who flashed her tattoos at every opportunity (and considering where some were, it was very distracting). The game lasted three hours and The London Flyaways won, which meant they would face Wesley's team, The Manchester Fountains for the cup.

"Now I've got something to impress the boys with," Cathy said, winking at Emily.

The Christmas holiday was over and Emily had just finished another early morning Dojo practice—the last one before they had to face Lintkie. She had just managed to get to Water Studies class in time and she joined the rest of the Ogragon team by the river in the forest. They were shivering in their thin training kits as Mr Waternham, a lanky, pale faced man with round glasses and a moustache was explaining to them about breathing under water.

"Although most have perfected the technique . . ." His eyes lingered on Emily, who rolled her eyes as soon as he looked away. "We're going to take ourselves out of the comfort of the tank and into the river. We're going to see how long you can breathe under water. Yes, Mr Notting?"

"What's the longest anyone has breathed under water for?" Jason asked.

"The longest on record is fifteen minutes, but Waterloons are warriors that can live under water and stay alive in ice." Emily put her hand up and Mr Waternham sighed, as if it was a big effort to answer her question. "Yes, Knight?"

"Did you just say someone can live in ice?"

Mr Waternham crossed his arms. "So you can't breathe under water *and* you can't listen? Let's form an orderly queue. No pushing!"

Emily placed herself at the back behind Nicky Johansen, who was complaining that she didn't want to get her hair wet. She had never thought that there could be a person alive under the ice. *But how did they get there? And what did they want? What could be so important that they needed me to see it?* But she would have to find someone who could speak Hariem. She made a mental note to tell Julian later. Thinking about Julian made Emily smile. She wanted to hear him call her beautiful again.

"Anytime today, Knight." Mr Waternham sighed.

Emily didn't realise she was now at the front of the queue. Slowly, she took off her baht shoes and walked into the freezing water. Emily groaned as the water soaked her training kit and she closed her eyes. She took a deep breath and went underneath. "You can do this, just breathe," she said to herself, but the idea of breathing made her panic. A sharp pain shot through her chest and she shot her head above the water and exhaled before going into a coughing fit.

Mr Waternham rolled his eyes. "Did you even try?"

Emily walked back to the class. The training kit was stuck to her body and she was shivering. "Yes," she stammered and Mr Waternham tutted and commanded Daisy Atam to go in next.

The next lesson was Mediation class with Miss Amity Roshi. Roshi was stretching out their aching bodies and instructing them to clear their minds. Emily found herself again thinking of the Hariem inscriptions on the ice.

"Emily?" Roshi called, in her singsong voice. She looked younger than the whole class with her petite body and pixie hair cut.

Emily looked around. Everyone was sitting on their zafu and Emily was still lying down with her legs over her shoulders.

"Sorry," Emily said, joining them.

The next day was the Ogragon vs. Linktie match and Emily was sitting in the Ogragon living room with Jason and Wesley, when Michella ran in with a letter in her hand and gave it to Emily.

"It's from Janette," she explained.

Jason and Wesley stopped their conversation and they watched in anticipation as Emily opened the letter.

Dear Emily,

Michella wrote to me about your upcoming match. The best way to beat a guy like Alan Fair is to rely more on your speed than your power. Tire him out before you attack. Warren is fighting

*Alan first, so hopefully he will defeat him. But regardless you'll be
fine. Good luck!*
  Janette x

"It's worth a try. Thanks, Michella," Emily said, folding the
letter. "I'll tell Warren."

"You'll do fine today," Jason said, rubbing Emily's back.

A loud rumble echoed throughout the room. They all
looked at Wesley.

Michella laughed. "Was that your stomach?"

Wesley smiled guiltily. "I guess I'm much hungrier than I
thought. I better get something to eat before the match starts."
He knelt down beside Emily's chair. "I'm not going to say
good luck because you don't need it. You're much stronger,
tougher and smarter than when you last faced Alan. If you
end up facing him, you can take him down. And please for
everyones sake, kick Tanya's arse for us?"

Emily squeezed his shoulders. "It would be my pleasure."

Michella opened up her arms and Emily stood up and
embraced her. "We'll be cheering from the stands," she said
in Emily's ear. She kissed Emily on the cheek and beckoned
at the boys to follow her.

As soon as they had left the room, Warren and Pete came
in.

"Morning, Emily," Pete said cheerfully.

"Morning, guys. Hey, Warren, Janette sent me a letter
about beating Alan. Here, take a look."

She handed him the letter and Warren read it to himself,
before screwing it up and throwing it over his shoulder, where
it landed perfectly in the bin.

"Don't listen to her," Warren said easily. "We've got a better way to beat him."

"You do?" Emily asked dubiously. "How?"

"We can't tell you, we'll have to show you," Pete explained.

Emily looked from one to the other. "I don't like the sound of this," she confessed.

"You'll love it," the brothers said in unison.

They led Emily out of the room and down the flights of stairs, past the dining hall where some of the Ogragon and Linktie Dojo team were still eating breakfast and out of the front doors of Osaki. They walked through Gilford's Walk and into the brightly lit stadium, where the scoreboard read, 'Dojo Champions-Pentwon' and underneath it read, 'Ogragon vs. Linktie.' Emily assumed they were going to walk on to the pitch, but instead she was led towards the changing rooms.

"Sit here," Warren instructed as Pete went into the little office that Lenny used.

Emily sat on the wooden bench, underneath the row of pegs. Pete came back into the room, holding a black rucksack that Emily remembered seeing in the summer.

"Do not freak out," Pete warned as he opened the bag and lifted out the surprise.

Emily jumped to her feet and Warren grabbed her and instantly put his hand over her mouth to stop her from screaming.

Emily pushed Warren off and pointed accusingly at the boys. "How did you even get that?"

"We brought it," Warren said simply. "Isn't it great?"

"Oh my gosh, oh my gosh," Emily chanted, walking up and down the changing room. "This is insane."

"Relax," Pete said, looking proudly at his surprise.

"Relax!" Emily shouted. "What the hell are you going to do with that thing? Bring it on to the pitch?" The boys smiled at each other and Emily collapsed on to the bench in disbelief. "We will get disqualified if we bring that out and it's seen."

"*If* it's seen," Warren said, sitting beside her. "It will be out, for a second and no one will see it but Alan."

"How is that possible?" Emily snapped. "Oh my gosh, Michella! With the mouse in her suitcase!"

Pete sighed. "I know, right. I thought we'd blown it."

"Because Michella would have told Lenny," Warren added.

"And Lenny, for sure would have told Mum," Pete said and Warren shuddered.

"If people see that—" Emily begun.

"That's a big if," Pete said, sitting down by her other side.

Emily looked at the brothers perplexed. She didn't understand how they thought this could work. She looked down at the bag that was on the floor and winced. "Why *that*?"

"We had a tip off last year that Alan has a big fear of these bad boys," Warren explained. "So after that embarrassing defeat against Linktie, Pete and I saved up. Mum helped out too, for 'Nicholas's birthday'." The boys laughed.

"So when we were at Sia's Avenue, we saw it, brought it, bribed Mike to keep his mouth shut and the boys in our room would never tell. We'll release it into the wild as soon as the match is over. They'll be no evidence, their word against ours. Warren, this was your best idea yet, honestly out done yourself, bro," Pete said.

"Cheers, Pete," Warren said, slapping him on the back.

Emily thought they had lost their minds. As calmly as she

could, she said, "I don't understand how you believe that a whole school watching the match will not see this . . . thing appear! What about Wesley and Harmony? If they see it and they say something—"

"They won't announce it because you're going to tell them not to," Warren argued.

"What?" Emily said outraged, standing to her feet. "I'm not a part of this! We don't even need to use it. We've trained so hard, we can beat him."

"Oh come on, Emily, this is a guaranteed win," Pete said, sounding frustrated. "We all said we want to win the championship for Lenny, so that's what we're going to do. Don't tell the hippy one, but tell Wesley because he'll listen to you. Just tell him to make sure that she doesn't see it. Easy."

"Easy?" Emily said bewildered.

"And what do you mean you don't want to be a part of this?" Warren demanded, rounding on her. "You're here, you're part of this. I mean, come on! You don't want to beat, Alan? You'll get to battle, Tanya." He put an arm around Emily's shoulder. "And we all know how much you dislike her. All we need to do is show Alan this, he'll piss himself, I'll knock him out and Tanya will be all yours. Easy."

Emily looked from Warren to Pete. It amazed her that these two scheming boys were related to Michella. Emily knew what she wanted to do, but she wasn't sure if it was a good idea, although the idea of facing Tanya was very tempting. Warren and Pete were nodding their heads and smiling at her as if they could hear her thoughts.

"I'll do it," Emily heard herself say.

The boys applauded her.

"You, Emily Knight, are a saint," Warren said, leading her towards the exit. "You've got five minutes to work your magic."

Emily stepped on to the pitch and hugged herself as the wind blew strongly. The sky was grey and cloudy. The stands were starting to fill up with teachers and students and at the very top in the commentators' box were Wesley and Harmony.

Emily looked around the stadium and saw that Roberta and Jenkins had just walked in and all eyes were on them. Ms Macay was in deep conversation with Ferguson Cloud. Whilst everyone was distracted, Emily ran to the middle of the pitch and shot up into the air. She hovered in front of the window until a surprised Wesley saw her and pointed towards the door to her right. Emily flew over and walked into their box.

"Emily!" Wesley said surprised, as he closed the door after her. "What are you doing? The match is about to start."

Emily was distracted by the room. There was a long table with soft drinks and snacks. To her left, was a giant well-known picture of the leaders of the Warrior Revolution. There was a stack of magazines in the corner, a bathroom, two giant armchairs and an excellent view of the entire pitch.

"Nice," Emily said, walking over to the table and grabbing a handful of chocolate covered pretzels.

"Cheers," Wesley replied, his eyes following her. "Now, what are you doing here?"

"Err," Emily said, feeling nervous. "I need to talk to you in private."

Emily looked at Harmony, who sat still watching them until it dawned on her and she hurriedly left the commentators' box. When the door shut, Emily informed Wesley of Warren and Pete's plans. Wesley stared at her shell-shocked.

"They're bringing what?"

"A snake. They're bringing a snake on to the pitch."

Wesley shook his head. "I need to sit down."

There were only a few minutes left till the match started. She hoped Warren and Pete were covering for her because Lenny would be fuming over her absence.

"Let me get this straight," Wesley said perplexed. "They're going to bring a snake on to the pitch and I can't announce it?" Emily nodded. Wesley gasped and pointed his thumb towards the door. "What about Harmony?"

"Do anything you can to distract her. She's in Jenkint, she won't care if we win or lose."

Wesley pulled a face. "How am I going to distract her?"

"I don't care," Emily said, glancing at the clock. "Amuse her with your card skills. Do whatever it takes. We need you to help us, Wesley."

Emily opened the door and Harmony jumped back looking guilty.

"I couldn't hear anything, I promise," Harmony said.

"Let's hope so," Emily replied before she flew down to the pitch.

Ms Macay caught her running and yelled, "Knight? What are you doing?"

"Sorry," Emily shouted over her shoulder and sprinted into the changing room. Everyone looked at her when she entered.

"Are you okay?" Lenny asked, looking concerned.

Emily glanced at Pete, who nodded at her. "Yes, I'm fine thank you," she said, trying not to sound uncertain.

"Do you need some painkillers, babe?" Raquel Davis asked. "When I get mine, I'm in agony."

Emily shot a dark look at Warren and Pete, who were annoyingly trying not to laugh. "I'm okay," Emily said, feeling uncomfortable.

"Glad to hear it. Now everyone make sure you're focused, control your energy, so that you can fight longer and let's win!" Lenny said and the team applauded him.

"Please tell me you didn't say what I think you said," Emily whispered to Warren and Pete, when they walked towards the pitch.

"Well, Lenny can't get angry about your time of the month, can he?" Warren said innocently before he burst out laughing.

"You're such an idiot," Emily said, thumping his arm.

"Did you do it?" Pete asked eagerly.

Emily nodded. "Is the snake with you?"

Warren shifted his Dojo kit. "He's safe in here. I'm just praying he doesn't make any sudden moves."

"And here comes the Ogragon team—Lenny Kinkle, Summer Wind, Raquel Davis, Rosa Martin, Jessie Kendaschi, Pete Kinkle, Warren Kinkle and Emily Knight!" Harmony announced, to a thunderous roar of applause from the crowd.

Emily looked into the stands and could see Michella and Jason waving excitedly at her and she waved back. In the stand below them, Gabriel Thompson was sitting next to Jasper Jones and Gabriel was staring straight at Emily. Emily waved at them, but only Jasper waved back.

"And the Linktie team—Josie Harrington, Lorlene Sims, Tan Matthews. Charlie Tendon, Craig Neon, Tony Welsh, Alan Fair and Tanya Frank!" Wesley announced, as the Linkties walked on in black training kits.

The Linktie side of the stadium seemed to be louder than

everyone. From the corner of her eye, Emily saw Warren fiddle with his kit. He saw Emily looking and shrugged sheepishly. Emily prayed they wouldn't get caught and disqualified.

"I want a clean match," Ms Macay said, eyeing them all. "Any outbursts like Gary Coles, and you'll be out of Osaki by the end of the day. Fly up on the whistle."

The whistle blew and the teams flew up. Warren had one arm pressed tight against his chest, holding the snake and Emily felt that everyone could tell what he was hiding. As usual, the captains started off the match. Josie Harrington, the Linktie Captain was a petite girl with buck teeth. Lenny was double her size, but Emily would bet Josie was one of their fastest Fighters.

"Kinkle charges towards Harrington and Harrington— where is she?" Harmony said, looking around the stadium. "She's behind Kinkle! Harrington grabs Kinkle around his neck—Kinkle's trying to swing her off, but it seems like a pretty tight grip. Ogragon Distracter, Rosa Martin has shot a fireball at Harrington—it's hit her on the back! That looks so painful! Harrington's let go—Kinkle's grabbed her arms and kneed Harrington in the stomach. Linktie Distracter, Lorlene Sims, elbows Kinkle in the back—she's teleported and so has Raquel Davis who's on the hunt for her! Harrington's punched Kinkle in the face, who's gone flying—Harrington's got a fireball in her hand. Summer Wind, Ogragon Distracter, has grabbed her arm and Harrington's punched Wind in the face!"

"Not allowed!" Wesley shouted into the microphone and stood to his feet. The stadium was a mixture of cheers and boos. "Ref, sort it out!"

Ms Macay blew her whistle. Her face was as red as her hair. "Fighters are not allowed to hit Distracters—" but before Ms Macay could finish, Summer charged at Josie Harrington.

"Don't be fooled by Summer Wind's pretty face—she's headbutted Harrington in the stomach—the Linktie Distracters are watching from a safe distance, so much for team work! Wind's retreated back, but she's spin kicked Harrington in the face—Harrington's been hit so hard, she's banged into the invisible wall—Wind's making a fireball—oh, Lenny!" Wesley fell back on to his seat, looking irritated.

Lenny had grabbed Summer around the waist and pulled her away from Josie Harrington.

"Whoa girl, I think you made your point," he said.

"I'm so proud of her," Warren said to Emily, who laughed.

Summer was breathing hard. Her long, blonde hair was a complete state and she resembled a bull ready to charge again.

"Wait for it," Lenny said to her.

Everyone's eyes turned to Josie Harrington, who started to slide, very slowly down the invisible wall, making a squeaky sound. She landed with a loud thump in the sand and Ferguson Cloud waved the red flag.

The stadium went wild with the Ogragon's cheering the loudest. Emily clapped with the rest of her team as the Linkties stayed sombre. Rosa and Raquel embraced Summer in a tight hug and Emily spotted the Linktie Distracters staring daggers at them.

Ms Macay blew her whistle and third year, Craig Neon, a tall, muscular white boy with brown hair and a faint moustache was next to fight Lenny.

"Neon's not wasting anytime," Harmony said. "He has

charged towards Kinkle–Linktie Distracters' Sims, Matthews and Tendon have gone for the Ogragon Distracters. I can't keep up! Kinkle's thrown a fireball at Neon who's caught it! And shot it back at Kinkle! Kinkle has blocked it and the fireball's rebounded, hitting the main Distracter for Linktie, Lorlene Sims in her back. She's taken the blow. She's falling—the flag's up—SIMS IS OUT OF THE GAME!"

Ms Macay blew her whistle loudly. She was waving her hands back and forth and beckoning for Lenny and Craig Neon to come down to the pitch. Lorlene Sims was back up and was shouting and pointing at Lenny.

"He's in serious trouble now," Jessie Kendaschi said.

"How come?" Emily asked, as she watched Ms Macay talking to them.

"Lenny hit a Distracter and we're not allowed to touch them."

"But it was an accident," Emily said outraged. "He was blocking the fireball."

Jessie shrugged.

They had to wait several minutes for a decision. Harmony flew out of the commentators' box to see what was going on. Emily couldn't tell from her expression whether it was good news or not. She flew back to the box and addressed the stadium.

"We all know that in Dojo, Fighters are not allowed to hit the Distracters. So as a result, Lenny Kinkle is disqualified for blocking a fireball that hit Distracter, Lorlene Sims. This is a—"

Whatever else Harmony was trying to say got blocked out by the loud boos from the audience, even Wesley was booing from the microphone.

"So the next Fighter is third year, Jessie Kendaschi."

Harmony had to shout on the microphone over the boos. "Jessie hasn't played for over a year because of a knee injury, so it's great to see him in action."

"Come on, Jessie!" Wesley shouted.

Harmony elbowed him as commentators weren't supposed to take sides, even though Wesley did it all the time.

"That was the most ridiculous decision ever!" Wesley moaned into the speaker. "I mean, what was Lenny meant to do? Take the fall. What a load of bull—relax, Harmony, I am behaving myself! Anyway, Neon's thrown the worst punch ever at Kendaschi who has teleported. Neon's swung a kick, but has missed by a long shot. Raquel Davis has teleported behind Neon—she's fired a fireball at him—yes, Raquel! But—hold up—Linktie Distracter, Charlie Tendon jumped in front of Neon and has taken the hit of the fireball—she's clutching her stomach—she looks in agony—Ogragon Distracter, Rosa Martin has teleported above Tendon. She's thumped her hard on the back and Tendon's soaring to the ground . . . and she's out! TENDON'S OUT OF THE GAME!"

The blue flag went up and Emily cheered with the rest of her team, but there wasn't much time to celebrate as Jessie had punched Craig Neon so hard in the mouth, that he started to bleed.

"Well, Jessie doesn't waste any time," Harmony continued. "Neon's clutching his mouth—there's blood everywhere—Neon's drawing his head back and has spat his bloody saliva in Kendaschi's face. Oh my gosh, that is disgusting!"

"Go on—beat him up, Jessie! No, I'm not taking sides Harmony, so shut up! Kendaschi's not holding back, punching Neon with so much force—did a tooth just fall out? Kendaschi's headbutted Neon, who's flown to the invisible wall and Neon's falling—oh yes—his touched the floor—the red flag's up. NEON'S OUT OF THE GAME. 2-1 TO OGRAGON."

Jessie wiped his face with his sleeve and the blood camouflaged with the red Dojo kit he was wearing. Beside Emily, Warren was again fidgeting with his kit. She couldn't wait till the game was done with.

The next Fighter for Linktie was Tony Welsh and he looked livid. Jessie rubbed his hands and grinned.

"Kendaschi's punched Welsh in the stomach and head-butted him—Welsh has staggered back—Kendaschi's thrown an uppercut and is punching him repeatedly in the face. I think it's an understatement to say that Jessie has missed playing Dojo." Harmony laughed. "Linktie Distractor, Tan Matthews is trying to interfere, but Rosa Martin and Summer Wind are making sure that she doesn't. Welsh has kicked Kendaschi . . . err . . . in the lower regions and Kendaschi's howling in pain."

"I can understand that pain," Wesley said. "What a bloody cheap shot! Welsh has punched Kendaschi in the face that has sent him flying and Welsh is going after him. Ogragon Distracter, Raquel Davis has teleported in front of Kendaschi and pulled Welsh's face down hard on to her knee—Welsh is clutching his nose and Davis has teleported again—Kendaschi looks ready to go—he's grabbed Welsh by the hair and is dragging him around the stadium! Do you hear that noise, Harmony? The crowd is loving this! But wait! Kendaschi has abandoned Welsh and flown up high into the sky. Welsh is floating limply in the air—what is Kendaschi up to?"

"I don't know, Wesley, but it seems like—can you see that? Jessie Kendaschi's fist is on fire! And he's charging towards

Welsh with it! Wow, how did he do that? Kendaschi's flying fast and hit Welsh with his fire-covered fist—that must be a pain beyond words—no surprise Welsh is falling—"

"But Kendaschi's falling too!" Wesley said surprised, standing to his feet. "Welsh has got Kendaschi by the ankle and is dragging him down—the Ogragon Distracters are trying to help, but the Linktie Distracters are blocking them. Kendaschi's trying to get free, but he can't—teleport! Aah it's too late, they've touched the floor. Poor Jessie! WELSH AND KANDASCHI ARE OUT OF THE GAME! 3-2 TO OGRAGON."

"That's not fair!" Pete hollered. "This crap shouldn't be allowed."

"It's Dojo, mate," Warren said, crossing his arms, then yelping when he remembered the snake was there.

The stadium was going crazy with a mixture of cheers and boos. Wesley was stomping up and down the commentators box and Harmony nervously watched him before continuing her commentary.

"Jessie Kendaschi is fuming down below, but all is fair in a game of Dojo. Yes, it is fair, Wesley—yes it is—yes it—oh whatever! Next to fight from Linktie is Alan Fair against Ogragons, Pete Kinkle."

Pete flew forward. His mouth was set in a thin line and his fists were clenched.

"This isn't good," Warren said, frowning.

"Why?" Emily asked.

"I didn't think our Fighters would be out so quick. I need to be the one to battle Alan." Warren coughed loudly and Pete looked at him.

Warren shook his head and Pete muttered, "I know, okay!"

Emily raised her eyebrows at Warren who tutted. "I didn't even think that Pete would be facing Alan. He has to lose the match. This snake isn't here to make my day more amusing."

Ms Macay blew the whistle and Pete floated into the middle of the stadium, not moving a muscle when Alan Fair flew over to him, gripped his arm and twisted it around his back. Emily watched Lenny pacing below them with his head in his hands.

"Kinkle . . . doesn't seem to be putting up much of a fight," Harmony said uncertainly.

Pete gritted his teeth, but he made no effort to escape from Alan's grip.

"Teleport, Pete!" Warren shouted.

Pete looked over at him irritated. "Make up your mind." Pete teleported out of Alan's arms, who look around mystified.

"Behind you!" Tanya Frank shouted.

"Kinkle swung a kick at Fair's head and Fair didn't even budge!" Wesley commentated. "Wind's teleported beside Kinkle and shot a fireball at Fair—it's hit his chest—but Fair's still up! What the hell is this guy made of? Fair seems to have shaken it off. Kinkle and Wind seem to be discussing tactics."

Summer looked over at Warren with narrowed eyes.

"Oh great, he told her," Warren moaned. "I'll never hear the end of it."

"Wind has disappeared and Kinkle's shot up into the sky with Fair behind him. The Ogragon Distracters are blocking Matthews, the only Linktie Distracter left, from flying up—I can't see where they are," Harmony said.

Emily looked up to the cloudy sky and saw no sign of them. The stadium fell quiet as everyone tried to catch a glimpse of the fight, and suddenly a body shot down into the sandy ground with a loud thump. Emily had to wait for the dust to clear to see it was.

"And it's . . . Pete Kinkle! KINKLE IS OUT OF THE GAME! THE TEAMS ARE TIED."

The audience burst into huge cheers. Alan flew back down and Emily couldn't help but laugh at his confused expression. She would have betted that Pete threw himself from the sky. Lenny was screaming at Pete below on the ground.

"Let's see if Warren Kinkle can take care of Fair," Harmony said.

Emily caught Wesley's eye and nodded. The Linkties were chanting Alan's name and Alan's quizzical expression was soon turned into a smirk. Warren floated in front of Alan, looking smug.

"Hey, you want to see something cool?" Warren asked.

Alan frowned, but moved closer to Warren.

"Now, what do you think is going on there, Wes—"

Emily looked up as Harmony stopped speaking and saw something that made her catch her breath. Wesley and Harmony were kissing. Emily felt as if someone had grabbed her heart and twisted it. She could feel the heat rising in her body. She wanted to stop it, but she couldn't. Her whole body was shaking and she felt like she was on fire. Wesley had finally seen her. He looked worried and hurriedly wiped his mouth with the back of his hand. He was pointing at her and saying something into the microphone, but all Emily could hear was her breathing loud in her ears. Harmony wasn't staring at her, but Emily saw it. She was smiling to herself. And that's when the huge energy exploded from Emily and the stadium disappeared in a blinding light.

CHAPTER NINE

Awakened

It was dark and cold and her feet were freezing. That's when Emily noticed that she wasn't wearing her baht shoes anymore. She didn't recognise her surroundings. The last thing she remembered was Warren flying forwards to fight Alan Fair. She looked down and noticed she was wearing a white nightgown which wasn't hers. There was a person dressed in black in front of her. She didn't know if it was the same man who had taken her before.

They walked down a long corridor until they came to a battered door. Emily knew what was behind the door and she tried to run, but the person had a firm grip on her. Emily squirmed until she felt a forceful hand slap her hard across her face. She instantly covered her sore cheek and fell quiet. The door opened and the beauty of the ice made Emily gasp.

Emily touched the tip of the ice with her toe, which sent a shiver up her body. The person grabbed Emily around the waist, with freezing hands and teleported her to the centre of the room. Emily looked up at the person, but their face was covered with a black mask. The chanting started, the same chanting said in a foreign tongue and it echoed around the room becoming louder and harsher. The inscriptions on the ice turned a bright blue and then a light ascended from it. The light was so bright that Emily had to shield her eyes.

"Yes," the person whispered gleefully beside her.

Someone was coming out of the ice.

Emily stared in astonishment as a man floated in front of her. The light from the ice began to fade and Emily could see that the man was very tall with pale skin. He was handsome with a strong jaw. His naked torso was lean, but toned and his bottom half was covered with fitted, white shorts. His long, brown hair was wet and stuck to his face and body. He looked at Emily with cold, icy, blue eyes.

He floated slowly towards her with water dripping down his body. Emily took a step back, but was blocked by the mysterious man in black. The ice man was coming closer to Emily, his eyes locked on hers. Emily felt frozen. He traced an ice-cold finger down the side of her face, below her chin where his hand flexed and he wrapped his strong hand around her neck. Emily pulled at his hand in a poor attempt to get him off.

"Not yet," the man beside her said, hitting the ice man's arm and he dragged Emily back.

Emily wrapped her arm protectively around her neck and breathed heavily. She glanced at the man in black. She recognised his voice, but she couldn't place a face to it.

The ice man nodded and then everything seemed to merge into one. Everything went dark and Emily closed her eyes, but when she opened them, the ice room was gone. She was surprised and confused to be in the sick bay and she noticed that every bed was occupied with sleeping students. She looked down at her body and the white night gown was stuck to her. Her neck felt sore and bruised.

"You're awake," Nurse Hilda said. A plump woman with a tight blonde bun walked towards her. "You knocked yourself out."

"I did? Why is it so busy?" Emily asked.

Nurse Hilda stopped walking. "That's all thanks to you, Miss Knight."

"Me?" Emily said in disbelief. "I didn't do . . ." Then she remembered. The kiss and the fireball that came out of her and everyone screaming. Emily put her head in her hands. "Was anyone seriously hurt?"

Nurse Hilda shook her head. "Nothing that I can't handle. They've just repaired parts of the stadium."

"Oh my gosh," Emily whispered and gasped when she noticed Tanya Frank and Alan Fair opposite her. Wesley, Warren Kinkle and Harmony Loving-Dale were to her left and a few other students that she didn't know were asleep on her right. Emily shook her head. She thought she had gotten better. *Who was going to believe they were safe with me when I can't control my own powers?*

"Did I just leave the room?" Emily asked Nurse Hilda, who shook her head.

"Must have been a dream because you were asleep the whole time. Oh, Roberta Taniana left you a message. She said she and Jenkins have gone to chase up a lead about the missing warrior and Ruth Walker and Mr Davon want to see you ASAP."

"I bet," Emily muttered. She slowly got out of the bed. She was a bit unsteady, but felt okay. It was only starting to get dark outside. "Can I go and see Ruth now?"

Nurse Hilda hesitated.

"I feel fine and I'll come back and stay the night here if you want," Emily promised.

"Okay," Nurse Hilda said reluctantly. "I'll phone home and let them know that you're alright. Don't take long and change into this." She handed Emily a spare blue Osaki uniform, which Emily put on.

The door to room 102 was already open. Emily peered in and Ruth Walker, a big, middle-aged woman with her Afro in a bun, was organising her books. Emily knocked on the door. Ruth turned around and peered at Emily over her small glasses and smiled.

"Emily, how are you?" Ruth asked. She beckoned Emily to come in, greeting her like an old friend.

Emily closed the door and sat in the seat that Ruth gestured to.

"Did we win?" she asked and Ruth laughed.

"Yes, you did. That's the great thing about Dojo, it doesn't matter how you knock someone out, just as long as you do and you, missy, knocked out two Fighters with one fireball . . . and a few other people."

"Ah man," Emily said, shaking her head. "I don't know what happened."

Ruth clasped her hands on her lap and stared intensely at Emily. "Do you have feelings for Wesley Parker?"

Emily raised her eyebrows, surprised at the bluntness of the question. "Err . . . well I care about him. He's one of my best friends."

Ruth chuckled. "It's always a sign when they avoid the question." She crossed her legs, looking serious. "You have to be more careful. You gave an amazing speech about people being safe if they put their trust in you, but how can they? When this is how you react over a kiss! There was a student I used to counsel and she was confused whether to finish school at Osaki, or play professional Dojo. There was a story that my grandma used to tell me about an eagle and a buzzard. Have I mentioned this?" Emily shook her head.

"An eagle is stronger and more powerful than a buzzard. Native Indians believe that the eagle is a symbol of leadership and great strength. It's also a symbol for hope. A buzzard is a poor imitation of an eagle, but can easily be mistaken for one if you don't know the difference."

"Janette Kinkle said something along those lines to me, but I didn't really understand," Emily confessed.

"Yes! Janette was the student. Okay, you need to ask yourself, are you going to step up and embrace this role of leadership? Are you going to believe that you're destined for greatness? Or are you going to keep hoping that someone else can take over the role?"

"It's not that easy." Emily sighed. "I can't even control myself sometimes. It's a lot of pressure. I didn't put my hand up to do this."

"I know, but that's why we're all here, to help you be the best you can be. I guess arguably the most important question right now is, are you going to admit that you have feelings for Wesley? And that's why you created that incredible energy, or are you going to keep pretending that you don't? Until the next time he kisses someone else?"

Emily didn't know whether to laugh, clap, or be offended. "Is that what people think? That I lost it because he kissed someone?"

Ruth shook her head. "It wasn't a long kiss, most people didn't even notice."

"It had nothing to do with him kissing anyone," Emily lied. "Besides I fancy Julian. I don't even like Wesley like that."

Ruth looked at her over her glasses. "There's no point lying to me. I'm telepathic, so I could hear every thought you were having."

Emily groaned. "This is so embarrassing."

Ruth laughed. "Don't worry I've seen and heard worse and with Julian, I wonder if you would have reacted the same way if he had kissed someone." Emily opened her mouth and then closed, it lost for words. "Now, what else is on your mind? I haven't seen you for quite a while. How are you doing?"

"Something strange has been happening and this sounds silly, but I don't know if it's real or not," Emily said, looking at her hands. "I've been having these visits. I think someone is teleporting me to this ice room that's here in Osaki and there's a man, who lives in the ice, but he came out of it today and wanted to hurt me."

Ruth didn't respond. Emily didn't realise she was holding her breath waiting to hear her thoughts. Ruth took off her glasses and cleaned them on her turquoise jumper. "And this has happened more than once?" she finally asked.

Emily nodded.

Ruth ripped up of a piece of paper from her notebook which was by her feet and scribbled something on it. She folded it up and handed it to Emily. "Do not read that. Go to Mr Davon and give him that note."

"Okay," Emily said, standing up. "Aren't you going to give me some advice?"

Ruth smiled. "On this occasion, Mr Davon is the right person for that."

Before Emily reached the door, Ruth called her name.

"When you're ready to talk about that kiss, my office is open, but you can go," Ruth said, before Emily could protest.

Emily had only been to the headmaster's office twice last year. The first time was when he had told her that her powers were controlled by her emotions and the second time was when she had teleported herself and Lox to his office when they escaped from Neci. She typed in the pin 060888 and rested against the cool oak doors. She opened up the note that Ruth gave her.

You were right.

Emily frowned. *Right about what?* She folded it back up into its creases and walked up the stairs until she was outside his office. She knocked on the door and entered.

Mr Davon's office looked the same as it did last year. On the right side of the room were his different coloured training kits and on the left side was a huge painting of the leaders of the Warrior Revolution. Emily closed the door, but this time, she avoided looking at the Five Warriors picture that hung on the back of the door. She didn't want to see her absentee father's face.

Mr Davon was seated behind his desk, with his chin resting on his clasped hands, not looking the least bit surprised to see her. Emily wondered if Mr Davon was also telepathic.

"Hello, Emily," he said. "Come, take a seat." Emily sat down in the chair opposite him. She noticed that Mr Davon looked more tired than usual. He had heavy bags underneath his blue eyes that weren't there before. "How are you feeling?"

Emily shrugged. "Okay I guess. I kind of feel embarrassed because I thought I was getting better at controlling my powers."

Mr Davon nodded. "Yes, I thought so too. You injured a lot of students today and damaged school property. This is something you need to learn to control, especially now when all eyes are on you."

"I know, I'm sorry. I'll try harder—oh here, this is from Ruth Walker," Emily said.

He opened up the note. Emily studied his expression, but it didn't change as he read the short message. He crumpled it up into a small ball. "So tell me about these visits."

"How did you—" Emily began and Mr Davon tapped his head. "So you are telepathic!"

"I have many secrets, Emily." Mr Davon smiled. "Now, these visits?"

Emily explained about the ice room and that it was a teleporter who was behind it. Mr Davon listened carefully until Emily finished.

"Have you told anyone else apart from Ruth about the ice room?"

"Michella and Julian," Emily said.

"Okay, please don't tell anybody else." He glanced at the crumpled piece of paper. "I'm guessing you want to know what I was right about?"

"How do you know I read it?"

Mr Davon laughed. "Because you're fourteen. This really

fits in with what I've been sensing. As you know, students aren't allowed to use their powers in school, only in lessons, or Dojo and only third years and upwards know how to teleport. I know you teleported last year, but again that was due to your emotions controlling your powers." Mr Davon stood up and paced around the room. "I've been sensing teleporters with great powers coming into the school."

"Teleporters?" Emily said shocked.

"Yes, there has definitely been more than one. But I can only sense them, for a split second before they're gone. With Osaki, anyone can teleport in here, but people usually don't, as there are so many strong warriors, it would be stupid."

"You mean Neci could come here?" Emily gulped.

"Neci isn't stupid," Mr Davon said. He stopped walking and looked at Emily. "But only desperate people do stupid things. Now we know Neci and her team want to find this missing warrior before anyone else, but I'm starting to wonder if there is someone closer to home, who is also desperate for something."

"Do you mean someone is playing for both teams?" Emily asked confused.

"It's possible," Mr Davon said. "Is there anything else unusual that you have noticed?"

Emily hesitated. "Well, a while ago, I heard Gabriel Thompson talking to someone. It was a female and he got really angry with me when I tried to help him. He didn't like when I questioned him about it."

"Yes, Gabriel—he's very different from Niles and the strange thing about Gabriel is, I can't get into his head. It's like he has this block keeping me out."

"That's what Niles said," Emily added. "Do you think it's Gabriel who's the desperate one?"

Mr Davon sighed heavily, making him seem older than he was. "Well, the question is, what would he be desperate for?"

Mr Davon made Emily promise to not tell anyone else about the ice room and to make sure that Michella and Julian kept it to themselves. He said he would investigate the room and if anything else happened, she should tell him first. Emily reluctantly promised. She had wanted to show Michella and Julian, but now she couldn't.

It took several days for everyone in the sick bay to be released. When Emily was questioned by the other students and her family on what had made her so angry, she ran with the story that Mr Davon suggested; she was angry that Lox hadn't come back. It surprised her that everyone believed the lie.

Everyone except Wesley Parker. The first thing he did when he came out of the sick bay was ask Emily to go for a walk. A part of her was angry at him that he had kissed Harmony. Wesley had kissed her first. Did it even mean anything if he was going around kissing other girls? She told him to distract her, not to kiss her! The last thing Emily wanted to do was be alone with him, but if she refused, then it would look like she had something to hide.

They walked along the curved bridge, covered with snow that went over the koi pond. It was one of Emily's favourite places at school. She wished she was walking with Wesley under different circumstances. Emily tucked her hands into her coat pockets as she watched the exotic fish darting through the water, deliberately avoiding Wesley's gaze. Wesley sat with his feet hanging over the bridge and tapped the space next to him, where Emily sat down nervously. She noticed that Wesley didn't look as confident and was also looking down at the water.

"Sorry about the . . . you know," Emily muttered, breaking the agonising silence.

"It's cool," Wesley said. "I didn't mean to kiss Harmony, it just kind of happened. I panicked. I was trying to distract her." Wesley looked at Emily. "But I didn't know that you would get that mad about it." A slow smile spread across his face. "It's cute."

Emily laughed, but even to her own ears it sounded forced. "I wasn't mad about that, I was mad about—"

"I'm not buying the Lox story, I'm not stupid," Wesley said harshly, making Emily recoil. "If you like me enough that they have to re-construct parts of the stadium, why didn't you say?"

Emily stayed silent.

"So you like me *and* Julian?" Wesley demanded, his hazel eyes stared accusingly at her.

Emily wanted to respond, but she didn't know how.

"Why aren't you talking?" Wesley asked annoyed. "So you're allowed to crush on Julian and I deal with it, but I kiss Harmony for a second, and you send me to the sick bay for days? You can't have it both ways, Emily."

"I'm sorry," Emily said.

Wesley glared at her. "Sorry for what exactly?"

"I'm just sorry, for . . ." she trailed of miserably. She wished Wesley would just drop it.

"So you still can't admit that you like me?"

Emily wanted to tell him how she felt, but the words felt stuck in her throat. She did like him and she was jealous and felt betrayed that he kissed Harmony, but she knew she was being selfish because she also liked Julian. Wesley got up and Emily looked at him surprised.

"Where are you going?" she asked.

"To find Harmony," he said, dusting off his school uniform.

"Why?" Emily demanded.

Wesley stared at her coldly. "Because she doesn't do this! I like Harmony. Harmony's cool, but best of all she's honest and she doesn't play silly games." Wesley turned away from her and stormed off, leaving Emily feeling rejected and confused, alone on the bridge.

Emily sat on the bridge, until her bottom was numb from the cold. She stood up and dusted the snow of her training kit. She pulled on the hood of her coat and hurried back to Osaki. She climbed the stairs and entered the Ogragon team room. Wesley was sitting with Michella and Jason. They were in mid-conversation, but they stopped when they saw Emily. Without a word, she grabbed her backpack that she had left earlier by the coffee table and hurried back outside. She knew they were talking about her and it irritated her. She walked to the willow tree and sat under it, taking out her history notes that she spread across her legs.

"Didn't you hear me calling you?"

Emily looked up from her notes and Michella was standing in front of her.

"I'm guessing Wesley told you?" Emily said, as she placed her notes on top of her bag.

Michella nodded, siting down beside her. "Why didn't you just tell him how you feel? I mean, that was some jealousy-filled fireball. I'm surprised it wasn't green."

"I hate that you notice everything," Emily said, before she sighed. "I don't know, I was nervous, I guess. And a part of me is just so mad at him. You know he kissed me?"

"What?" Michella said flabbergasted. "Why didn't you tell me?"

"I didn't tell anyone. I mean, it was the corner of my mouth, not a full on snog. Now I'm thinking it didn't mean anything."

"But you know Wesley likes you!"

"How do you know that?" Emily argued.

Michella scoffed. "Please, Emily, it's painfully obvious." Michella hesitated. "I saw him holding hands with Harmony."

A sharp pain shot through Emily's heart. "Oh," she said in a nonchalant tone. "He can hold hands with whoever he wants."

"Look out," Michella whispered.

To her dismay, Harmony Loving-Dale was approaching them. She waved and Emily groaned. Michella elbowed her and smiled at Harmony.

"Hey, girls," Harmony said.

"Piss off," Emily muttered at the same time Michella loudly said, "Hi."

Harmony stood in front of them, nervously playing with the long plait in her hair. "I just wanted to make sure that . . . I mean, I know you guys are all really close and I didn't want to step on anyone's toes," she said, glancing at Emily. "Wesley and I are . . . well I guess we're dating and he said I was being silly, but I just wanted to check it was okay?"

Emily and Michella glanced at each other.

"Well actually it's n-"

Michella coughed loudly, startling Emily, so that she didn't finish what she was about to say.

Michella smiled sweetly at Harmony. "It's cool. We're all just friends."

Harmony instantly looked relieved, which annoyed Emily. "And you're okay with it too, Emily?" she asked.

Michella discreetly nodded at Emily and Emily glared back at her.

"She's fine," Michella answered for her.

"Oh great!" Harmony said, smiling beautifully. "I guess I'll see you guys later. Great game, Emily."

Michella nudged her as soon as Harmony walked away. "You can't tell Harmony how you feel and not Wesley. That will only make him more annoyed with you."

"Is she taking the piss? Great game, Emily," Emily said, imitating Harmony's voice.

"No, she's just being Harmony."

"What does he see in her anyway?" Emily asked, aggressively stuffing her notes into her heavy backpack.

"She's pretty, loves Dojo, weird in a quirky way . . . oh," Michella said, when she noticed Emily was glowering at her. "You wanted me to lie?"

Emily rolled her eyes. "So what about you and Jason?"

"What do you mean?" Michella responded, a little too quickly.

Emily smirked. If Michella was going to challenge her, she was going to be challenged also. "I notice a lot too. Are you dating?"

"No," Michella said, picking at the grass.

"Why?"

"Jason is really good-looking. I just don't feel that I . . ."

"You what?" Emily prompted.

Michella looked at her sadly. "I don't feel that I measure up."

"What?" Emily said, pushing Michella roughly. "You are an idiot."

"I'm not! Oh come on, Emily. He can have his pick of any girl, why would he want me?"

Emily stared at Michella surprised. "Michella, how could he not like you? You're amazing."

"I'm not," Michella said, turning away. "I'm nothing special and if we ever got together, I know everyone will think, why is he with her?"

"Who cares what anyone thinks? You should be with the person you like," Emily said and then laughed, when Michella looked at her knowingly. "I guess I'm not one to talk."

They stood up and Emily swung her backpack across her shoulder.

"When are we going to hunt for the ice room, now that the match is over?" Michella asked.

"There's no point, it was definitely a dream. I haven't even dreamt about it since," Emily lied, and when Michella didn't argue, she added, "Come on, we're going to be late for Water Studies."

They walked with their arms linked towards the forest

at the back of Osaki. Wesley and Jason were already there, talking close together.

"When did it start with you and Jason?" Emily whispered.

"You know we went out before? It didn't really work. We still liked each other though and then we spoke about everything before he went to France, but I don't know if anything will actually happen. He hasn't asked me out yet," Michella whispered back.

"There you two are," Jason said.

Wesley held Emily's gaze and smiled. She tried to smile back at him, but it felt like her mouth wasn't working properly. Wesley tutted and turned away.

"Today, we will be learning how to use our powers under water," Mr Waternham called from the front of the class. Everyone cheered, which confused Emily. She didn't understand how anyone could enjoy being under the water.

"Mr Waternham, sir," a small voice called from the back. Xavier Jenkins appeared wearing a white training kit, waving his hand to draw attention to himself.

"Are you lost, Xavier?" Mr Waternham asked, sounding sincerely concerned, which fascinated Emily. She had never heard him be anything but sincerely rude.

"I need to take Emily and Jason. My mum needs them for something." Xavier looked at Emily. She mouthed 'thank you' and he smiled, making him resemble his handsome father even more.

"Very well," Mr Waternham said, dismissing them.

They waved goodbye to the class and went to walk back to Osaki, when they noticed Xavier walking in another direction, further into the forest. Xavier wasn't a big talker and he was impatient, so he was silent and moving fast, making Emily and Jason run after him. He led them to a part of the forest where Emily had never been. It had a trail running along the floor.

"Ah, there they are," Roberta said. She was wearing a red training kit that hung like a second skin to her curves. She was holding Antonio's hand, who jumped happily when he saw them.

"Any luck with the missing warrior?" Emily asked and Roberta shook her head. Emily noticed that there was one person missing. "Where's Gabriel?"

Roberta looked embarrassed and cleared her throat. "Err, well Gabriel is . . . we don't currently know."

"What?" Jason said in disbelief beside Emily. "Gabriel doesn't seem the type to bunk of lessons."

"No, he doesn't," Roberta agreed. "But Niles is trying to get in touch with his parents to see if they know where he is."

"What, he's missing? Did he run away?" Julian asked.

Alice laughed. "Ran away from what?" at the same time, Xavier asked, "Shouldn't we be looking for him?"

"How long has he been gone for? Who saw him last?" Emily asked.

"Guys, please," Roberta said, holding up her hands until it fell silent. "Gabriel can't have gone far. No one has seen him since yesterday. We have many people looking for him, but we have to keep this quiet, or people will panic."

"And what if he teleports?" Emily asked.

Everyone looked at her.

Alice rolled her eyes. "He's in the first year. He doesn't know how." She spoke slowly, as if Emily would find it hard to understand.

"How do you know?" Emily rounded on her. "What if he can? How well do you know him? How well do any of us really know him?"

They all looked at Roberta.

"If he can teleport, it will take a bit longer to find him. Why do you think he can?" Roberta looked suspiciously at Emily.

"Just laying up the options."

"Hmmm," Roberta said, not looking convinced. "Right, today is about endurance. Everyone pick up a backpack."

Emily hadn't noticed the seven backpacks to the left of them. She dropped the one she had and picked up one from the seven. She instantly dropped it due to its weight. She watched as the boys struggled to put them on their backs, masking their discomfort. Emily picked one up again and quickly swung it on. Her knees buckled, but she gritted her teeth and stood up. Roberta put hers on as if was weightless.

"I want you all to follow this trail. Keep the backpack on and run at a steady pace. This is not a race," she said, looking at them sternly. "This is building up your stamina. Go."

Emily struggled to walk, let alone run with the backpack. The weight of the bag made sharp pains shoot across her back, but she practiced the breathing techniques Roshi showed them in Meditation class and it helped. She ran at a steady pace behind Jason, watching his blond hair flop up and down as he ran.

"Emily!" Julian called behind her.

She glanced over her shoulder and ran on the spot until he caught up with her and they began to run side by side.

"What was that back there? About Gabriel teleporting?" he asked.

"I think that Gabriel's hiding something," Emily said truthfully.

"You think he's the one taking you to the ice room? That he teleported you there?"

Emily stopped in her tracks. "What makes you say that?"

Julian beckoned for them to keep moving, so she did, but she kept her eyes on him. "Because I've been watching Gabriel ever since we spoke at Christmas and I think I've seen him teleport."

"What?" Emily exclaimed, shocked that she had got it right. "Why didn't you say anything back there?"

"Because I don't know, for sure. I was at Dojo practice with Mentorawth and he was watching from the top of the stands. I remember seeing him there, then a second later, he was on the first stand next to the pitch and I remember thinking, no one can move that fast without teleporting."

Emily stopped running. She was breathing hard, but her brain was trying to piece everything together. Gabriel acting strange towards her, his cold hands, the person who was threatening him and his family.

"But if it is Gabriel, I don't understand why? Aren't we fighting for the same thing?"

Julian kneeled over with his hands on his lap. Sweat poured down his forehead. "What's down there? In the ice room?" he said in between breaths.

Emily bit her lip. Mr Davon told her to keep quiet, but Julian already knew half the story *and* believed her. Emily told him about the inscriptions in Hariem and the ice man.

Julian stared at her open-mouthed. "A man lives in the ice?"

Emily nodded. "Maybe Gabriel's releasing the man, but then he would know how to speak Hariem and I thought it was a dead language that no one knew."

Julian fell silent, looking up at the sky as he collected his thoughts. "Do you think that the ice man is the missing warrior Neci wants?"

Emily gasped. "I didn't even think that. But if Gabriel is releasing him then . . . then we're going to have a war." Emily buckled and Julian caught her before she fell.

"Ooh, I'm telling." Antonio Jenkins was smiling cheekily at them.

"Antonio?" Roberta's voice called in the distance.

"I'm here, Mummy," Antonio called back.

"Quick, before she comes," Julian said, grabbing Emily's hand. They ran off leaving Antonio behind.

"We have to find Gabriel," Emily said urgently.

"We'll find him—together?"

Emily noticed they were still holding hands. It felt good.

"Okay," she said gratefully.

After the agonising run with the backpacks, which turned out to have nothing inside them, (Roberta had mind tricked them into thinking they were heavy) she made them do five hundred push ups in a handstand and five hundred sit ups before they were dismissed. Emily felt shattered and the day only got more intense when Lenny called a Dojo practice.

The Ogragon Dojo team treated Emily like a hero when she first returned back to training, even urging her to get angry at every game. Warren was the only one unhappy with Emily because he felt she had stolen his snake thunder.

The Ogragons would be facing Pentwon for the cup. Lenny

was even more stressed than usual as this was his last chance to win the cup before he graduated, so it came as no surprise to Emily when she asked him for a 'light' session that Lenny shook her roughly by the shoulders and pleaded with her to 'cooperate.' Emily didn't have the strength to argue, so she trained hard with her team. She barely kept up with them and that evening when she finally crawled into her four-poster bed, she slept deeply, with no nightmares.

The next few weeks began to resemble a pattern of classes, training with the secret group, Dojo training and revising for exams. One evening during dinner, Emily had excused herself from the table saying she had to go to the toilet and when she walked into the hallway, Julian was already there. They walked around the corner and saw the knights in suits of armour, standing in a line side by side.

"I remember that Gabriel knocked on the hand of the armour and it moved," Emily said.

"Which suit of armour was it?" Julian asked, looking from one end of the corridor to the other.

"I don't know," Emily confessed. "I don't remember if it was the right or left hand. Let's start on either side and meet in the middle."

"Should we have a signal?" Julian suggested and Emily frowned. "You know in case someone comes and we need to abort the mission."

"Okay, let's whistle. If you hear that, run."

They ran in opposite directions and Emily stood in front of the tall knight. The metal was glistening as if it had been freshly oiled and it was holding an axe in its right hand. She found it creepy looking at the empty space where a head should be. Anxiously, she knocked quietly on the hand holding the axe and waited. Nothing happened. She then knocked on the other hand and again nothing happened. Emily moved on to the next one. She had got through a quarter of the knights when she heard Julian whistle and she sprinted back down the corridor and hid around the corner.

Julian's voice carried and she could hear him saying that he was doing research for History class, then the unmistakable voice of Mr Waternham followed. "As much as I do admire your eagerness to learn, Mr Kena, all students should be in the hall for dinner."

Their footsteps echoed away and Emily counted to twenty before she went back down the corridor towards the dining hall. She made her way back to her table and caught Julian's eye. They both shook their heads at each other.

Gabriel had been missing for several weeks now and somebody had leaked it to the press. The media were questioning if Osaki was a safe place for warrior children to stay. Some of the students had started to travel in daily to school, rather than board and the amount of letters from parents to their children had doubled, to the point that they were getting handed out at every meal. Mr Davon continuously reassured the concerned students that no harm would come to them at Osaki and they would find Gabriel Thompson.

There was a huge reward money for anyone who had information, and posters of Gabriel's face were plastered everywhere. There was a news conference with his parents, where his mother cried the whole way through. The media brought back the slogan, 'Where is our Knight?' and the faith people had in them was wavering. Roberta and Jenkins had to release a statement saying that everything was under control and Gabriel would be found alive and well.

One day, when Emily had arrived at Osaki, warriors from S.U.D.W had been placed around the school to stop any of the media talking to the students, as well as capturing any unwanted warriors from entering the school. The rumour floating around the students was that Neci had Gabriel captive.

It didn't help that after breakfast, at their secret training session, Jenkins had held up today's newspaper and on the front page was Neci. She was dressed in all black with a white mask covering her face and behind her were Scarlett, Maggie, a gangly, white woman with short, brown, curly hair and frog-like eyes and Dion, a short, black man with a black, Mohican—but what made Emily horrified was seeing the thousand man army dressed in black behind them. The slogan read, 'YOUR MOVE, KNIGHT.'

"What the hell?" Alice said, pointing at the newspaper. "We can't fight all of them."

"We have been securing our own allies," Jenkins said calmly. "Roberta is with some of them now."

"And we're equal in numbers?" Alice demanded. When Jenkins stayed silent, she said, "Didn't think so." She stood to her feet with her hands on her hips. "We cannot beat her. I'm done with this."

"Alice!" Jenkins called. He threw the newspaper on the floor as he ran after her.

Julian picked up the newspaper and stared at it in silence. Xavier and Antonio sat beside him to get a closer look.

"Crazy, right?" Jason said as he sat next to Emily.

"My brother told me we shouldn't fight. He said we can't win this."

"You saw Lox?" Jason asked with his blue eyes wide. "When was this?"

"Just after the speech. Maybe he's right."

"We can't think like that," Jason snapped, drawing the attention of Julian, Antonio and Xavier. "There's always a chance and she said she wouldn't go to war without her missing warrior. As long as we find the person first, there won't be a war to worry about."

Emily and Julian caught each other's eye, both thinking the same thing. They had no more time to waste in finding Gabriel.

A depressed Niles Thompson floated around Osaki and students stopped him to share their condolences with him. Emily watched him feeling guilty—if only she had challenged Gabriel more, it may not have come to this.

Mr Davon called her into a meeting, to tell a bewildered Emily that he couldn't find the ice room that she had described.

"What?" was all Emily managed to say as Mr Davon explained that he had followed Emily's instructions and knocked on every knight in the hallway, but nothing had happened. He reassured Emily that even though he hadn't seen it, he believed that it existed.

Emily left the meeting perplexed. The knight in the suit of armour was the only way to the ice room. *How was I going to find Gabriel now?* She headed towards Meditation class and almost walked into Niles, who was floating in the middle of the empty corridor, staring into space.

"Hi, Niles," Emily said softly. Niles smiled sadly when he saw her. "I'm sorry about Gabriel, but you know Roberta and Jenkins will find him."

"I know." Niles sighed.

"Niles, I wanted to ask you something about Gabriel. It's kind of random, but did he know Hariem?"

"Yeah," Niles said miserably.

"Huh?" Emily said thrown.

"Yes," Niles repeated, looking at her. "Our granddad taught us. Why?"

"Oh my gosh!" Emily said.

"What is it?" Niles asked, looking alert. "Do you know something?"

"I have to go," Emily said, running in the opposite direction.

Niles called out her name, but Emily ignored him. She tried to remember what lessons the Mentorawths had when she was in Meditation. She was almost certain they had History. Emily sprinted to the History room, grateful that no one was in the corridors to question why she wasn't in class and even more grateful that Niles wasn't following her.

She knocked loudly on Mr King's door.

"Come in," he drawled.

Emily opened the door and wasn't surprised that the Mentorawths were doing whatever they wanted in the classroom. Mr King's supervised visits only happened a few times and as soon as they stopped, he went right back to his fashion magazines. Julian Kena was talking to a blond-haired boy with a nose piercing called Jerry Austin and he looked surprised to see Emily at the door.

"Sir, I need Julian," Emily said to a bored Mr King, who didn't even acknowledge her.

The room could have been on fire and Mr King wouldn't have taken any notice. Julian looked at Emily quizzically and gathered his books. Some of the boys wolf whistled and playfully nudged Julian.

"She *needs* you," one of the boys said and Julian laughed it off.

As soon as he closed the door, silencing the classroom, Emily told him what Niles had said.

"So where are we going now?" Julian asked. Emily explained what Mr Davon told her and Julian sighed. "Great, now what do we do?"

"I think we should look again. Maybe Mr Davon missed one. That is the only way into the room, it can't just disappear!"

They hurried down the silent corridors until Emily stopped in front of the suits of armour.

"Do you know where you got up to before?" Emily asked and Julian nodded. "Okay, and whistle if anyone comes."

Emily ran to the last knight she had knocked on. Every time one didn't move, she started to lose hope. She could see Julian on the other side of the corridor. There wasn't many left. Emily knocked on the one in front of her, holding the axe and stepped back in shock, when it slowly moved to the left.

"Julian, I found it." He ran over to her and gasped when he saw the tunnel. "Mr Davon must have missed it." Emily took a step forward and Julian grabbed her arm.

"Are you sure about this?" he asked, looking at it uncertainly. "Shouldn't we tell someone? Just in case."

Emily didn't want to ask what the just in case was. She

shook her head vigorously. "It will waste time. He must be in the ice room. It all makes sense now. Something bad must have happened to him. He's been missing for weeks. He could be dead, Julian."

"You're right." Julian's face looked paler than usual.

Emily took a deep breath and held out her hand. Julian looked down at it before he grabbed it and together they walked into the darkness.

CHAPTER TEN

The Ice Man

They walked in silence. The only sound they could hear was their breathing and the squeaking of their baht shoes. The tunnel seemed much longer to Emily, but she realised that this was the first time she wasn't being dragged. Emily didn't want Julian to know, but she was frightened.

The further down they went in the tunnel, the colder it became. Emily glanced at Julian, who was hugging himself. It didn't dawn on her till now that they should have grabbed jackets to put over their school uniform.

"We're here," Emily said, stopping outside the battered door. "Are you ready?"

Julian nodded and Emily opened the door.

"Oh my gosh," she heard Julian exclaim, as he looked at the ice room. "This is unreal."

There was a certain beauty about the room that briefly made Emily forget about the ice man who existed there. She stepped on to the ice first and slipped. Julian caught her before she touched the ground.

"Thanks," Emily said, as he helped her up.

They walked slowly across the ice, holding on to each other for support. Emily couldn't put her finger on it, but there was something different about the room. They walked past a huge mountain of ice and Emily stopped and pointed at it.

"That wasn't there before—neither was that," Emily said, pointing out the giant blocks of ice that were scattered around the room.

"Where is he?" Julian asked, looking around.

They continued to walk, slow and careful when they stopped and looked at each other. Emily gulped. "Can you sense that?" she whispered to Julian.

He nodded. "It might be, Gabriel." He pointed to where the energy was coming from and as silently as they could, they walked towards it.

There was a giant block of ice that took up a large amount of the surface area. They walked around it and when they got to the other side, Emily almost fell over when she saw who was there.

The ice man was no longer trapped. He was standing bare foot in front of them. He was still topless, in the same white shorts. His muscled arms were crossed and his blue eyes stared coldly at them.

"Is this the guy?" Julian asked in a shaky voice.

Emily couldn't respond, she couldn't move. The ice man smirked at them. It was a slow, sinister smile that made Emily wish she was safe in Meditation class. The ice man took a step towards them and they instantly took a step back, wanting to be as far away from him as possible.

"Where's Gabriel?" Julian asked and Emily looked at him

surprised, that unlike her, he had the confidence to address him.

The ice man stared at Julian for ages, looking staggered. Emily wasn't sure if it was because Julian had spoken to him, or because he was expecting Emily to come alone.

"You look very familiar," the ice man said to Julian. He had a deep, gravelly voice. "What's your name?"

"Julian Kena," Julian said boldly.

The ice man looked taken aback and then chuckled to himself. He raised a long, bony finger and pointed it to the right of him. Emily and Julian glanced at each other before they slowly walked around the ice, keeping an eye on the ice man, who stared blankly at them. Trapped in the middle of the ice was Gabriel.

A loud, piercing scream echoed around the room. It took a while for Emily to realise it was coming from her. The room began to shake as Emily's voice vibrated and some of the giant blocks of ice broke and fell down to the floor with a loud bang. Emily and Julian looked around panicking while the ice man didn't move. The room stopped shaking as quickly as it begun.

Emily ran her hand over the ice and Gabriel stared back at her. His eyes were wide open, his glasses were on the edge of his nose and his mouth was open in a silent scream. He had one leg in front of the other, with his body leaning forward as if he was going to run, but it was too late.

"Gabriel?" Emily called.

"Is he dead?" Julian asked.

"Not yet," the ice man said. "He put up a good fight, but he'll be dead soon."

"Who are you?" Emily demanded. She whipped round to face him.

"Max, but I would prefer to be called by my fighting name, Blade."

"Why are you here?" Julian asked.

Blade looked around the ice room as if taking it all in. "I've been here for many years," he said softly. "Trapped. I was working with a warrior called Rose."

"Rose?" Emily asked confused.

"Yes, but she had another name. Her fighting name was Neci." Emily gripped Julian's arm hard and took a step away from Blade, who noticed Emily's reaction. "So you know of her?"

"Of course we do!" Julian snapped. "And we know you're her missing warrior."

Blade looked surprised. "Missing warrior?"

"He doesn't know," Emily hissed at Julian. "He doesn't know what's been happening." She released Julian's arm. "How do you know, Neci?"

Something changed in Blade's eyes. They seemed to soften at the mention of her name.

"We trained together. Well, we trained each other. We never came to a training school," Blade said. "In fact your grandfather, Tainwo Keno taught us how to make light beams. Small world, isn't it?"

Julian stepped forward, but Emily pulled him back by his arm.

"We wanted to take over the world. We both had very complicated childhoods. We met at school when we were young. Rose and I both wanted to prove ourselves as warriors, for different reasons. Mine was to show off my new power." Blade smiled to himself.

"How did you find out about Osaki?" Emily asked.

"There was this group of warriors that was formed here. I remember them being all over the news and everyone said they were destined for greatness. I don't know if they're still fighting. They were called the Five Warriors."

"You fought the Five Warriors?" Emily asked surprised. "All of them?"

"No, just one. Do they still battle?"

"Not as a full team because Cecil and Niles were murdered by your friend, Rose," Julian said aggressively. "But she couldn't defeat them all."

Blade's eyes widened. "Rose fought them by herself?"

"She lost," Julian said. "You two were way out of your depth."

Blade smiled. "Maybe. We wanted to test how strong they really were. I didn't believe they could be stronger than Rose and I. She warned me not to come without her, but I didn't listen. I was young." Blade's face suddenly hardened. "As I was exploring the school, testing my powers out, I ran into one of those warriors. I attacked him, but he was very strong. I remember running away and he chased me. I found this room and I put the ice here to block him." His pale hands clenched tight into fists. "But he managed to get in and we battled. I thought if I hid under the ice, I could surprise attack him, but when I tried to get out, I couldn't. He had found a way to trap me in my own powers."

"Hold on a minute," Julian said, holding his hands up. "Who trapped you here?"

"A warrior named Thomas Knight," Blade said.

"What? My dad put you here?" Emily said taken aback. She looked at Julian whose shocked expression mirrored hers. "I didn't know he could speak Hariem."

"Thomas Knight defeated Neci as well," Julian said and Blade shot him a dark look. "I wish he had killed her."

"He should have," Blade said simply. "Because Rose doesn't take defeat well and neither do I."

"You're a Waterloon, aren't you?" Emily asked. "You can survive under water and in ice."

Blade mockingly applauded her and she glared at him.

"What has all of this got to do with Gabriel or Emily?" Julian asked frustrated.

Blade glanced at the frozen Gabriel and Emily panicked. *How long have we been talking for? What if he's dead?*

"Not yet," Blade said, looking at her.

Emily desperately tried to stop thinking and clear her mind. She had no idea if Blade was telepathic.

"Gabriel knows Hariem. He said Rose sent him to release me. He was told to bring you here," Blade said, pointing at Emily. "He said it was a guaranteed way to get Thomas Knight's attention. Apparently your daddy has been hiding. He might come out if he found out his daughter was trapped in ice."

Julian protectively stood in front of her.

"She said I had a way out," Emily muttered, feeling betrayed and foolish.

Julian whispered from the side of his mouth, "You should know better than to trust, Neci."

"As you can see, Gabriel didn't do what he was told. He told us that you have been asking him a lot of questions."

"Whose us?" Emily demanded.

"Scarlett," Blade said and Emily caught her breath. "Oh, didn't you know that they have been talking with each other all year? She was convinced that if Gabriel disappeared, you would try and find him."

Emily looked frantically around the room, trying to find a hint of red. *Was Scarlett also here?*

The ground began to rumble. Emily watched in horror as a long crack appeared in the ice and it broke in half, separating them from the door.

"Go!" Julian yelled. He grabbed her hand and forced her to run with him. Emily half-skated and half-ran beside him.

She looked back to where Blade was standing but he was gone. "Julian—"

"We'll get help and come back for Gabriel," Julian begged. "Come on."

"Blade isn't there!"

Julian looked over his shoulder and then from left to right. "Where is he?"

They were almost at the door, but Blade teleported in front of them and they skidded to a halt.

"I thought we were getting to know each other?" he said, before he soared up towards the ceiling with white objects circling him. Emily squinted as she tried to see what they were.

"Move!" she yelled at Julian, at the same time Blade shot the icicles.

They flew to the other side of the room, over the crevice, barely dodging Blade's attack as Emily felt the icicles breeze past her. She landed on all fours, trying to catch her breath, when a white beam soared towards them from across the room. Emily and Julian darted in different directions, but the ice beam split in half and followed them. They weaved in and out of the giant pieces of ice that were around the room, but they couldn't lose Blade's ice beam. Julian was in front of her, flying towards her.

"Now!" he yelled.

Emily gathered her energy and shot a blue fireball at the ice beam following Julian. At the same time, Julian shot a yellow fireball at the ice beam behind her. There was a loud bang as the ice and the fireballs collided. Emily and Julian quickly flew towards the floor and crouched down behind a piece of ice.

Emily had a good view of Blade from where she was. He was standing by the door, looking up at the explosion they had caused. When the ice and fireballs had disappeared and Blade couldn't see Emily or Julian, he threw back his head and roared, "Where are you? Show yourselves!"

Emily looked behind her but Julian wasn't there. She looked up but he wasn't there either. Then she saw him, flying low towards Blade, whose back was facing them, with a fireball in his hand. Julian stopped a few metres behind Blade and shot his fireball. Emily held her breath as the fireball soared towards Blade, but Blade teleported at the last second. Julian looked around frustrated.

Emily saw a streak of white and cried out, "Behind you, Julian!"

Julian spun around and Blade punched him hard in the stomach. Julian kneeled over and groaned. Blade looked down at Julian smugly and Julian punched Blade across the face. Blade soared across the room and went through a thick piece of ice, where he appeared on the other side of it. He collapsed on to the floor and the ice crumbled around him.

"Emily?" Julian called. His arm was wrapped around his stomach. "Go to Gabriel and try to unfreeze him, but keep your energy level down, or Blade will sense you."

"Got it." Emily stood up from her hiding place and skated down to where Gabriel was trapped. She looked back and Blade was still knocked out on the floor.

"I hope you're okay," Emily said to Gabriel's frozen body. She turned around again to make sure Blade was still out cold, but he was gone. She sensed a huge energy above her and looked up to see Julian and Blade fighting. The speed with which they were attacking each other was so quick that they looked like they were teleporting all over the room.

Emily took a step back from Gabriel and shot a fireball. It hit the ice loudly. Emily stopped and waited to see if the noise attracted any attention, but they were still fighting. She shot multiple fireballs at the ice, which chipped away second by second. It was making a lot of noise, but the battle was even louder. It wasn't long before Gabriel's head and neck were free from the ice. He was still for a split second, before he took a long breath in and coughed aggressively. His face was tinged blue. Emily put her hand on his cheek and Gabriel stared at her. She pushed his glasses down until it sat comfortably on his face.

"Hey," Emily said softly.

"I'm so sorry, I'm so sorry," Gabriel said, with tears streaming down his face.

"Ssh," Emily said. "Let's just get you out of there."

Gabriel looked down at his frozen body and at the fireball

in Emily's hand. "Emily, I could . . . I mean I think I can teleport out of the ice."

Emily frowned. "Are you sure? Do you have enough energy?"

"Yeah," Gabriel said weakly. "Just give me a minute."

Emily closed her fist and her fireball disappeared. She watched fascinated as Gabriel's body seemed to become one with the ice until it disappeared and a second later, Gabriel was laying on the floor, shaking and coughing.

A chunk of ice soared above their heads and crashed not far from them. The fight was still going strong. She didn't have anything to offer but herself, so she laid down beside Gabriel, ignoring how cold it felt when the ice started to seep through her training kit. She wrapped her arms around him, holding him tight until he stopped shaking.

"As soon as you have enough energy, you get some help," Emily whispered. "I need to—"

She could sense Blade a second before Gabriel whispered, "Behind you."

Emily gently released Gabriel and swept her leg across the floor, tripping Blade up, so he landed painfully on to his back. Across the room, she could see Julian shooting fireballs at the ice that had trapped his leg.

Emily flew up into the air, above Blade and shouted, "ANYOSINGH!" Her giant red fireball shot down and hit Blade in the pit of his stomach, forcing the ice beneath him to break. The water splashed up dangerously and Blade sunk below it.

Emily floated in the air, feeling anxious, waiting for Blade to jump out, but he didn't. Julian flew towards her looking down at the hole in the ice.

"Good job," he said breathlessly, when he reached Emily.

"We don't have much time. He's a Waterloon remember?"

They flew down and landed next to Gabriel, who was staring at them both in awe.

"Hey buddy," Julian said, placing a hand on Gabriel's shoulders. "How are you feeling?"

"B-b-better," Gabriel stammered with his teeth chattering.

Emily and Julian looked at each other worried.

"Let's go get help," Julian said. He picked Gabriel up easily in his arms.

They walked slowly and carefully towards the door in an attempt to keep their energy level down.

"As soon as we get out, I'll get Roberta and Jenkins and you take Gabriel to—" Emily was cut off by the sound of ice breaking. She spun around and watched in horror as the ground around them began to crack and break apart. "Go! Go!" she screamed.

They jumped over the crevice and ran towards the door. They weren't far from it, when the ground beneath them collapsed and they fell into the icy cold water.

Emily tried hard not to take in any of the water. Her head began to throb and she felt dizzy. She thrashed around, trying to hold on to something, but there was nothing to grab. She felt strong hands pin her arms to her side. She opened her eyes and Julian was floating in front of her. His long, black plait looked like a serpent in the water. He was gesturing at Emily to breathe and she shook her head vigorously.

He held her waist and swam them upwards to the surface, but they hit something solid. Julian rubbed his hand against the surface and there was ice. He swam them along the water, but there was ice everywhere. Emily's head was spinning and her lungs ached. Her eyes felt heavy and everything looked blurry. She wished she had told her friends how much they mean to her.

She could faintly see Gabriel floating beside them, looking more alert under the water than he did above it. Julian pointed at Gabriel and then upwards. Gabriel gave him the thumbs up and teleported.

Emily felt like her head was going to explode. She began to fight of Julian, wanting, needing to get some air. Julian held her tighter and pulled her close, so their lips touched. He opened up her mouth with his own and breathed into her. Oxygen rushed into Emily's lungs, making everything stop spinning. She stopped thrashing around and wrapped her arms around Julian's neck as he held her tightly. Time seemed to stand still as they floated and kissed in the water and she didn't want it to stop. Only when Julian let go of her, did she realise that she was breathing under water. She was finally doing it.

Julian pointed his thumb upwards and Emily nodded. She held on to him as he raised up his right arm above his head. His arm was glowing and Emily looked at it in awe. She hadn't mastered how to use her powers under water yet. Julian flew up and they broke though the ice. They collapsed on to each other, breathing hard with their hair matted to their faces. Emily's head was resting on Julian's chest with her ear against his racing heart.

"Thank you," Emily said.

"Anytime," Julian responded.

The door to the ice room opened and Mr Davon, Roberta, Jenkins, Cecil and Niles appeared.

"My goodness," Cecil Archinia said, looking at the room in amazement.

Roberta saw them lying on the floor first. She teleported and appeared next to them. She was on her knees and pushed back their hair of their faces. "Are you both okay? Is anything broken?"

"Never better," Julian croaked, which made Emily laugh. She instantly wished she hadn't because her throat felt like sandpaper.

"Where's Blade?" Roberta asked, looking around the room. "We can't sense him."

"He must be under water still," Emily said, slowly sitting up. "How did you know it was him?"

"Where's Gabriel?" Niles demanded, floating towards them.

Emily and Julian looked at each other puzzled.

"He teleported to get you, guys," Julian said uncertainly.

Everyone fell silent. Mr Davon glanced at Jenkins, who dived gracefully into the water. Roberta and Mr Davon helped Emily and Julian up.

Julian looked at them frustrated. "How did you know we were here then?"

"It was me," Niles said, looking troubled. "A few minutes ago, I managed to get inside Gabriel's head and read his thoughts."

Emily wrapped her cold arms around herself to stop shaking. She had a gut feeling that Gabriel was with Blade. Jenkins flew out of the water and shook his head solemnly and Emily groaned. *Why Gabriel?*

"Read his mind again, Niles," Cecil urged.

Niles closed his eyes and winced as if he had been hurt. "I can't. He has blocked me again."

"Let's get you two out of here," Mr Davon said. He held on to Emily and Julian and the ice room blurred into a white light. She closed her eyes and when she opened them, she was standing in the sick bay.

"Let's get you changed," Nurse Hilda said, walking up to Emily. She took her behind a screened curtain where Emily slowly removed her wet training kit. Her teeth were chattering uncontrollably and Nurse Hilda wrapped her in a soft white robe.

"Drink this," Nurse Hilda said, handing her a steaming hot cup.

Emily took a sip of something sweet and instantly felt weightless before everything turned black.

A few hours later, when Emily awoke, she looked around the room confused at first where she was. She turned to her left and saw Julian sitting up, also wearing a white robe. He didn't notice she was awake. He jumped off the bed and walked to the other side of the room. Emily's eyes followed him and she saw Mr Davon, Roberta and Jenkins, and sitting on the bed was Gabriel Thompson, in a fresh training kit.

"Where were you?" Emily asked, marching up to him and everyone looked at her surprised. "Where's Blade?"

"Emily, please," Mr Davon said, standing in between them.

"I almost died for you!" Emily shouted. "Did you take him to Neci?"

"I'm sorry," Gabriel said quietly.

"What's new?" Julian said annoyed, crossing his arms.

Gabriel's face turned red as he shouted, "Yeah, well what would have done if they said they were going to kill your family? She would have killed them if I didn't follow through.

What would you have done?" Gabriel's outburst made Emily and Julian fall quiet.

A bewildered Niles floated towards his brother and at the sight of him, Gabriel began to cry.

"I'm sorry, Niles," he said. "They threatened me all year. They blew up the house. They were going to kill Mum and Dad. I-I couldn't lose them too. I'm sorry."

Mr Davon sighed. "I need a moment alone with, Gabriel."

"Oh no, I want to hear this," Emily said defiantly.

"Emily, come on," Jenkins said, pushing her towards the exit.

"No," Emily said shrugging him off.

"I had no choice," Gabriel said sadly.

"YOU HAD A CHOICE!" Emily roared, charging towards him.

Julian blocked her and Jenkins lifted her up over his shoulder and walked them out of the sick bay. Students stared perplexed at a furious Emily, who was hoisted over Jenkins shoulder. Julian followed behind them with Roberta.

Jenkins took them up to Mr Davon's office and dumped Emily on an armchair. He sat in Mr Davon's chair and stared at Emily.

"You of all people should know what it's like to lose your family," Jenkins said softly and Emily felt all the anger that was in her instantly depart. "What would you have done if you had a chance to help, Lox? You would take it in a second." Emily crossed her arms stubbornly. "He didn't do the smartest thing, but he was scared."

"Do you know that part of this plan was to trap me under the ice?" Emily spat at Jenkins. If he was surprised by the news, he didn't show it. "I am so sick of people putting me on the firing line. I get it. My dad has a lot of enemies, but I am not Thomas Knight!"

Roberta placed a steaming cup in front of Emily.

"What is this?" Emily asked suspiciously, remembering that Nurse Hilda had given her a drink in the same looking cup and she had fallen asleep.

"Hot chocolate," Roberta said innocently.

Emily reached for it and took a sip. The hot chocolate burnt her tongue, but she didn't care, she embraced the warmth that ran through her body.

"I get why Gabriel did it," Julian said, glancing at Emily, who glared back at him. "But I don't think it's cool. He let down the team. How are we all meant to fight together when he betrayed us like that?"

At the word fight, Emily almost dropped her cup. If Blade was reunited with Neci, then there was going to be a war and there was nothing she could do any more to stop it. Julian, Roberta and Jenkins were talking and Emily tuned them out. She looked down into her cup and felt her anger rise again. People were going to die because Gabriel wanted to protect his family. Well, congratulations, except they would probably die anyway.

Emily chuckled at her own logic and everyone looked at her stunned. She placed her cup on the desk and looked at them. "I'm not going to fight in this war," she said calmly.

"What?" they chorused.

"I'm not," Emily said simply. "No one seems to care about me, so why should I care about anyone else?"

"That is not true, Emily," Jenkins protested.

"Really? Yet here you are defending, Gabriel!"

Julian slammed his cup on the desk so hard that his hot chocolate spilled over it. "I believed you about the ice room. I came with you. I stopped you from drowning yourself and now you won't fight? You won't fight with me like I just fought with you?"

Emily opened her mouth but was lost for words.

"Let's give these two some privacy," Roberta said to Jenkins, who couldn't look more relieved and walked out quickly.

Emily slumped into her chair and stared into space. "I just feel like I can't trust anyone."

"Including me?" Julian looked so hurt that Emily wanted to run and embrace him. Instead, she walked over to him and got on her knees and leaned forward, so that her head was under his.

"I do trust you," she said and she watched him until he looked at her. She leaned back, so she was sitting on the back of her feet with her arms slumped to the side. "I can't help that I'm Thomas Knight's daughter, but I get punished for it all the time. He's not here to clean up his own mess. Lox is...God knows where, and I can't keep taking everyone's crap. Gabriel let them use me as bait. Yeah, okay, Neci lied about giving me a way out, but before I knew that, I didn't take it, even though I wanted to." A tear raced down Emily's face and she wiped it away aggressively. "Gabriel has opened up a door that we can't shut and Neci is going to kill all of us." She put her head in her hands, as she tried to stop the tears from flowing down her face. "I don't want to die."

"Oh, Emily," Julian said, joining her on the floor and hugging her. "Gabriel might not have taken Blade to Neci, but if he did I promise that I'll fight with you. I promise you."

Emily stayed in Julian's arms until her tears dried up and their bodies went limp. They fell entwined on to the soft carpet and fell asleep.

Emily felt a warm hand holding on to hers. She turned towards it, smiling, opening her eyes, expecting to see Julian but it wasn't him.

"Hi," Emily said to Michella, who was holding her hand. Wesley and Jason were standing beside her.

"How are you feeling?" Michella asked softly.

"Like I just lost a Dojo match," Emily croaked. She was back in the sick bay. Julian was asleep a few beds away from her. There were some people from Mentorawth standing by his bed. Ambria Appleton was holding his hand and stroking his head, causing a possessiveness to rise up in Emily. It took all of her energy not to punch Ambria.

"Please remind me to never take a drink from, Roberta," Emily said.

"Why?" Jason asked confused.

"Because I think she drugged us. Last thing I remember, Julian and I were talking in Mr Davon's office."

"I'm sorry we weren't there for you," Wesley said, gently stroking her cheek.

Emily quickly glanced over at Julian who was facing them, but his eyes were shut.

"I'm sorry I didn't believe you when you first told me about the ice room," Michella gushed. Her braids were unravelling from its neat bun. "I'm just so grateful that Julian was there."

Emily smiled weakly. "It's okay. So how much do you guys know?"

The three of them looked at each other.

"Roberta and Jenkins led a press conference, explaining that Gabriel was being threatened by Scarlett. They said that Gabriel released Blade, who was the missing warrior Neci was talking about. But no one knows yet if Blade is back with Neci, but if he is, we have to prepare for war," Jason said, looking distressed. "Did Gabriel really do that?"

They looked at Emily with desperation in their eyes. She could see their hope fading with every second she stayed quiet. Emily nodded and Michella gasped and covered her mouth. Jason's face got paler as he digested the information and Wesley grabbed Emily's hand and held it tight, as if scared that she would leave him.

"It'll be okay," Emily said, with fake confidence. "We still have a chance to win this."

Michella choked back her tears and nodded as Jason rubbed her back.

Nurse Hilda walked into the sick bay and ordered everyone to leave Emily and Julian in peace.

"I left you some cards on the bedside table, in case you get bored," Wesley called before Nurse Hilda shut the door.

Emily was relieved they were gone. Her eyes felt heavy and all she wanted to do was sleep and forget about everything. Her eyes searched the room and she noticed that Gabriel wasn't in the sick bay.

"Nurse Hilda," Emily called. "Where's Gabriel?"

Nurse Hilda fluffed up Emily's pillow and said, "He's with Ruth Walker—poor boy is traumatised."

"This is all his fault," Emily said, annoyed that someone else was defending him.

Nurse Hilda looked at her and smiled sadly. "Emily this is all Neci's fault and don't lose sight of that." She patted Emily's leg and walked back to her office at the far end of the room. Out of the corner of her eye, she saw Julian Kena sit up in his bed.

"You're awake," Emily said happily.

"I was always awake," Julian confessed. "Just couldn't face everyone asking me what happened."

"Fair enough, but you missed Ambria looking adoringly at you whilst she held your hand."

Julian laughed and then moaned and rubbed his chest. "You know how girls act with a wounded hero."

Emily scoffed.

"But seriously, Emily," Julian said, looking at her in disbelief. "I can't believe we fought with an ice man. How crazy is that?"

"About as crazy as a bunch of kids fighting in a war," Emily said flatly.

They both fell silent.

Julian asked in a nonchalant tone, "So what's up with you and Wesley?"

"What do you mean?" Emily asked, as she pulled her ponytail to her nose. She pulled a face at the unpleasant smell.

"I mean is there something between you two? I saw the way he stroked your face."

"I thought you were sleeping," Emily said, looking at her hands.

"Pretending," he replied.

Emily found it funny how it had all worked out. At the

beginning of the year, she seemed to have this internal struggle between Wesley and Julian and now here she was feeling closer to Julian than she did Wesley. They still hadn't spoken properly about their status, but Emily hoped that Wesley would still be her best friend and it wouldn't be weird between them anymore.

"No, Wesley and I are just friends."

"Good," Julian said, putting his arms behind his head.

Emily raised her eyebrows. "And why is that?"

"Because when we go on our date, we don't have to feel bad about it. Remember the ice room was the pre-date."

"That's your idea of a good time?" Emily asked but she was relieved that he remembered. "When will this date be?"

"Well, the war could start at any time. What about right now?"

"What?" Emily laughed and then groaned, when a sharp pain shot through her torso. "You do know we're in the sick bay, right?"

"So?" Julian said, slowly getting up from his bed. "This can be our sharing our feelings kind of date." He walked slowly towards her and Emily budged over in her bed, so he could sit beside her. He gritted his teeth when he sat down and Emily patted his hand sympathetically. "I think I need more Reviving Water."

"Do you play cards?" Emily asked, reaching over to the bedside table and grabbing the pack Wesley left for her. "I could do with a bit of Black Jack right now."

"You see, I didn't know you played that. I'm learning something new already," Julian said.

Emily smiled and shuffled the cards. She yawned loudly and Julian raised his eyebrows. "Tired?"

"I'm okay," she said, even though she could feel sleep coming over her.

"How are you feeling about everything?"

"Scared," Emily said truthfully. "I have a gut feeling that Blade will reunite with Neci, whether it be today, or next week. I don't think Gabriel actually took him to Neci because I think she would have killed him, or kept him to blackmail us. We're nowhere near ready to help in the battle and there is still no sign of my dad."

"He'll come," Julian replied. "I can't imagine a fight with Neci and Thomas Knight not being a part of it. Do you know where your brother is?"

"No," Emily said sadly. She dealt out the cards. "Would your grandfather come out of retirement to fight?"

"I think so. No one can shoot a light beam like Tainwo Kena." Julian looked at his cards and frowned. "What's up with this? I've got the worst hand."

"Sorry." Emily laughed. Her own hand was pretty good. "Do you ever hate the expectations put on you? Just because of your last name?"

Julian nodded. "My granddad created light beams, my mum battled in the warrior tournaments and won. Being an only child and having to carry that legacy is a lot of pressure— different league than you, I don't know how you handle it."

"I don't," Emily said half-joking. She yawned again and Julian watched her bemused.

"Tired of our date already?"

"Not at all, but I am just tired," Emily confessed. "Can we put a pause on the date?"

"Of course," Julian said. He took the cards out of her hands and put them on the bedside table. He pushed Emily gently down, so she was leaning back on the bed and he placed the bed covers over her. "We'll continue later."

Emily nodded with her eyes already shut, and a few minutes later she was fast asleep.

Scarlett and Blade were in front of her and the forest was covered in bright amber flames. The dry leaves crinkled and withered as they were licked by the fire. The air was covered in grey smoke that caused Emily to cover her mouth and cough harshly as her throat dried up. The fire was surrounding them.

Blade shot an ice beam at Emily, but she jumped over it and in her place were sharp icicles. Scarlett and Blade looked at each other and with a seductive smile, Scarlett flicked back her red hair and shot Sino at Emily. This time, Emily bent her knees to fly, but she felt someone pushing her down. She looked up and saw Gabriel with a manic look in his eyes. Emily wanted to scream, but she couldn't. The white, killing fireball soared towards her, getting brighter and brighter— Emily opened her mouth to scream.

Emily sat up breathing heavily. It was dark except for a dim light from the moon. She looked frantically around the sick bay, but all she could see was Julian asleep. She wiped the sweat across her forehead. She could still taste the smoke in her throat. She reached over to the bedside table, ignoring the pain in her side, and turned on the lamp. There was a jug of water, a cup and an envelope with her name on it. Abandoning the water, Emily reached for the envelope and studied the writing. It looked vaguely familiar. She opened it up and scanned to the bottom of the letter and gasped when she saw her dad's name on it.

My darling girl

I'm sorry this letter is short. We're in difficult times and I'm cautious that this may get into the wrong hands. I'm so proud of you. The fact that you went over and beyond to help Gabriel and battle Blade shows that you are growing into an amazing warrior. There is so much I need to say to you, but I promise, when I see you, I will explain everything. I am sorry for putting you in this position and I hope one day you will be able to forgive me. Thank you for L. I know you all went to great lengths to get his attention. It worked. I'll see you very soon.

I love you

Dad x

It worked? Emily re-read the letter a few more times before she hugged it to her chest. *Did this mean he was coming back? Were him and Lox together?* Emily put her hand over her mouth to stop herself from screaming with joy. He was coming back to her.

"Julian?" Emily called, but there was no response. "Julian?" she said louder, but this time he snored.

Emily folded up the letter until it was small and she could hide it in her clenched fist. Slowly, she climbed out of the bed. On the floor were her slippers, that she slid her feet into and walked towards the door. She carefully opened it, so that it wouldn't creak and alert Nurse Hilda.

"Where are you going?" a deep voice called and Emily jumped. A burly warrior in all black was standing beside the door. Emily recognised him as one of the guards from S.U.D.W which have been based at Osaki. "You're not allowed to leave the sick bay."

"I just need to see Mr Davon about something," Emily

said, as she tried to walk past. The guard stepped in front of her, blocking her way. "It's late, Miss Knight. It will have to wait until the morning. Unless you want me to pass on a message?"

"Can you tell Mr Davon or Roberta and Jenkins to come and see me?"

"Yes, that's not a problem." The guard gently guided her back into the sick bay.

"Who was the last person to come in here?" Emily asked.

"No one has been in since Nurse Hilda told your friends to leave," he said. "Why?"

"Nothing," Emily replied quickly. She shut the door behind her and climbed back into bed. She opened the letter and re-read it. *Maybe he teleported here and gave this to me himself?* The thought made Emily smile. She placed the letter under her pillow and fell into a dreamless sleep.

The next day, Nurse Hilda told Emily and Julian they were allowed to leave the sick bay. They didn't have time to finish their date, so Julian said they should meet up in the weekend to hang out and Emily was ecstatic.

Julian went upstairs to the Mentorawth team room, whilst Emily stayed behind to see if her message had been delivered. In the end, she decided not to tell Julian about the letter from her dad, not until she had shared the information with Roberta, Jenkins or Mr Davon.

Roberta arrived in a grey training kit with her long black hair pulled back into a tight, high, ponytail, showing off her sharp cheekbones. She smiled when she saw Emily and sat beside her on the bed.

"You're looking much better," she said.

"I feel better." Emily smiled. "How's Gabriel?"

Roberta hesitated. "He's getting there. He has been in regular counselling sessions and escorted home to see his parents. He's still on edge, but Mr Davon is going to call a meeting in a few days, so Gabriel can explain himself to the team."

"Any news on Blade or Neci?"

"Nothing yet. I was told you wanted to see me? But I was coming anyway to check on you. Nurse Hilda said you've been discharged?"

Emily nodded. She removed the letter from under her pillow and handed it to Roberta, who opened it and read it.

A slow smile spread across Roberta's face. "Well, well, well, I guess Lox came through."

"Do you think they're together?" Emily asked.

"I'm not sure, but they've definitely been in contact. This is a good sign, Emily. Have you told anyone about this?"

Emily shook her head.

"Not even your close friends?"

"I haven't seen them yet," Emily said.

"Okay, well let's keep this between us for now. Knowing Thomas, he'll arrive back making sure everyone knows."

"If Lox stopped running, that means he's on our side, right?" Emily asked anxiously.

Roberta stroked her cheek affectionately. "I really hope so. Come on, let me take you home."

Emily hadn't been back to Legends Village for a few days and Roberta teleported her outside of her house, so she avoided the press outside the gates.

Rosy, Yvonne and James had made a 'Welcome Home' banner for Emily that was taped to the dining table because they couldn't reach the high ceiling. Michael, Sally and Cathy sat with Emily around the table, whilst the kids played outside. Michael sat opposite her and demanded to know everything that had happened. They winced and gasped as Emily told them the full story of Gabriel's visits, the ice man and the dreams about Scarlett.

"Why didn't you tell us about any of this?" Sally asked, reaching across the table and holding Emily's hand. "After last year with Lox, I thought we would have no more secrets."

"I'm sorry," Emily said, feeling guilty. "I don't know why I didn't say anything. I guess a part of me thought that I could just deal with it myself. Also, I never had any concrete proof. I didn't want people to think I was making stuff up, or that I couldn't handle the pressure. I'm just thankful that Julian was there to help me. I couldn't have done it by myself."

"Ooh, Julian," Cathy teased. "I need to meet this sexy beast."

"Not when you say things like sexy beast."

"Well, I think we should invite the Kenas round for dinner as a token of our appreciation," Michael suggested.

"Yes," Sally and Cathy said, at the same time Emily said, "No, gosh how embarrassing."

"It's the least we can do," Michael insisted.

The three of them looked at Emily who crossed her arms. "Okay fine! But it'll have to be in the holidays after exams. And speaking of exams, I need to revise and seeing as you aren't doing anything, can you help me?" she said to a startled Cathy.

"Boring," Cathy sang.

"Cathy!" Sally exclaimed.

Michael and Sally looked sternly at her and Cathy let out a dramatic sigh, huffed and left the table. Emily waited for her footsteps to fade before she said to her godparents, "I know there hasn't been any confirmation that Blade's with Neci, but I know that this war is inevitable and I will have to fight in it."

"I just can't believe this is happening," Sally said in disbelief. "To be honest, I thought Thomas would be back by now."

"Nothing from him?" Emily asked, thinking of her letter.

"No, honey," Sally said. "I can't let you do this. I can't let you fight."

"Sally," Emily said, embracing her. "I have to and I think I'm okay with it now."

"You're only fourteen years old!" Sally cried. "You haven't even lived yet. I'm going to tell Roberta and Jenkins right now!" Sally stood up and Emily stumbled back.

"Why don't we just wait to see what happens?" Michael suggested, putting a hand on Sally's arm and gently wiping the tears off her face. "Roberta and Jenkins will have a plan. Emily, go upstairs and do your revision."

"Are you sure?" Emily hesitated as Sally flopped on to the chair and placed her head in her hands.

Michael nodded. "We just need to have faith." He sat down beside Sally, murmuring quietly into her ear and reluctantly Emily went upstairs.

CHAPTER ELEVEN

Gabriel's Story

Emily was standing outside the dining hall between Michella and Jason holding her History book and cramming in as much information as possible before the last exam began. They had already completed their Flying exam, which was a harder obstacle course than last year and had to be completed under a minute, but Emily found it a breeze. In the Foughtgon exam, they were tested on their sparring techniques, breaking a tree trunk with a single punch and successfully shooting the 'Anyosingh' fireball. Waterstudies was breathing under water, for up to five minutes, and for extra marks, shooting a fireball under water. Emily noted Mr Waternham's baffled face when she managed to breathe under water for the whole time and sent a mental note of gratitude to Julian for his teaching methods

"What's the guy's name?" Michella asked aloud and when no one answered, she added, "The guy who took the thing to that person?"

"What?" Emily asked perplexed.

"It's Rydan Butterworth," Jason said, not looking up from his textbook. "He's the guy with the thing."

"Thanks," Michella said gratefully.

Emily looked at them both mystified.

"I'll see you later."

She looked up at Wesley's voice and saw that he was hugging Harmony Loving-Dale. Emily felt an ache in her heart, but it wasn't as bad as before. She smiled to herself, as she thought of Julian's lips on hers.

"Déjà vu, right?"

Emily jumped as Wesley interrupted her memory. "What?"

Wesley pointed at her text book. "Last year? We were cramming it in."

"Right," Emily said, relieved. "And like last year, it's going right over my head."

Wesley laughed. He looked at Emily uncertainly. "We're cool?"

"Yeah," Emily said. "I've got a date with Julian Kena."

Michella, Wesley and Jason looked at her, stunned. She didn't plan for it to come out, but a part of her wanted to see how Wesley reacted. He was staring at her as if he had never seen her before and she instantly felt guilty for her impulsive comment.

"Good for you," Michella said, squeezing Emily's arm before going back to her revision. Not even an announcement like that could distract Michella from exams.

"Maybe you both should double date," Jason said, stifling his laughter.

Wesley shot him a dark look, but he didn't say anything. Emily looked up and briefly saw the hurt in Wesley's eyes before he silently turned away from her and looked at his notes.

They were called into the dining hall by the teachers and they walked past the guards that were standing outside the doors. Emily sat down at a wooden desk with a piece of paper reading 'Knight. E.' She could feel Wesley's eyes boring into the back of her neck. She turned around and he was sitting near the back of the hall, staring at her. He looked away when she caught his eye.

"You have two hours to complete the paper. Begin," the same bald examiner from last year said.

Emily flicked through the paper, catching questions that she knew the answers to. Feeling confident, she began the test.

Michella and Jason wished Emily luck as they went to sit by the koi pond and relax before the Dojo final, as Emily and Wesley walked down Gilford's Walk to the stadium. There was an excitement around the school that even the looming threat of war couldn't completely erase. Exams were officially over and the Dojo final between Ogragon and Pentwon was about to take place. It had almost been cancelled because some of the teachers thought it would be a perfect opportunity for Neci's team to attack, due to the number of spectators, but Mr Davon said it would be fine. He felt with the added security in the school, everyone would be safe and the championship should still happen. Warren and Pete Kinkle were also planning a party that they claimed would be *the* party, but it would only happen if Ogragon won.

Emily and Wesley walked in silence with a tension hovering between them.

"Emily!" Jasper Jones from Mentorawth ran up towards her.

"Hi, Jasper," Emily said, noticing that he held an Ogragon banner in his hand.

"Hi, I just wanted to say that it was pretty cool how you rescued, Gabriel."

"Oh thanks," Emily said humbled.

"Anyway, good luck for today!" he said, waving at them as he ran off.

Emily and Wesley hadn't taken a few steps when someone else called Emily's name. Emily couldn't hide her surprise when she saw Alice Archinia walking with Tanya Frank. Alice whispered something to Tanya, before running up to Emily. Wesley looked Alice appreciatively up and down in her fitted training kit and Emily nudged him in the ribs for how obvious he was being.

"Hey, I wanted to visit you and Julian at the sick bay, but I have a thing about hospitals," Alice said, swiping her blonde hair behind her heavily pierced ears.

"It's not really a hospital," Emily retorted.

"Yeah, so it's, you know, cool what you did with Gabriel," Alice continued as if Emily hadn't spoken. "Even though we're probably going to die because of that idiot, but you did good."

Emily's mouth dropped and Alice folded her arms over her ample bosom, looking defensive.

"Thank you," Emily said and Alice lowered her arms.

"If you're lucky I might even cheer for you today," Alice said cheekily and Emily laughed.

"I won't hold my breath. Oh, Alice, do you know, Wesley Parker?"

Alice smiled at Wesley flirtatiously. "You're the best commentator I've ever heard."

"Thanks," Wesley said. "I really liked your show. I was upset when it got cancelled."

Alice's green eyes shone and in a husky voice she said, "Well if you're lucky, I might give you a private show."

Wesley grinned cheekily back. "It better be the best show I've seen."

"Okay," Emily said, feeling uncomfortable. "That is so inappropriate. Alice you're sixteen, let's aim for your age."

Alice threw back her head and laughed, showing off her perfect teeth. "Ooh, feisty." She winked at Wesley before she hurried back to an irate Tanya.

The stadium had been filled with students and teachers, long before the match began, but now they were down to the two last Fighters. The crowd's cheering was deafeningly loud and Emily tried to tune them out as she faced Aaron Collins, a sixth year Fighter in Pentwon. He was a tall, muscular, dark-skinned boy who had a lot more power than speed. Pentwon had no Distracters left and Emily had Summer Wind.

Emily charged at Aaron and he teleported. She looked around wildly and found him on top of the commentators' box.

"I've got him," Summer shouted.

She teleported and appeared behind Aaron. She kicked him in his back, so that he fell forward. He teleported again and appeared above Emily, but so did Summer. Emily had no idea how Summer was tracking him, but she watched on impressed. Aaron was getting more and more frustrated because he couldn't retaliate.

"Come on, right here," Summer mocked, pointing at her cheek.

Aaron balled his hands into fists. "You'd love that."

They all knew if Aaron laid one finger on Summer, that he would lose and Ogragon would win the cup.

"I would," Summer said, blowing him a kiss.

"Let's see how much you love this," Aaron said. He closed his eyes and out of his body flew two identical versions of himself. When he smirked, they all smirked.

"What is that?" Wesley announced, standing up in his seat. "Oh, no wonder that's Pentwon's last Fighter! Collins is a Trisime—he can split himself into three!"

"Okay, don't panic," Summer said, flying over to Emily, as the Aarons flexed their arms, which the crowd went crazy for. "We just need to figure out which one is really him, then boom it's over."

"Boom?" Emily said doubtfully, looking at the Aarons. "And how do we know which one is him?"

Summer bit down on her lip. "Well . . . just attack!"

"There goes Knight and Wind, throwing punches at the Collins, who are dodging them effortlessly," Harmony announced. "I've never seen anything like this—Knight has shot a fireball at one and it's gone right through! One Collins is gone! Only two more to go."

Summer noticed what Emily's fireball did and she shot fireballs one after the other at the two Collins. Smoke appeared in the centre of the stadium as the fireballs hit Aaron. Emily covered her mouth, trying not to breathe in the smoke. Summer stopped shooting and was breathing hard, her face shiny with sweat.

Emily watched the smoke begin to clear, but then she felt the heat of a fireball soar past her body, missing her by inches. Emily ducked at the same time as Aaron swung a punch. He went to uppercut her and Emily caught on to his hand holding it tight, crushing it. Aaron yelled and was swinging his other arm, trying to get Emily off, but she held on. Emily looked around the stadium and there were no other versions of Aaron.

"Sleeper, Summer!" Emily yelled.

Summer flew behind Aaron and grabbed him tight around the neck. Aaron's eyes bulged as Summer gripped him harder.

"Remember how we practiced?" Summer asked Emily, who nodded.

Emily flew back. She could hear Lenny shouting directions from the pitch and she ignored him and everyone else. She took a deep breath and charged at Aaron. Emily held him with one arm wrapped around his waist and flew them up high into the sky, until the stadium was hidden underneath the clouds. Summer's legs were locked around Aaron's torso, and her grip on his neck didn't loosen.

"Ready?" Emily yelled.

Summer nodded as Aaron half-heartedly tried to fight them off.

Emily placed one hand behind Summer's back and shot down like a rocket. Everything was a blur. The wind made her eyes water. Summer was holding on tight with her blonde hair covering her face.

Emily let go of Summer's back and Summer teleported. Emily dropped Aaron and his body slammed deep into the sandy pitch. The whistle blew and Emily fell on top of Aaron, who was out cold. Sand went into her mouth and she spat it out. She wiped her mouth with the back of her hand before someone lifted her up from the hole she had created. When she was on her two feet, Lenny raised her hand up into the air. The noise in the stadium was deafening.

"OGRAGON WON! OGRAGON WON!" Wesley screamed over the microphone.

The last thing Emily remembered was Lenny, Warren, Pete, Jessie, Raquel, Rosa and Summer sprinting towards her, cheering and crying and the weight of them all on top of her, then everything went black.

Someone forced open her mouth and poured water down her throat. She felt a tingly sensation as the Reviving Water energised her. She opened her eyes and the worried looks on her Ogragon teammates' faces were immediately replaced with ecstatic expressions.

"Come on," Summer said, helping her up

Ms Macay walked over holding a big, gold trophy with a handle on either side. At the bottom of it, it read, 'Dojo Champions Ogragon.' Emily looked around the stadium, taking in all of the people on their feet, waving Ogragon banners. The scoreboard now read, 'Congratulations to Ogragon—our new Dojo Champions!' Emily looked at the commentators' box where Harmony Loving-Dale was clapping for them. Wesley held up his arms and loudly cheered.

Lenny took the trophy from a smiling Ms Macay and held it up high for everyone in the stadium to see and Emily was glad that she was part of the reason why they all had something to celebrate.

A few hours after the Ogragon team had won the Dojo match, Warren and Pete hosted a celebration party in the Ogragon living room. Warren had led an emotional speech, thanking Lenny for being a great captain. Lenny had excused himself, hiding his face from view. All the other teams came, dressed up and partied hard with them.

Ms Macay turned a blind eye, but warned if there was any alcohol she would shut the party down. There turned out to be a lot of alcohol that had been snuck in. Emily poured herself a cup of punch. She took a sip and almost gagged because it was straight vodka.

She held out her cup to Michella, who pulled a face.

"Not after what happened last year."

Emily laughed. "Oh my gosh, your shoe in the toilet!"

Michella laughed also. "I know, it was awful. Emily, I wasn't completely honest with you."

"Oh?" Emily said, putting down her cup. Warren Kinkle immediately picked it up and chucked it back in one go.

"Last year's party, I kissed Jason."

"What?" Emily said surprised.

"I know, but I was drunk! Well, I wasn't that drunk, but I blamed it on the alcohol in case he hated it."

"But he didn't hate it," Emily said, wrapping her arms around Michella's small waist. "He liked it so much that he wants to be with you."

"I know." Michella sighed. "I just wish I could see what he sees."

Emily grabbed Michella's hand. "Come on."

She led Michella through the masses of people either dancing, talking, or kissing. It was so loud and packed that no one noticed them slip into Michella's bedroom. Emily placed Michella in front of the full-length mirror and stood behind her.

"Let me tell you what I see," Emily said. "I see a beautiful, smart, kind girl, who expects the best for everyone, but not for herself." Michella looked away from her reflection. Emily gently pulled her face back to the mirror. "And if you could see this same beautiful, smart, kind girl then you would completely understand why a catch like Jason would be so into you."

Michella hugged Emily tight. "Thank you."

Emily pulled away, smiling. "Give me a minute, wait here."

Emily left the room and went back to the party. It wasn't hard to find Jason. He was standing near the snack table, with a drink in his hand, talking to Wesley and a group of girls. Harmony Loving-Dale was watching from a distance, looking possessively at Wesley. Lisa Fowler was twirling her hair, hanging on to Jason's every word.

"Excuse me," Emily said, pushing past the girls, who scowled at her.

"The girl of the night!" Jason said, hugging her and the scowling girls instantly gushed over her.

"Michella's waiting to talk to you in her bedroom," Emily whispered to Jason.

He lowered the drink that was almost at his lips and raised

his eyebrows. "Be back in a bit, guys," Jason said, leaving his drink on the table before he walked away.

"Where's he going?" Lisa demanded, with her hands on her hips.

"Where he wants to be," Emily said.

The girls pouted and walked off, leaving Emily and Wesley alone.

"Is he with Michella?" Wesley asked and when Emily nodded, he said, "Good, I'm glad."

"Me too," Emily said, smiling to herself, praying that Michella would be as honest to Jason as she was to her.

"So where do you want to be?" Wesley asked casually.

Emily didn't answer immediately. Instead she looked around the party. It was nice that people from the other teams came to celebrate with them. Julian was on the other side of the room with some boys from Mentorawth. As if he could feel her presence, he looked in her direction and held up his drink to her. His friends followed his gaze and loudly applauded Emily, who gave them the thumbs up.

"Wesley," Harmony called, beckoning him over.

Wesley glanced at Harmony and then at Emily.

"First, you tell me where you want to be," Emily said to Wesley.

"Touché," Wesley said, sipping his drink.

Emily smiled, aware that neither of them moved away from each other.

After the celebrations of Ogragon winning and the end of

exams came an air of anxiousness. There had been so much going on at school, it was easy to forget about Neci and just live in the moment. Now everyone was on edge, waiting to hear what Neci would say. There was a chance that Blade never reunited with her. It was a slim chance, but still possible.

Mr Davon asked Emily, Jason, Julian and Alice to come to his office after lunch. The four of them walked together and Jason had a spring in his step because Michella had agreed to be his girlfriend.

Roberta, Jenkins, Xavier and Antonio were seated on one side of the office and Gabriel was opposite them. Cecil and Niles were floating beside him and Mr Davon was sitting behind his desk.

"Please come and sit," Mr Davon beckoned.

Emily sat in the armchair offered, her eyes never leaving Gabriel, who had the good grace to look uncomfortable.

"Hey, Granddad," Alice said, moving her seat, so that it was beside Cecil.

"Hello, sweet pea," Cecil said, patting Alice's head with his ghostly hand.

"Thank you all for coming. I felt it was important for all of us to hear what Gabriel has to say. He has been through a terrible ordeal and he needed time to process what had happened." Mr Davon turned to Gabriel. "Whenever you're ready."

Niles nodded encouragingly at his frightened brother. Gabriel stood up. He looked even paler with everyone staring at him. "First of all, I want to say sorry for what I've done. It was selfish and stupid and I'm really really sorry." He stopped and looked at Niles.

"Go on," Niles said encouragingly.

In a quiet voice, Gabriel said, "In the summer, I had a visit from Scarlett. She works with Neci and she said that she wanted me to find Blade and release him. I asked her why did it had to be me and she said it was because I know Hariem. I don't know how she knew that. I refused and told her I could never help someone who killed my brother and she left. I thought it was over, but then she set fire to my house. I watched her trap me with her powers. I know I should have told someone, but I thought the worst had been done."

Gabriel's voice croaked towards the end. He took a deep breath and continued. "Scarlett came back and told me she would kill me and my family if I didn't release Blade. So I panicked and said I'd do whatever she wanted. We teleported to Osaki in the summer, whilst no one was here and she led me to Blade. I had to release him, so she could see that I could, but she made me put him back—she said it wasn't time yet. She said Neci would let her know. Neci wanted us to believe that we had a chance if we found the missing warrior first, but she knew all along where Blade was. She wanted everyone to be anxious and scared so people would go to her for protection. Then Scarlett told me to get, Emily." Gabriel glanced at Emily, who stared at him blankly. "I asked why and she said because Neci wants Thomas. If you disappeared, she believed that Thomas would come back. I asked what I was meant to do with Emily and she said Blade would deal with her. From there, I teleported to your house, to your bedroom, just for a second."

"My house?" Emily said confused. Then she remembered, that night in the middle of summer, she felt so cold even though the windows were closed. "Why?"

"I needed to remember what you looked like. That's why I was so off with you all the time because I knew what I was doing. I couldn't have you being nice to me because it made me feel worse. Every time Scarlett gave me the go-ahead, I couldn't do it. She was angry that I was taking so long. I was just so scared. Every day I was frightened I was going to hear that my parents were dead."

"Why didn't you just leave me in the ice when you had the chance?" Emily asked. "When I first saw Blade, you told him not yet, when he grabbed my throat. Why?"

"Because I hoped that you would tell someone about him and the ice room and they could stop everything!"

"But I did," Emily protested. She looked desperately at Mr Davon.

"Scarlett sealed the door," Gabriel said sadly. "She found out that Mr Davon knew from Ruth Walker."

"Ruth?" Emily asked bewildered. "What has she got to do with it?"

"Ruth keeps a folder of notes from her counselling sessions. She had written down that you knew about the ice room and you were coming to see, Mr Davon," Gabriel explained. "Scarlett saw the notes."

"Who taught you how to teleport?" Julian asked and Gabriel looked guiltily at Niles.

"I did," Niles said, looking awkward. "I taught him when he was young. I was always travelling with the Five Warriors and I wanted him to be able to come to me wherever I was. I'm sorry, I should have told you." He looked at Mr Davon, who gave him a look that he understood.

"Why did you get trapped in the ice?" Jason asked.

"Scarlett," Gabriel said. "She felt I was dragging my feet, so she came to my room and teleported me to the ice room, so Blade could freeze me. She thought things would move quicker if I disappeared. She knew there would be a massive search for me—the only downside, for her, was the security in the school was stronger, so she couldn't get in and out anymore. Scarlett knew Emily was on my case and that she would come to me. She told me once I was released, I was to drop Blade at Mount Gregory and if I didn't, she would kill my fam-family." Gabriel put his face in his hands. His shoulders shook as he cried nosily.

Roberta ran up to him and pulled him close to her. She murmured softly in his ear and stroked his dark hair. After a few minutes, when his sobbing had stopped, he pulled away from her. His face was blotchy and red.

"After watching you train Emily, I honestly started to believe that you could defeat Blade if it came to it. You're so talented and I thought you would be okay. I know it's not an excuse."

"Hold on a minute," Alice said, frowning at Gabriel. "So Blade might not have made it to, Neci?"

"No one was there when I dropped him, so I don't know for sure."

Emily felt relieved. Although slim, they still had a chance. The door to Mr Davon's office burst open.

"Sir," Laton Chin said, looking unnaturally untidy. "Come quick. It's Neci."

Mr Davon immediately left the room. Jenkins picked up Antonio and held on to Xavier's hand. Emily and Julian exchanged worried glances as they followed everyone else.

The relief Emily had felt a second ago went as quickly as it came.

"I will make this up to you, Emily," Gabriel promised. He was walking beside her. She noticed he was walking taller and bolder as if holding on to that secret all year had lifted a giant weight of his shoulders.

"Good," Emily said, but she smiled at him, to let him know that she understood why he had done it.

They hurried down the corridors and into the dining hall, where there was a giant television set up. Michella and Wesley saw them enter and gestured to Emily and Jason to come over.

"Why is the television up?" Emily whispered, sitting next to Michella.

"I think Laton Chin got a call saying Neci's making an announcement. It's obviously about the war. Why else would she want everyone to be watching?"

"And there's no match to interrupt this year," Wesley added.

The screen was facing a black room that was empty apart from a wooden stool in the middle of the floor. Everyone was whispering amongst each other, at times, Emily caught the odd glance her way. Mr Davon was standing at the front of the hall, with his arms crossed, staring sternly at the television.

There was a rustling sound and then a person in a black cloak and white mask sat elegantly on the stool. The hall fell silent. Surrounding Neci were five other warriors, all of whom Emily recognised: the beautiful redhead, Scarlett, who had threatened Gabriel, a short black man, with a gold tooth named Dion, Maggie, a froggy-eyed, white lady and Blade, the ice man, who was now wearing a long white cloak.

But the person Emily couldn't take her eyes off was her brother. He was staring coldly into the camera and Emily automatically reached out and held on to Michella's arm.

"I know," Michella said softly.

"I have thousands of people that want to fight with me. Smart people who know that I will win," Neci said in her gentle voice. "They have been branded to show their support for me and to those who refused to have the microchips—because I am a fair person, I will give you one last chance to come over to my team. The Five Warriors, or shall I say the Three Warriors will not save you. I have some of the strongest warriors in the world behind me and of course my missing warrior, Blade, which means . . . we're going to war."

The hall erupted into screams and shouts, blocking out whatever Neci was saying.

"SILENCE!" Mr Davon yelled.

And the hall fell quiet.

". . . and you all know, Lox Knight. Do you think we can claim his missing persons reward?" Neci said and the warriors laughed. Emily noticed that Lox's laughter didn't reach his eyes. "And so I must stress," Neci continued. "That a lot of people are going to die, but only if—"

The lights in the room began to flicker and Neci and her warriors looked around the room baffled. Emily studied her brother closely. He was the only one staring at the camera.

"What is going on?" Neci demanded.

The whole room went black. Everyone in Osaki began to talk and point at the screen.

"He knows something," Emily said to no one in particular, but Michella, Wesley and Jason heard her.

A loud piercing scream came from the television and echoed throughout the dining hall, sending a chill through Emily's body. The camera that was filming toppled over, so that there was a sideways view of the rooms floor. There was a bright light and then a loud boom as if a fireball had been shot. The warriors were shouting amongst each other. There was another scream and everyone in Osaki gasped as someone collapsed to the floor. It was Scarlett and her face was in front of the camera, with her eyes closed and her mouth slightly open. Someone at the back of the hall applauded. Emily turned around and saw Gabriel smiling as he clapped his hands.

Emily looked back at the screen and Scarlett was being pulled away from the camera, her face sliding against the floor, her red hair leaving a trail. A black shoe was in front of the camera blocking the view. A deep voice was speaking and there was a conversation happening that didn't sound clear. A pair of dirty, grey, ripped trousers was in the camera shot and then a face appeared up close to the screen. His brown eyes, chiselled face and strong chin were magnified for a second before it went black.

Emily caught her breath and gripped Michella's arm tight. She looked slowly towards Michella, who was already looking back at her, shell-shocked, as the hall exploded into noise.

Emily's voice shook as she asked Michella, "Was—was that my dad?"

Michella nodded her head, clearly lost for words.

Someone from the other side of the room yelled, "He's back!"

Emily watched as some students hugged each other, whilst other threw their hands up in the air and cheered loudly. She caught Roberta's eye, who was grinning back at her. Emily slowly smiled as it sunk in. Her dad was back to fight beside her. She knew that together, they still had a fighting chance.

About the Author

A. Bello is a 29-year-old author who was born and raised in London, where she still lives and works. She wrote her first novel at the age of eight—she fought monsters and dragons on a daily basis—and experienced her first taste of 'being published' after winning a school poetry competition at the age of 12. Seeing her words in print fuelled a passion for writing that remains to this day. A. Bello first began writing the Emily Knight saga shortly afterwards (still only 12 years old!) with the intention of filling the gaping hole in children's fiction for an inspirational, strong, black female, young protagonist. This gap, nearly 18 years later, remains in the publishing world despite continued calls for more BAME background authors and diversity within characters and plotlines.

A. Bello received rave reviews for her debut book, 'Emily Knight I am . . .', as well as outstanding success with her Emily Knight Warriors pop-up book, which went viral in 2015 when it was gradually released online throughout the month of August. She is the founder of The Lil' Author School and co-founder of The Author School. The Author School was shortlisted for The Great British Entrepreneur Awards 2016.

A. Bello is regularly called to talk at literary events and within the media, she has appeared in Female First Magazine and The Mirror to name a few.

Find out more at www.a-bello.com
Follow her on Twitter: @EmilyKnightIAM
Instagram: @abiolabello @emilyknightiam
Facebook.com/EmilyKnightIAM